Not into Temptation

Not into Temptation

SIÂN JAMES

St. Martin's Press
New York

 For information, address St. Martin's Press, 175 Fifth Avenue, New York, N.Y. 10010.

Library of Congress Cataloging in Publication Data

James, Siân.
Not into temptation.

I. Title.
PR6060.A474N6 1984 823'.914 84-2135
ISBN 0-312-57957-8

First published in Great Britain by Century Publishing Co. Ltd. under the title *A Dangerous Time*

10 9 8 7 6 5 4 3 2

PART 1

Chapter One

The train left Leeds at a few minutes past seven. It was July but a cold morning; Laura shivered and pulled her old brown cardigan tightly round her shoulders.

She would not be home before night.

Home was a tall isolated grey house on a hillside in Warwickshire. Home sweet home. Home is where the heart is. Home is love is rest is peace.

But there was no peace. It was 1941. Soldiers were embarking for battlefields in Africa and Greece. Bombs had fallen the previous night in Birmingham, earlier in the week in Liverpool, London and Hull.

When she got home she'd clean the windows for Susan, she'd scrub the flags in the kitchen and the hall, she'd brush the carpets and polish the table and chairs, all for the joy of being back; back out of harm's way.

The garden was heaven, tall grasses the colour of new apples, and buttercups and wild scabious and the smell of orange blossom and elderflower. Butterflies; tortoiseshells and peacocks by the dozen, the peacocks very dark on the underside, the females larger than the males. She knew nothing about butterflies a year ago, nothing about gardens.

Susan would make her a cup of tea and a sandwich when she got back. 'How was your dad?' she'd ask and Laura would talk about his cough, his weak chest and about her step-mother's problems at the shop; all the shortages and the coupons and points for this and that and how she felt like giving it all up. And she'd tell Susan how shocked she'd been to see the city centre after the bombing; the ruined cathedral and the art gallery and the shops. She wouldn't mention her trip to Leeds. Susan was easy to deceive.

The train was unheated. Laura had hoped to catch up on sleep but she was too cold, too uncomfortable.

There was an unpleasant smell in the compartment. Over the usual acrid smell drifting back from the engine, there was a sickly-sweet smell of sweat and dirt. It seemed a familiar combination, very familiar, yet she'd somehow mislaid the key.

When the train entered a tunnel she closed her eyes and sniffed her way back into the past.

Her grandmother's house, that was it, her grandmother's dirty house in Longworth, near the gasworks and the tannery and the canal.

If she thought back far enough she could remember her mother taking her there on an afternoon's visit. Her grandmother didn't like her daughter-in-law but she got as much out of her as she could; her mother would clean the house for her and then go out to do some shopping. 'Thank you Molly,' her grandmother would say in her low whining voice. 'Only you've brought the wrong tea again and you never remembered the candles.' 'I'll get you some candles next week, Ma. I only managed to save a couple of bob this week; Harry had to have his shoes mended again.' 'And what did you get for the little girl, eh? More books, I dare say, and another new pinafore.'

Laura hated her grandmother, couldn't understand why her mother bothered with her; her father never did and after all she was *his* mother.

Laura's mother was a country girl but she'd left her home at fourteen to go into service in the town. She'd often tell Laura about the country; the village she used to return to once or twice every year until she was married. 'I used to tell everyone about all the fine sights of the city but I liked the fields and hedges better. I could take you to the very spot in Brook Lane where the white violets grew and the kingcups and the little spotted orchids. Of course primroses and cowslips were everywhere, common as grass.'

But she never did take Laura back to her old home, though it was only twenty miles away, money was always short, there were always more pressing things to do.

Her mother had died when Laura was eleven.

For a time, afterwards, her grandmother had had to stir herself to help them. Laura could remember her coming over on the bus, doing a load of washing, some perfunctory cleaning and a great deal of grumbling.

Her father hadn't been able to stand it for long. 'We'll be all right now,' he'd said. 'Laura's getting old enough to make herself useful and Mrs Dunn next door is going to help us.'

Laura had soon learned to cope with simple meals and the day to day cleaning and shopping while Mrs Dunn did the washing and ironing and a weekly clean-through for half a crown, 'Which I can't afford,' her father used to say. 'How can I afford to pay wages out of my pay-packet? You won't be able to go to that fancy school of yours much longer I can tell you that; I can't afford the uniform nor the bus fares.'

'But I've got the uniform.'

'I can't afford more when you grow.'

'I won't grow, I promise.'

There had followed two miserable years when her dignity at the grammar school had plummeted. What did high marks count when you hadn't got shorts and shirt for PT and the teacher made you do it in your navy-blue knickers which had faded to a dull plum colour and a darned and yellowing vest? Laura would never forget those humiliating PT lessons, nor the teacher, a graduate of the Chelsea College of Physical Training; her piercing upper-class voice and her chilling insensitivity.

The other girls, too, from homes very different from hers could be unwittingly cruel. 'But *why* do you bring sandwiches every day?' 'Do you mean you don't *possess* a mackintosh?' 'Well, why not *buy* an atlas, they only cost five shillings.'

Even Susan Wilkins, her best friend ever since they'd started school together at Eversley Road Infants', used to giggle occasionally, about her short gym tunic and her tight blouses.

Once Laura had burst out crying. 'Oh, don't be a dope,'

Susan had said. 'I didn't mean it, did I? Look I've got my sixpence pocket money, I'll share it with you, you can have a ha'penny.'

Laura didn't get any regular pocket money though her father was occasionally generous when he came back from the pub.

Her father spent a lot of time at the pub; that was only natural, she supposed. And it was only natural, too, that he should have no idea what she went through when she was on her own late at night, her mind full of ghosts and vampires and werewolves, shadows everywhere. And she never complained in case her father sent her to live with her grandmother as he often threatened to do.

When she was about fourteen he started staying out later and later, occasionally all night. He gave her less money, too, for shopping. Things got worse and worse. And then better.

Annie. Even on that cold and miserable morning the thought of Annie warmed Laura to the bone.

Miss Florence Horsefield, senior History teacher at St Winifred's Grammar School for Girls called Laura Brown over to her desk. It was the beginning of the summer term 1934. School was over for the day.

'I'll let you into a secret, Lucy,' Miss Horsefield said, her pale, short-sighted eyes skimming over her fourteen-year-old pupil. 'We have something in common you and I, you and I and Snow-white. Can you guess, dear? Yes, a step-mother.'

Laura Brown, thoroughly disconcerted by the simpering attention she was receiving from a normally dignified form-teacher, wondering what she could say, how she could get away - her friend Susan Wilkins would surely leave without her, she might even miss her bus - turned her head feebly in the direction of the door and escape.

Miss Horsefield, interpreting the sign as dumb misery, motioned the girl to sit.

'Why don't we have a little heart-to-heart talk,' she said. 'After all, a trouble shared is a trouble halved.'

'Please, Miss Horsefield, what about my bus?' Laura managed to stammer out.

'Don't worry about your bus, child. If you miss it, I'll drive you home in my motorcar. Sit down my dear.'

'The headmistress asked me to have a word with you, Lucy. You've always been such a good girl, such a hard worker; a prize-winner, I believe, in your first and second years; she wanted you to approach your new life in a mature and philosophical way. So many things, you see, are quite beyond our control, and the wise course of action is to endeavour to make the best of them.'

Florence Horsefield looked across at her pupil. On the whole the scholarship element at St Winifred's was not altogether reliable but Lucy Brown, or was she Lorna, was an honourable exception; neat and industrious and thoroughly likeable.

Laura met her teacher's pale watery eyes. What had possessed her father, she wondered, to involve her in this hideous embarrassment.

'I'm not pretending it will be easy for you, Lucy. You see, all women have their own ideas about running a house and so forth, your step-mother will want to change many institutions which you feel are rather sacred, but try to remember, dear, that she probably doesn't realise that she's stepping in your own dear mother's shoes.'

Miss Horsefield sniffed, her eyes and her nose becoming rather red. She was faring badly. In attempting to preach forbearance she was only managing to reveal how much she had suffered, indeed was still suffering, from the second Mrs Horsefield. All the same she persevered in her duty.

'Your father will seem . . . preoccupied for a time. He may seem to have grown away from you, to be less lavish of his affection. Dear child, try to bear with him patiently. If you reproach him he will begin to feel guilty and any man who feels guilty invariably loses his temper. Try to be patient, Lucy, both with your father and your new step-mother. Try to be patient and brave. Remember that you have in me a friend and well-wisher. I may not be able to do much in any practical sense, but a sympathetic ear is often of great value, don't you agree? Remember that I have myself gone through the same difficulties, so that I shall understand. There, Lucy. I hope you've found our little talk has been of some help.'

'Oh yes, thank you, Miss Horsefield,' Laura said. 'Thank you very much.'

As soon as she realised that she was being dismissed she scuttled from the classroom - running was not allowed - and along the corridor to the cloakroom to fetch her coat and hat. Susan Wilkins had not waited for her. She would have half an hour, now, before her next bus. But, thank goodness, Miss Horsefield had forgotten about taking her home in her car. That would really have been the end.

'Why ever did you write to my school about Annie?' she asked her father over tea.

'I didn't, lass. Your Headmistress came in to the garage, that's all, and we had a little chat about you. She said she hoped you'd be staying on for your school certificate or summat. I said I didn't rightly know about that. "Oh Mr Brown," she says, "I hope your circumstances haven't altered." "Not exactly," I said, "only I am reckoning to be getting married again in the Easter holidays." That's all I said.'

'You fool,' Annie said. 'Why should that make any difference? If she wants to stay on at school for her certificate, then good luck to her. Don't you dare say she can't because of me.'

It was impossible to regard Annie as someone stepping into her mother's shoes. She was so unlike her mother, for one thing, so unlike anybody's mother. She seemed a big sister or a lodger but not a mother or even a step-mother. She was young, good-natured, easy going, warm and vivacious. She was a working girl and didn't intend to give up her job; she was a cleaner in one of the big car factories and she earned twenty-five shillings a week. Laura had taken to her at first sight; loved her.

After Miss Horsefield's talk, it had seemed necessary to vindicate her total capitulation to Annie. Laura had tried to recall her mother's face, but that night she couldn't, not in any real sense. She could only remember the face in the wedding photograph downstairs, soft round eyes, straight nose, bobbed hair gently waved, but that wasn't the face she wanted to remember. Her mother's body, that was easier; she was tall, neither thin nor fat, she wore flowered overalls in the house and black pointed shoes with a strap and a button.

She was shy. When she came to meet her out of school, she stood a little apart from the other mothers and hurried her away so that she didn't have to talk to anyone. She had a long brown coat and a small brown hat and she carried a shopping bag made from squares of leather because she got one or two things from the corner shop on her way to the school. The elementary school was on the common, it was a pleasant walk. Her mother had come to meet her every day until she was nine or ten; until she had fallen ill.

Like a teacher, she would point out things on the way home, the fat buds on a lilac tree in someone's garden, the crocus, 'look, the yellow ones are always the first,' the gargoyles on St Luke's church, the clouds, 'those rounded ones are called cumulus,' an Elizabethan doorway, 'look how short and wide it is. Do you know why?' She loved facts. She got Laura books from the library, usually educational ones about nature or architecture; she didn't get any for herself but liked to read Laura's. She would sometimes buy books from a stall in the market, they were a penny each, sometimes twopence. She'd got *Little Women* once for a penny; they'd both enjoyed that.

When Miss Talbot, Headmistress of Eversley Road Elementary, had said Laura was clever enough to win a scholarship to the local grammar school, her mother had been quiet for several days. 'Don't you want me to try?' Laura remembered asking her. 'I don't mind.' Other children laughed and whistled at the Grammar School crowd and called them stuck-up.

'Oh, I do,' her mother had said in a low, fervent voice. 'I want it more than anything.'

To Laura the thought of travelling on a bus every day was alarming, so was the navy blue and scarlet uniform and the satchel bulging with books. 'The scholarship class has to work very hard,' she'd said. 'They have to have pens and rulers and exercise books for their homework.'

'I'll get you whatever you need.'

'Did you ever go to Grammar School?'

'No.'

'Why not? You were clever.'

'I had to leave school when I was fourteen. My mother was poor; she was a widow.'

'Shall Laura try for the Grammar School, Harry?' she'd asked her husband the next Friday evening.

He'd looked crossly at her, as though he would have liked to have refused. 'As you like,' he'd said. 'Why ask me? I don't know nothing about schooling do I? I had a job when I was thirteen and kept it too. Up every morning at six, summer and winter, but people are soft nowadays. Don't ask me nothing about it, I'm off out.'

Laura tried to remember how things had been between her mother and father; she could only recall the unease, her mother becoming tense, a different person, when her father was expected home. Everything had to be ready for him. She remembered the cooked meal being laid on the table within minutes of his arriving in the house. Her mother didn't eat with him, she'd had a piece of toast and cheese or a boiled egg earlier on with Laura, but would always sit at the table with a cup of tea to keep him company.

Laura would be reading or crayoning by this time, often on the other side of the table. She used to try not to hear her mother persuading him to stay in. 'You won't be going out tonight, Harry? It's a dirty night and there's such a good fire. There's a good programme on the wireless. Didn't you want to mend that puncture in your front wheel?'

When his meal was over and the dishes washed up, it would be time for her bed. Had he stayed in or gone out? She'd always tried to keep out of the conflict; tried to go to sleep as soon as she could. She didn't want to find out.

On Sunday mornings her father would stay in bed while she and her mother went to church, but on fine Sunday afternoons they sometimes went out for a walk together to the park or to the town centre.

When her father was with them her mother was quite different, saying less, seeming less interested in things around her. They seemed to talk a great deal about the time he was in the army; he'd been in the trenches for three years.

Laura hated hearing about the war, the same old stories about improbable people called the Boche and an improbable place called No Man's Land. She also hated the fact that her mother, who must have heard the same old stories even oftener than she had, would appear to be completely enthralled, looking amused, apprehensive, relieved in all the right places. Was it because her mother loved her father, Laura wondered. Was it love which made her seem so simple-minded where his war-time reminiscences were concerned? 'Did I ever tell you about the night Nobby, Frank and me . . .' Laura couldn't bear to see her mother looking so eager to hear the anecdote she must know by heart. Couldn't she tell that her father was exaggerating and boasting?

'Your father's chest has never been right since the trenches,' her mother would say whenever he coughed his smoker's cough in the morning. And almost every week she bought him some new medicine to try. If only she had looked after herself as she looked after him.

But she hadn't. Laura had failed to understand, even in the last few months, how serious her mother's illness was. Even when she had to stay in bed for the greater part of the day, she'd struggle to get up before Laura came home from school. 'How are you today, Mum?' 'I think I'm a bit better today, love. I've managed to make a few scones and a pie for your father's tea.'

She seemed to have willed herself not to give way before Laura's scholarship examination at the beginning of May.

She'd died in hospital ten days later, still insisting to the last that she felt a bit stronger every day.

Laura had cried herself to sleep for six weeks or more. 'You've still got your father,' neighbours and friends used to tell her, but her father hardly counted, she'd never felt close to him.

Her father had been very uneasy when he first told her about Annie. 'A man gets lonely without a wife,' he'd said. 'I don't think your mother would want me to live alone for the rest of my life, do you?'

Laura had thought earnestly about it. 'No, I don't think so,' she'd said. 'I don't think she'd want you to be lonely.'

*

When he'd first brought Annie home, Laura had almost cried out with relief. Somehow she'd been expecting a shrunken, middle-aged woman like Mrs Dunn, their next-door neighbour. Mrs Dunn was small and colourless, she suffered from rheumatism and toothache and spoke so slowly and carefully that you knew what she was going to say the moment she started and could hardly wait for her to finish. 'Take this to Mrs Dunn,' her father would say every Friday night handing her half a crown from his pay-packet. 'If I go in she'll keep me half the night.'

'Oh, I don't want it,' Mrs Dunn would say as she had said every Friday night for the last three years. 'I do it for love not for any financial reward. I do it for friendship. I had a lot of time for your mother, Laura. She'd have wanted me to keep an eye on her house. Not that I can keep it in the way she did, poor soul, I can't kneel, you see, not with my back. Your mother was a wonderful housewife, Laura. "Mrs Brown's got her bedroom curtains on the line again," I used to tell Albert, regular as clockwork. Every spring and autumn she washed every pair of curtains in the house. There was never a fine summer day but she had a blanket on the line. Your house was turned out like a palace, Laura. I can't pretend to do things the way she did. I can't clean windows or polish the furniture, not any more, not with my back. All I can manage now is to brush the carpets a bit and flick a duster over the front room and mop the kitchen out, but I dare say it helps a bit. Oh, but I don't like taking money for it,' she'd say, putting the half-crown safely into her large, leather purse.

When Laura had first seen Annie, her dark eyes, her dark curly hair, her fine body, her bright clothes, she thought there'd been some mistake. She couldn't imagine why such a lovely woman would want to marry her father.

'Come on,' her father had said, 'can't you say anything to each other, have you both been struck dumb or what?'

'You leave us alone, you,' Annie had said. 'We'll get on all right in our own time. How can we talk when you're watching us.'

Laura had cleaned and polished the front room and put

some daffodils in a blue jug on the table.

'Where did you get the flowers?' her father had asked her, another note of complaint in his voice.

'I bought them,' she'd said defiantly, 'they were only sixpence.'

'And they're lovely,' Annie said. 'I like flowers in a room, they brighten things up.' She'd smiled at Laura.

'What's sixpence,' she'd said to Laura's father. 'You mean devil.'

'What do you think of the front room?' her father had asked.

It was a pleasant room, tastefully furnished; the carpet floral, brown and fawn, pink and blue, the curtains a faded indigo, three easy chairs with wooden arms and cocoa-brown covers. His wife had been proud of it.

'You can change whatever you like. A woman doesn't want to live with another woman's things. I got some money.'

'Keep it then,' Annie had said. 'I'd rather have a holiday than new furniture any day; I've never had a holiday. This room looks fine to me, what do you say Laura? It's a jolly sight better than anything I've been used to anyway, I can tell you that, and it's been cleaned lovely.'

'We're going away for a few days next week,' her father had told Laura, his eyes fixed on the floral carpet. 'We're getting married private in a registry office on Tuesday morning, then we're going to Blackpool for a few days.'

'And I'm going to Grandma's on Monday,' Laura said. 'And coming back on Friday. That's what you said, wasn't it?'

'Where does your grandma live?' Annie asked. 'I hope you don't mind having to go.'

'In Longworth. It's only twenty minutes on the bus. I often go there during the holidays. I don't mind a bit. Would you like a cup of tea now? I've made some cakes.'

'Oh, lovely.'

'Would you like to come to see the kitchen? Or would you prefer to stay here?'

'I'll stay here, please, and be waited on. I'll be a lady for once.'

Annie's laughter rang out, loud and reassuring.

Everything she did was right.

'I can imagine just what she's like, thank you very much,' Grandma Brown had said when Laura had tried to describe Annie. 'Oh yes, I've met her sort before.'

She disapproved of her son's second marriage. She thought everything was fine as it was, Laura growing up fast and little Mrs Dunn next door so ready to help and not even a widow.

'My Dad gets lonely,' Laura had said.

'Well, he's no call to get lonely at his age. Ain't he forty-five next birthday? Men never thinks of anything but theirselves, that's the trouble. When does he ever think what you want?'

'But I'm glad he's getting married again.'

'Well, that's a nice thing. Don't you mind this scheming young hussy taking over all your ma's nice things?'

'Well, *she* doesn't want them, does she? Not now.'

Grandma Brown had regarded Laura severely. She hadn't liked her daughter-in-law but she'd respected her. '*You* should have your ma's things,' she'd said, 'not another woman.'

Laura wondered what 'things' her grandmother was so concerned about; the silver dressing-table set, perhaps, that her mother had had as a wedding present from Mrs Johnson-Wright her employer. She must remember to find it for Annie as soon as she got back.

'Your mother gave herself airs but she was careful of her things. I've never said anything against her as a housewife. She knew how to manage, how to make the most of a few bob.'

'Annie's going to go on working,' Laura had said. 'She's got a good job in a factory.'

'Well, she's no right to take a man's job when she's married, that's for sure. There's plenty of men wanting work. Anyway, what about when she gets in the family way?'

'What do you mean?'

'When women get married they get babies, don't they? Haven't you thought of that?'

Laura, though she was fourteen, hadn't thought of it. 'She's not so young as all that,' she told her grandmother. 'She's probably twenty-eight or thirty. And anyway my Dad is quite old, you said that yourself.'

'She'll have a baby this time next year, you can be sure of that, and perhaps a lot earlier too. Then you'll have to leave that fine school of yours and go out to work.'

'I won't mind. I like babies.'

'She's got you where she wants you and no mistake.'

Laura didn't like Grandma Brown. Grandma Wells, her mother's mother, whom she could only just remember, had been a pretty little woman with a tiny face and white hair. Grandma Brown was fat and dirty, her face was large with loose hanging chins. Her dark skin was lined like a map, its rivers and roads deep and silted. She had two bedrooms but she always wanted Laura to sleep with her to save having to make up another bed. 'Let me do it,' Laura would beg. 'Just give me the sheets and I'll get it done in two minutes.'

'It ain't aired. It ain't been slept in for years. You'd be much better off sleeping with me.'

But she wasn't. Laura hated the nights. Her grandmother snored and her sheets were grey and smelly.

And the days weren't much better. She never had a proper meal while she was there. Her grandmother kept hens but she sold all the eggs; Laura was never given anything but bread and margarine with fish paste or plum jam to hide the taste. Even the tea she made was grey; grey as dust, grey as funerals.

Her father, on that occasion in a mood of rare generosity, had sent a ten shilling note for her keep, but her grandmother, instead of sending her out to the shops with it, had immediately put it away in the tin box on her mantlepiece.

One morning when her grandmother was down at the bottom of the garden feeding the hens, Laura had taken a peep in the tin box. It was full of notes, twelve or fifteen pounds in all: the rotten old skinflint was rich.

'I lost my 'usband when I was only twenty-five,' her grandmother had said when she'd got back to the house, as thought sensing Laura's disapprobation. 'He was took bad and taken off to a sanatorium. I lost two lads in the war, your Uncle Jack and your Uncle Ernest. I've only got your Dad, your Dad and you. You wait till you're an old woman and on your own.'

I won't whine about it, Laura thought. At least I'll wash myself and treat myself to some butter and some decent tea.

'Shall I do some cleaning for you, Grandma?' she asked, weakening in spite of herself. 'If you give me some soap and a rag I'll wash the sink and the paint-work for you. I'll scrub the kitchen floor.'

Even as she offered to help, her heart sank. The kitchen floor was covered by many, many small pieces of greasy lino, some of them frayed at the edges, some of them completely disintegrated, forming hideous brown messes like large cow pats on the floor.

'Just sweep it over,' her grandmother said. 'It only needs sweeping. Your mother came here one day and wanted to take up all this lino. She said there was good red tiles underneath. But once you have red tiles there's no end of trouble, scrubbing and polishing. Your mother didn't understand old age; how stiff you get. Well, she'll never 'ave to go through it. She's well out of it and no one left to miss her.'

'I miss her,' Laura said, poking angrily into filthy corners with her sweeping brush.

How dare you say I don't miss her, you whining old cow, she thought. I miss her every day. Just because I like Annie it doesn't mean I don't miss my mother.

She watered the floor with her angry tears and brushed them away. The truth was that she'd almost forgotten her mother; she existed only as a pretty picture in the back of her mind. Annie was alive and an ally.

When Laura returned home on the Friday of that week she was worn out by lack of sleep and food. As she sat in the bus she felt sure that she could smell her grandmother, even her grandmother's chickens, on her clothes and her body; she'd hardly been able to wash, there was only the greasy sink in the kitchen and cold water and a dirty old towel. She hoped she'd arrive before her father and Annie so that she could have a good wash before they came.

She was home first. She got the key from Mrs Dunn, boiled water, washed herself all over and changed her clothes.

For the first hour or two she was so busy that she didn't worry that they were late.

By eight o'clock she had begun to worry but she busied herself lighting a fire in the front room, dusting, cutting bread and butter and making sandwiches.

By ten o'clock she was tired and frightened, wondering if she should go to the police station; they'd said they'd be home by half past five.

It was almost half past eleven by the time they arrived. They'd missed the train, that's all, and had had to get a later one.

'It doesn't matter a bit,' Laura said. 'I wasn't worried.'

'Why didn't you go to bed?' her father asked her. 'Fancy waiting up till this time of night.'

'Don't be so daft,' Annie said, putting her arms round her. 'As though she'd go to bed before we came home. Don't you think she wants to see us?'

'I've made you some sandwiches but they've all curled up.'

'I don't want anything,' her father said, 'we had a pie in the station.'

'I'm ever so hungry,' Annie said. 'I'll eat them all. Hand them over.'

'Do you like your tea weak or strong?' Laura asked her.

'Strong,' Annie said. 'Strong with plenty of sugar.'

When they'd eaten, Annie brought out a bundle of presents for her. A beautiful Easter egg, a cup and saucer with 'A present from Blackpool' written on it in gold, a French doll dressed in a black and white satin dress and a black velvet hat, a blue leather purse, some red ribbon, a mirror in a red suède case, sugared almonds, a clockwork mouse.

'A load of rubbish,' her father said. 'I kept telling her you wasn't a kid. She thinks you're a kid. I kept telling her that all you liked was books.'

'They're lovely. I've never had so many presents. Thank you very much.'

'A big girl, rising fifteen,' her father said. 'A working girl by rights.'

'Now you're making her cry, you great bully. Come on, carry her up to bed. She's tired out. It's gone midnight.'

'I can't carry her.'

'Of course you can. You can carry me, can't you, and she's half my size. Come on, pick her up. I'll bring her presents and she can look at them in bed. Come on.'

Her father was angry and embarrassed, Laura could see that, but at last he did as he was told.

'Here we are then,' Annie said when they reached her bedroom. 'Didn't I say you'd manage it.'

Her father left without even saying goodnight, but Annie stayed on, helping her get undressed and talking to her about all the wonders of Blackpool until she fell asleep.

Chapter Two

Annie wasn't perfect, of course she wasn't. She wasn't always reliable. She'd promise to get something from town on her way from work, something Laura urgently needed for school, and she'd come back without it; she'd promise to be home early for a special meal and she'd be half an hour late; but as far as Laura was concerned she was very nearly perfect. She was always good-tempered, always affectionate, always full of high spirits.

She was extremely generous with her money. She bought Laura new clothes, school uniform, PT wear and anything else she needed, from her club or from the market stall. Sometimes Laura could tell that they were second-hand but they were never out of fashion – Annie knew about fashion. Nobody in school made fun of her any more.

Laura's mother had been gentle and devoted but undemonstrative, shy. Annie kissed and hugged exuberantly. Laura stopped envying other girls their well-dressed, quietly-spoken mothers; suddenly they seemed prissy and artificial. Annie wasn't the sort to offer her face blankly for a kiss, she didn't measure out her love in little pecks; all day it bubbled over in sudden quick hugs and endearments, often rude words Laura had never heard before; sweet words like fanny and titty were to remind her of Annie for the rest of her life.

Even when she was rushed in the morning – and she always was – she never lost her temper. 'Where's me gloves? Who's got me scarf? Shift your big bum out the way, you're sittin' on me bleedin' scarf. Useless bloody kid, what 'ave you done with me fags? Give us a kiss and hurry off to school and don't forget to work hard. Now where the 'ell's me shopping-bag?'

Every evening after tea she embarrassed Laura's father by sitting on his lap and ruffling his hair. 'Get off, you,' he'd say. 'Can't you see I'm reading my paper? Whatever's made you so rough?'

'Having five sisters and three brothers, I suppose,' she'd said once, suddenly in a quieter mood. 'There was always a rough and tumble in our 'ouse. We lived like piglets round a trough.'

Perhaps if Laura's father had given his daughter too much of his attention and love, it might have made Annie a little resentful. As it was she was always critical of him. 'Fine sort of a father you are,' she'd say. 'Beasts of the fields are better fathers than you are. No, *you* come and wipe the dishes, thank you, she's got her school work.'

Annie regarded Laura's school work as something holy. She cleared the table after their tea, laid a clean cloth on it and then set out her books in rows. 'We'll go to the pub, now, to give you a chance to study,' she'd say, hugging her.

'I haven't got any money,' Laura's father would say grumpily.

'I may have a bob or two. If not we'll just have a nice walk past C & A's windows.'

'You just like to be out gallivanting all the time. Laura's work is nothing but an excuse.'

'Perhaps you're right,' she'd say amiably. 'I do like seeing people. I do like a bit of life.'

When they came back she was always anxious to know how much work Laura had done.

'I've only done some reading tonight.'

Reading disappointed Annie. She liked to see page after page of small, neat writing. 'That's good,' she'd say. 'That's very good. Isn't this good work, Harry?'

'It's OK,' her father would say, picking up his newspaper.

She'd point to the teacher's comment at the end of the previous piece of work, an inch or two of even smaller writing in red ink. 'Read this out to me,' she'd say.

Any hint of criticism on the teacher's part angered and upset her.

'"Not fully explored." What does she mean "not fully explored"? That woman's got it in for you. What's her name? Miss Campbell? Crabby old spinster. I know her sort. Three pages of neat writing and she's still not satisfied. *Her* writing's like a butcher's bill, not meant to be understood. You tell her that from me, will you, Laura. "Not fully explored" indeed. I'll Miss Campbell 'er. A mean old bitch, that's what she is.'

Only 'excellent work' satisfied Annie.

'"Excellent work," eh? Yes, she's right. What teacher was that? Miss Salmon? All right, you can introduce me to old Miss Salmon any time you want to, I wouldn't mind shakin' her hand. She knows a thing or two, and she's like me: not afraid to be generous. I'd get along fine with old Miss Fishpaste.'

'You're superior, Laura,' she said one night when she and Laura's father had been out in the pub longer than usual and were both a little the worse for it. 'It's great to have brains. You're a cut above, you are. You're like your mother. Your mother was a lady.'

'Did you know my mother?'

'No, I didn't know her. But Mrs Dunn's told me things. So 'as Harry's mother.'

'Grandma didn't get on with her at all.'

'Well, she wouldn't, would she?'

'She wasn't a real lady you know. She was in service before she got married.'

'A lady's maid. Oh, you have to be very smart and lady-like to be a lady's maid. She was clever too, I bet.'

'Yes, I think so. She loved books.'

'You 'ave your brains from her. Your Dad's not too bright, is he, or 'e wouldn't 'ave taken up with a dummy like me.'

'You're not a dummy. You're the most intelligent person I know.'

'Intelligent? That's a laugh, that is.'

'You enjoy life, don't you? You make the most of things. Isn't that intelligence? When I grow up I want to be just like you. I want to be free and happy, I want to swagger through life like you do, enjoying myself and wearing street-walker's clothes.'

Her father put his newspaper down and came towards her. 'What did you say?' he roared.

But he didn't give her time to repeat herself. He struck her hard across the face, so hard that she fell backwards against the sideboard, scattering dishes and cutlery as she fell.

She lay on the floor, her hand across her mouth, looking up at him.

'You're a brave one, you are,' Annie said quietly, getting down on her knees to Laura. 'She doesn't even know what a street-walker is. It's something she's probably heard from your mother. "That woman dresses like a street-walker," can't you just hear her? And you hit your own flesh and blood for repeating something she doesn't even understand.'

Annie helped Laura up and sat her on a chair by the fire. She put a handkerchief on her mouth which was beginning to bleed.

'You call her a clever girl one minute,' her father was saying defensively, 'the next minute you say she doesn't know what a street-walker is. I hit her because she said you were like a street-walker.'

'Don't you dare hit her again, whatever she calls me. She can call me whatever she likes, do you hear me, and most of what she'll say might be true. If you ever hit her again I'll leave this house and take her with me, too. I mean it.'

Laura let Annie take her upstairs to bed.

'Don't quarrel with Dad any more,' she said. 'I don't like it. I'm sorry I was so daft. I suppose a street-walker is a prostitute; I should have thought. What a dreadful thing to say about you. I thought it was just someone smart and rather grand.'

'Anyway, prostitutes are not too bad, you know. There's plenty of people worse than prostitutes.'

'I suppose so.'

'Oh yes, plenty of people. People who make money out of other people's misery and 'ardship are much worse than prostitutes.'

'But anyway, don't quarrel with my Dad any more. He looks so hurt when you shout at him.'

'Don't ever be sorry for a man, Laura. Hurt or not, they always have the last word, don't you forget that.'

*

Her father came up later on and apologised to her. He looked very miserable as he stood at the door looking at her sitting up in bed, her lip cut and swollen.

When she accepted his apologies he became self-pitying again. 'You turn against me,' he said. 'You like Annie much better than your old Dad, don't you?'

Laura said nothing. It was true, of course. Blood wasn't thicker than love.

'We're women together,' she said at last.

Should she have felt sorry for her father? Annie certainly didn't pander to him as her mother had done. When he coughed his trench cough Annie only advised him not to smoke so much. She didn't even get him a cup of tea in the morning. When Annie brought home a tea-time treat he got his share but no more; if one piece chanced to be bigger than another, that was always for Laura. She made fun of his war-time exploits. 'Men are such heroes, Laura, when they're off playing war together. Pity they're so small-minded and soft when they come back 'ome.' He soon learnt that to interest Annie he had to talk about what had happened at work that day, she wasn't interested in yesterday, let alone in the events of twenty years ago. Well, she was right, Laura thought. He'd had too much of his own way.

Her father left the room and went downstairs.

A year passed; a happy year for Laura, punctuated by regular treats like tea and doughnuts in the market café on Saturday afternoon after looking round the shops, breakfast in bed; bacon and egg and sausage and fried bread, on Sunday morning and best of all pictures on Friday night.

On Friday, every Friday, Annie would rush home from work, light of step and bursting to be off. 'I won't be two shakes getting changed. 'Ave you got me cup of tea ready? It's a double-feature tonight, Myrna Loy, she's me favourite, and Sabu in "Jungle Adventure".'

They walked to the bus stop arm-in-arm, Annie giving her a hopelessly involved but spell-binding account of some previous film on the way. 'No, I forgot to say that before she met this man, she'd been friendly with this other man who'd once been engaged to her best friend's cousin, and this other man, whatever was his name, he wasn't exactly a crook, but he certainly hadn't led a blameless life, well, who has, and it was him that put the spanner in the works, only in the end of course it turned out a blessing in disguise because . . .' Laura, though unable to follow the convolutions of the plot, loved the adult intimacy of it; Annie squeezing her arm to press home some point too delicate to put into words, 'You understand don't you,' the dark around them; Laura anticipating her life as a woman, complicated and rich, as well as the film they were going to see.

In the splendid, red-carpeted foyer they had to decide whether to have a box of chocolates, 'Magic Centres', or fish and chips on the way home. 'Fish and chips,' Annie would say at last, 'and a tu'penny bar of chocolate between us for now, you choose which.'

They always sat in the cheapest seats.

Annie talked her way through the film, advising the women, admonishing the men, always foreseeing the consequences, but even so crying copiously at the end, squeezing Laura's arm again and again as her large, warm shoulders rose and fell and her perfume, Devon Violets or Attar of Roses, scented the warm darkness like real violets or roses in summer rain.

Walking home afterwards, they were silent but satisfied, and the fish and chips, liberally sprinkled with vinegar and salt, seemed the taste of fulfilment.

At this time, Laura's other friends counted for very little. Susan Wilkins was good enough for the working day, but whenever she suggested that they met in the evening or at the weekend like other girls of fourteen and fifteen, Laura would always prevaricate; she had to visit her grandma, do the shopping, run errands. The truth was that she wanted Annie's company, wanted Annie, and moreover wanted her to herself. Susan was bright and pert and lively, everyone's favourite. If Annie met Susan, might not she, Laura, seem awkward and dull by comparison? She took great care to keep them apart.

*

The only difficult part of her life, now, was when she had to visit her grandmother in the school holidays. And to make it worse, she had the feeling that she was made to go, not so much for the old woman's sake, but because her father enjoyed a greater freedom when she was away.

Her grandmother seemed dirtier each time she visited her, the tea weaker, the margarine cheaper, the bread more unpalatable. Each time, too, the kitchen - and her bed - smelt more strongly of chickens. Laura could hardly bear to stay there even for one night.

She mumbled now, and sucked her cheeks instead of eating. In the night she sat up in bed and complained and shouted; someone, everyone, had cheated her.

''E didn't give me the change for the coal. I counted the bags. 'E was two short. 'E still owes me three bob.'

'I'll tell him,' Laura would say. 'I'll have it out with him in the morning. He must be a rotten sort, cheating an old woman. Where does he live . . . ? In Wicklow Road . . . ? Why don't you tell me?'

''E's dead now, you stupid girl. 'Is son's 'ad the business twenty years. Only I 'as mine from Oughtons; the son was as bad as his father; the best Welsh coal was nothin' but slack.'

Her voice would change again. 'I tapped on the window. "Hey you," I said. "You can't get away wi' that. Think I can't bleedin' count? 'Alf a ton is ten bags and 'alf a ton I paid for. Think you can cheat me because I'm a widow. That's it, ain't it? I'll get the police, see if I don't."'

Sometimes the thought of the police seemed to pacify her; she'd lie down quietly and let Laura pull the bed-clothes over her shoulders.

At other times she'd side-step to another ancient wrong. 'It was Billy 'Opkins's mother. She knew it were mine, but she sold it to the rag an' bone man. "It was in my garden," she said. Aye, it was 'er boy, 'im that used to play with our Jack, as took it to 'er garden. Don't you ever play with that Billy 'Opkins again, do you 'ear me?'

'She should be in a Home,' Laura had told Annie when she came back after the Easter visit that year.

'Oh no, she's happier in her own house.'

'Annie, she can't be. Her legs are so swollen she can hardly walk. She doesn't eat. She hoards her money; she keeps it all in that tin she's got on her mantlepiece.'

'But she gets pleasure from it just the same. Old people love money; well, what else 'ave they got? My grandma used to 'ave a great big 'andbag and she used to spend 'alf an hour at a time looking through it; counting the coppers, unfolding some little pieces of paper with some words or figures scribbled on 'em. "Where's me bag?" she used to ask whenever she fell asleep and it had slipped down the side of 'er chair. "Who's taken me bag?" "Here it is, Gran. No one's taken it." "They better not an' all," she used to say. After she died we were all afraid to open the bleedin' thing. We should 'ave buried it with 'er, by rights.'

'She's filthy, Annie.'

'Would be she 'appier, though, in a hospital where they'd wash her every day and keep her tucked up in a clean white bed? We could 'ave 'er here for a week or two if you'd like to, but who'd look after her chickens if we did?'

'She doesn't sleep at night. She sits up and storms at people all night; Dad and you and the vicar and the rent-man, and other people who've been dead twenty or thirty years.'

'Old age is criminal I know, but she's got her freedom, Laura.'

'Freedom? What freedom? Freedom to hobble down the garden two or three times a day, a once-a-week excursion to the corner shop in her slippers.'

'When I was there last she showed me some primroses down the garden, she seemed pleased as Punch with them. "Come and see me flowers," she said.'

'Yes, and she said you stole some of her mint.'

'Oh Lord, I took her some best tea and a quarter of nice cooked 'am, and yes, I did pinch one stem of her bleedin' mint. She's still an old bitch, isn't she?'

'I'll go to see her every Saturday afternoon, but I'm not staying with her again. I can't, Annie. It's the smell. It's the decay.'

In September that year, Laura's father got a job in a car factory. It was better paid than the garage and the hours were shorter. Unfortunately, though, he occasionally had to work nights. He didn't mind this too much, but Annie did.

She took to going out on her own.

'I must let you work, love, because of your School Certificate.'

'Oh blow my School Certificate. Did you do your school certificate, Annie?'

'Don't be silly.'

Towards the middle of October Mrs Dunn next door let Laura know that her husband had seen Annie in a pub down-town with a strange man.

'It's her brother,' Laura said. 'He's a commercial traveller. He's home all this week and next.'

Mrs Dunn pretended to believe her. All the same she said she couldn't, any longer, manage their washing. 'It's getting too much for me, Laura,' she said. 'And you know I've always done it for love, never for financial reward. It's my back, you see. I can't cope any more, not with other people's sheets.'

Laura said that she quite understood.

Laura told Annie about the washing but not about the 'strange man'.

'Well, your Dad will have to pay the laundry bills, won't he? He's getting more money in the new job.'

'Didn't you even try to persuade her to change her mind?' her father said when he heard about it. 'Laundry indeed. Laundries charge the earth. I'll go over and plead with her a bit. I'll say we can't manage without her.'

'Of course we can manage without the old bag,' Annie said. 'We'll send the sheets to the laundry and I'll do the rest.'

'I'll help you,' Laura said. 'Don't go to see her, Dad.'

'Did she give any reason for giving up? Look, I'll go and offer her three bob a week; she'll do anything for money.'

'She can't cope any more; she gets rheumatism.'

'I'll go and offer her three and sixpence.'

'I'll go tomorrow if you like,' Laura said. 'I think she's off you because you got a new job and her husband's still on the dole.'

'Is that what's biting her?'

'I think so. It might be.'

In bed that night, Laura realised that she'd become an accomplished liar. And this in defence of a step-mother who was going out with another man and letting her father down. Well, women had to stick together, as Annie often said.

All the same, she tried to persuade her not to go out the following night.

'I wish you'd stay in tonight to keep me company. I could do with someone to talk to; I've got the curse coming.'

'You've got your work to do, Miss.'

'I don't have to work every night.'

'Oh yes you do. Your Headmistress said so. Three hours every night; that's what she said in that letter. You've got to come top, you know that, don't you. One 'undred per cent.'

'Stay in with me, Annie.'

'Whatever will I do stuck in all night while you're busy working? I can't even listen to the wireless when you're working.'

'Yes you can.'

'It'll disturb you. Nobody can work with 'Ippodrome on.'

'Why don't you read?'

'I can't read. Only things like Exit and No Smoking and Public Bar. I never learnt to read books.'

'Haven't you got any ironing to do?'

'Ironing! I'll tell you what. I'll just go out for half an hour. I'll pop in to "The Three Bells", have one little drink and bring back a nip of brandy for you; that'll be much better for your fanny than aspirin. All right?'

'All right.' (What else could she say?) 'Only don't be longer than half an hour.'

She was much longer than half an hour. At eleven o'clock, realising how ashamed and contrite she would be when she came home, Laura decided to go to bed. She heard her creeping in about an hour later. When Laura got downstairs in the morning Annie had already gone to work. There was a chocolate bar on her plate; a peace offering, she supposed.

*

Laura didn't try to prevent her going out after that. Every night, though, she was frightened of the consequences; she was sure Mrs Dunn would soon find an opportunity to let her father know what Annie was up to; something catastrophic was bound to happen; occasionally fear would almost choke her.

But nothing disastrous happened. Day followed day, week followed week.

And when her father came off nights a month later, Laura balanced things up with God by going to her grandmother's for the weekend.

She found the old woman surprisingly quiet. Her hair was combed, she'd had the district nurse in to bandage her leg and she invited Laura to open a tin of soup for their tea.

'How's that woman?' she said, when they were sitting at the table.

'Annie? She's very well. She's sent you some chocolate mints; the ones you like.'

'How's she behavin' to my 'Arry?'

'They get on fine.'

'That's not what I asked. I said, how's she behavin' to 'im.'

'I don't know what you mean.'

'Yes you do. I know the answer too . . . I always did. You know what she is, don't you? A bad woman.'

The old woman sucked at her cheeks - she had left her soup - and Laura felt a stirring of pity for her, and for her father.

They had a moment's communication.

'I love her,' Laura said then.

The storm of invective she had expected didn't materialise. Her grandmother only went on looking at her and sucking at her cheeks.

Laura - and her father - visited the old woman again on Christmas Eve.

On this occasion, to Laura's great relief, she didn't mention Annie; the ' 'er' she mentioned, ' 'er keeps saying I should eat greens' and ' 'er comes 'ere and puts polish on the lino, 'er wants to kill me off I reckon', seeming rather to refer to Laura's mother.

She seemed fairly comfortable; she had an adequate supply of coal and paraffin, though not much food apart from what Annie had sent over. 'I 'as bread-an'-milk twice a day,' she said when Laura tried to get her to eat a piece of Christmas cake, 'I 'as cocoa and digestion biscuits at night and I don't want nothing else.'

'Shall I make you a cup of cocoa now?' Laura asked her.

'Does the little girl manage the kettle?' she asked Laura's father.

'Little girl! She's taller than me,' he said. 'She's nearly seventeen. Of course she manages the bloody kettle.'

He wouldn't be convinced that his mother's mind was crumbling. Thinking it was another of her tricks, he kept shooting sly questions at her. 'What was the name of that brother of yours that went to Australia?' 'For Go' sake, what you want to know that for? He died in February 1908.' She then reeled off the names of his seven children and his various addresses in Victoria and New South Wales - and in the next breath asked her son when he was leaving the army.

Too exasperated to go on talking to her - he realised that he hadn't really talked to her for over twenty years, if ever - he went upstairs to mend a rattling window pane she'd been complaining about, while Laura tried to rid the kitchen of various remnants of decaying food and the worst of the grease and grime.

'Thur, I've drunk it right down to the dirt,' the old woman said, handing back her cocoa-cup to Laura.

'I don't like to think of her spending Christmas Day on her own,' Laura said as she and her father walked to the bus stop later. 'I should go back tomorrow to keep her company.'

But of course she didn't.

They had a lovely Christmas. Annie had managed to get herself an extra job as a waitress in the preceding weeks and had bought them all expensive presents and delicious food.

It was a cold Sunday morning three weeks after Christmas when the blow fell.

Laura was late getting up. When she went in to the living

room she found Annie already there dressed in her outdoor clothes, two suitcases at her side. She looked like someone on a stage-set.

'I'm leaving your Dad,' she said. 'We're splitting up... your Dad and me... I'm leaving... I 'ave to leave.'

Laura had imagined all manner of dreadful consequences; terrible quarrels, even violence, but never that one.

'No,' she said. Her voice sounded like someone warding off physical assault. 'No.'

It was beyond belief.

She burst into tears; she didn't try to control herself. 'You mustn't leave me, Annie, you can't leave. You must take me with you if you go. I can't bear you to go.'

Annie paled at the girl's passionate sobbing. 'You don't understand,' she said.

It was some time before Laura could answer.

'I do understand. I do understand. You've got another man, you've got a man-friend. I do understand. I've known for a long time. Mrs Dunn told me ages ago, oh, last October it must have been. I don't care. Why should I care? It doesn't matter. I only care about you.'

'Oh, Laura, you must care. You must care about your Dad. He's upset as well, love. You must care about him.'

'I don't care about him. Why should I care about him? What has he ever done for me? He's only my father. You're the one I care about. You're everything to me: you love me.'

Annie had never really analysed her feelings for Laura; she was a nice kid, a good kid; she did love her, perhaps.

'I do love you,' she said. 'Of course I do. But I can't stay here any longer. I can't. It's impossible.'

'You're pregnant aren't you?' Laura asked.

Annie shivered and seemed about to break down. 'Yes,' she said.

'And it's not Dad's baby? Is that it?'

'I don't know. I think it is. But I 'ave got another man, you're right; it could be his... I'm not sure... Anyway that isn't the point, not really.'

'What is the point?'

'I'm not going to have it in any case. I'm much too old to have a baby.'

'You're not old, Annie. You're young. You're young.'

'Laura, I'm thirty-six. That's much too old to have a baby. That's much too old to settle down. I don't mean to. I don't mean to give up my work. I can't.'

'Dad wouldn't mind, would he? He wouldn't mind if you gave up your job and had a baby? He's getting more money now, you know he is.'

'It doesn't matter how much money he's getting; that's his money, Laura. I've had my own money too long to settle for hand-outs from him. A woman, a woman like me, can't be happy unless she's her own boss and has her own money. I couldn't flatter a man for every shilling I want, I never could. I've always been independent.'

Laura had a sudden vision of her mother, how she seemed to fade in her father's presence.

'I can leave school and get work,' she said. 'I'm nearly seventeen. I can get a good job. You can have my money; all of it. I can get a job in a shop.'

'Never. You'll stay in school and get your certificate and a job as a secretary in an office. That's what your mother wanted for you and that's what you'll do. How do you think I'd feel if you threw away all your schooling for me?'

They looked sadly at each other.

'Do you mean to have an illegal operation?' Laura asked.

'You know too much all of a sudden.'

'I know they're very dangerous.'

Ever since her foolish mistake about the street-walker, Laura's reading on the various facts of life had been thorough, even formidable. She suddenly flung her arms round Annie. 'Seventeen per cent of all back-street abortions are fatal,' she said. 'Oh God, seventeen per cent.'

Annie loosened Laura's grip. 'Well,' she said, 'if you do your sums properly . . . wait a minute . . . that means that eighty-three per cent of them are perfectly safe. Those are very good odds, you know; much better than fifty-fifty.'

'Oh Annie, it's not a joke.'

'I've had one before, love, and more than one. I'm all right, aren't I? Only the good die young.'

'Will you come back when it's over?'

'No. Your father won't have me back. He doesn't want me

to have . . . an operation. If I do he won't have anything else to do with me.'

'He'll change his mind.'

'But he won't change his views. I'll be someone else in his eyes, someone he despises. And that won't do for me. I may be a bad lot but I've got me pride.'

'You're not a bad lot, of course you're not, don't be silly. If you must have an abortion then I suppose you must. But you mustn't let it break up your marriage. Oh Annie, doesn't marriage mean anything to you?'

'Not much, love.'

She looked bleakly at Laura. 'I am married, love,' she said, 'but not to your Dad. I'm sorry, Laura. We thought it best not to tell you. You were so young at the time. You were a little kid two years ago.'

'So you're not even my step-mother?'

'No, not really.'

'Oh, that's terrible. We're not related at all?'

'No. But we're friends aren't we; good friends. Won't that do?'

'But you're going away! I won't even have you as a friend.'

'Not right away. Not from the town.'

Annie hesitated. 'I'll let you have my address, Laura. I'm getting a room over the other end of town, not so very far from your grandma's. You'll be able to visit us both on a Saturday afternoon; two old biddies.'

'I can't believe you're really going. Does my father know?'

'Yes. He tried to throw me out last night but I wouldn't go without talking to you first. So *'e* went out somewhere.'

'Can't I make you some breakfast? Just some tea and some toast?'

'No, I've 'ad breakfast. I 'ad it hours ago. I never went to bed. I've just sat here waiting for you to get up.'

'Don't go. Please don't go.'

As Annie left at last she wondered if she had ever been loved so truly.

Chapter Three

The next morning, after a day and a night of weeping, Laura felt too ill to go to school. When her father came in – he was back on nights – she was lying in the armchair with a rug over her. He looked surprised to see her but said nothing. Later, when he was making breakfast for himself, he brought her a cup of tea, put it down on the table by her side and stood staring at her.

'I don't want to hear anything about that woman ever again, do you hear me. As far as I'm concerned, she's never been here. As far as I'm concerned she's dead. She's run me ragged, that woman 'as. She's made a monkey out of me.'

Laura wondered whether he was suffering. She examined him closely. He didn't seem to be. He looked the same as usual, a small, tough man, hard-hearted. She wondered how she could hurt him.

'I've lost two mothers,' she said.

'Don't be so bloody dramatic. Annie wasn't nobody's mother; wasn't fit to be.'

'You thought she was fit to be your . . . woman. "A man gets lonely" you told me before you brought her home. Won't you be "lonely" any more?'

'Perhaps I'll meet somebody decent.'

'Don't bring her here if you do. I hate decent people.'

'I'll bring her here if I want to. This is my house; don't you forget it. You're getting too big for your boots, my girl. You've never done a day's work in your life yet, and you almost seventeen. At your age I was up at six every morning and walking three miles to work, winter and summer. How much longer do I have to keep you in that school of yours?'

'You don't keep me. I have a scholarship.'

'That only pays your fees. Who pays for your food and your fancy uniform? Who pays for your books? Nearly five pounds this last year, don't forget that.'

'Annie paid for my uniform. You never give me a penny for clothes.'

'And I won't, either. Why should I? Go out and earn them.'

'All right I will. I'll leave school.'

'Please yourself.'

'I'll leave school and get a job in a factory. I'll go and live with Grandma.'

'You're stupid enough for anything. Two mad ones together. I'm going to bed.'

After the scene with her father, Laura managed to sleep for a few hours. When she woke, she packed some clothes, took half a crown from the rent money and went to her grandmother's. She had no intention of staying there for any length of time; her flight was merely a gesture of protest and defiance.

In the clean, white sunshine of the January afternoon, her grandmother's house looked more neglected than ever: the windows filthy, the curtains torn, the front yard full of swirling litter.

She knocked at the door but there was no reply. She knocked again and again. She banged on the front-room window and after a while her grandmother appeared in the bare unused room brandishing a stick. She didn't recognise her grand-daughter.

She went round to the back, but the door from the entry was locked. She got a stick and banged on the corrugated iron roof of the hen-house, hoping the noise of the hens would bring her out to investigate; it usually did. To her surprise there was complete silence from the hen-house.

At last she called on the long-suffering, long-estranged couple who lived next door.

'She's been took queer,' the old man said. 'She probably thought you was the district nurse; there's always trouble when the district nurse comes. Aye, they took away them hens because she can't feed them. *She* should be took away by rights, she's nothing but a nuisance here.'

'She's happier in her own home,' Laura said.

'Maybe so,' the old man said, his tone becoming less hostile. 'I takes her a loaf of bread, but she don't pay me.'

Laura gave him a shilling and promised to send more.

'I don't mind as long as she don't start shouting and raving in the night,' he said.

'Grandma,' Laura called through the letter-box. 'Grandma.'

The old man stood watching her. 'She thinks you're the nurse,' he said. 'The nurse 'as a terrible job. She 'ad to go away last time. My missus took her some tinned milk and some tea last week but she don't pay her.'

Laura promised to send his missus money. She banged on the door again. 'She'll starve to death,' she said.

'She's better mornings,' the old man said. 'You send some money and my missus will buy 'er sugar and tea and bread. You send a postal order. My missus leaves 'em on the doorstep and in 'alf an hour they're took in.'

Laura put her ear to the letter-box.

'What can you 'ear?' the old man asked.

'She's banging away at something.'

'She does that.'

'I may as well go then,' Laura said. 'I'll get my father to send you some money.'

She straightened herself up feeling a little more cheerful; she'd heard the unmistakable sounds of a hen - or two - coming from the back-kitchen: her grandmother had put one over on "them", "they" hadn't quite defeated her; not yet. She felt tears pricking her eyes.

'She's cussed,' the old man said. 'You ought to hear her shouting in the night. No one can do nothin' for her.'

After hanging about for an hour or so, again trying the front of the house and then the back, Laura gave up and went home.

The next morning she went back to school.

She felt more lonely than she'd ever felt in her life. Her friend, Susan Wilkins, had left the previous term, all the other girls seemed haughty and unfriendly, her home was cold and cheerless, she had nothing to look forward to, nothing to live for.

Her father kept out of her way. As soon as she arrived home from school at about five, he got up from bed and went out without even having a meal.

On Friday when he left ten shillings for her to get the groceries, she sent a five-shilling postal order to her grandmother's neighbours. She'd worried about having to ask for money but she didn't have to; neither she nor her father seemed to be eating, so there was no need to buy much food.

On Saturday afternoon she went over to the address Annie had given her; she had told her not to try to find her until the Sunday, but she could wait no longer.

She found the house without much difficulty. It was a Victorian monster in a run-down street near the canal, the smell of the canal hanging over it.

There were several bells on the front door. She tried them all but none of them seemed to work, no one answered. Some children ran past pointing at her and jeering; they called something after her when they'd gone some distance, she pretended not to hear.

She tried the door and to her surprise it opened. The tiled hall smelled of musty old cupboards, damp clothes, dampness, the canal.

She could hear no sounds of life from any of the rooms leading from the ground-floor hallway. She went up the uncarpeted stairs to the first floor, the noise of her feet echoing through the house.

She lost her nerve. She tapped on the first door she came to.

It was flung open by a large middle-aged woman who seemed to be expecting someone.

'Can I help you?' she asked. Her face was not made-up but painted; a painted lady like a butterfly. Her clothes, too, were brightly coloured, pink and purple and brown.

'I'm looking for . . . Annie.'

'Who?'

'Annie Brown. Do you know her?'

'I don't think so.'

'She's just moved in here. This week.'

'Then she must be up the top. Two floors up, ducky.' Her smile was unnerving; an illustration from a book suddenly smiling.

'Is she ill?' she asked, as Laura turned to go.

'I . . . I don't know.'

'There's been a doctor . . . Is it your mother, ducky?'

'Yes.'

'Call back if you want something. I'm in all afternoon.'

The surprising smile again. The smell of stale perfume.

'Thank you.'

Laura's legs felt stiff and painful as she went up the next two flights of stairs.

The house was very quiet. There was no sign of life, no sounds of children playing, no one shouting or quarrelling or singing. Nothing but the smell. It had changed now, it was salty like sweat, but warmer and darker.

Laura's heart was hammering. 'There's worse to come, there's worse to come,' it thudded against her ribs.

By this time she was expecting the worst.

When she found Annie she thought she was already dead. When, after a moment or two, she noticed a faint pulse in her neck, her instinct was to take her by the shoulders and shake her into life.

She got down on her knees by the bed.

'For God's sake don't wake her,' the woman said, pulling at her shoulder.

The woman was small and soft-spoken, perhaps Irish, and seemed to be looking after Annie.

Laura followed her to the other side of the room. 'Are you Laura?' she whispered. 'She said a Laura Brown might come.'

'What can I do? She can't stay here.'

The room had no furniture in it except the narrow bed, a deal table and a marble-topped washstand; no chairs or cupboards, no washing or cooking facilities. It was dismally cold; there seemed no heating.

'Is this all she has?'

'There's a kitchen of sorts along the landing and a w.c. on the next floor. I look after her. I could get an oil stove but it's five shillings deposit.'

'I've got five shillings.'

'She's warm enough in bed; she's got my quilt on her. You can get her half a bottle of brandy for five shillings; that's what she needs. She's very bad.'

'How bad?' Laura said quietly. 'Will she die?'

'She may do.'

'Has the doctor been? The woman downstairs said there was a doctor here.'

'He said he couldn't do anything unless... unless... she told him who...'

'Who did it?'

'That's right.'

'But that's wicked. That's torture, that is.'

'There's another doctor.'

'Where? Where can I find him?'

'It's a woman. Go to the hospital and ask for her address. It's a Dr Cunningham.'

Laura ran downstairs. As she passed the first floor landing the woman who had helped her earlier flung open the door again and looked at her questioningly.

'Can you lend me some money?' Laura said. 'I'll pay you back, I promise.' (She'd steal it if necessary.)

'How much do you want?'

'Two pounds.'

The woman hesitated, but not for long. Leaving Laura at the door for a moment, she came back, the notes held out in front of her. 'How bad is she?' she asked.

'Very bad.'

She got a bus to the hospital almost at once. It seemed a good omen. She got off at the gates and ran up the drive.

At the main doors, she breathed deeply to try to calm her nerves, drew herself up to her full height and advanced, very upright, to the reception desk. 'I've mislaid Dr Cunningham's address,' she said.

The receptionist gave it to her without question.

'And now, could you please call me a taxi. I have an appointment with her in half an hour.'

She'd never been in a taxi before.

Dr Cunningham lived in a detached house on the Warwick Road.

The brass plate on the gate gave the surgery hours; she was two hours early. She went up to the door and pressed the bell.

A tall, heavy, middle-aged man answered the door.

'I want Dr Cunningham, please.'

'I'm Dr Cunningham.'

'Dr Helen Cunningham, please.'

It was some minutes before Dr Helen Cunningham appeared; she was younger than her husband, about thirty, small and rather grave. She scrutinised Laura for what seemed to her an age, then invited her in.

She took her into a large oak-panelled room and pointed to a chair. 'Sit down,' she said. 'Sit down and tell me about it.'

Laura sat down: again she could feel her heart thumping.

'My mother is very ill; she's going to die.'

'What's her name? Is she one of my patients?'

'No.' Laura looked up at the doctor, her eyes glittering. 'But someone told me you'd help her . . . Only you.'

'I see. When did it happen?'

'I don't know. This week. Tuesday or Wednesday. Will you come to see her? I can pay you.'

'I can't. I'm very sorry. You see, I could be . . . well . . . struck off the register of doctors. You don't understand . . . You see, I've been involved too many times; I've been warned . . . I daren't come or they'd think I'd . . . I'm very sorry.'

'Can you give her tablets?'

'They won't cure her. I can't promise anything.'

'I know.'

'How old are you?'

'Twenty-one.'

'I'll give you six tablets. Give her two when the pain is very bad.'

'Won't I need more than six?'

'I don't think so. You can come back if you do. I can't give you more now.'

Dr Cunningham left the room and came back holding out a small white envelope. Laura handed her a pound note.

'I'll go then,' she said. 'I've asked the taxi to wait.'

'Where are you getting this money?' the doctor asked her. 'You look like a school-girl.'

'I'm twenty-one,' Laura said. It was quicker than trying to explain.

Laura stayed with Annie until she died at eleven o'clock the next morning. Annie, who was conscious some of the time, recognised her, squeezed her hand and even smiled at her once or twice.

She was in great pain while she was conscious; the tablets were of little use because she was too weak to swallow them.

On Sunday evening Laura went home.

Her father didn't seem surprised at her news. 'You shouldn't have gone over there. Do you want to involve me in it? I begged her not to do it; over and over again. You'll never know what a dance she led me.'

When she told him she needed money to pay some debts, he gave her ten pounds. She'd never held so much money before.

'It's your Grandma's,' he said. 'She died yesterday. She had twenty pounds in a tin on her mantlepiece and I'm giving you half.'

He got to his feet and walked to the door. 'Get yourself some clothes or some books; whatever you like.'

She listened to him walking upstairs to bed.

Chapter Four

For almost three months Laura went through a period of horror, living and re-living Annie's death, her mind so full of pain that she couldn't even concentrate on her school work.

Spring. By this time she was able to cry and then, gradually, her grief became manageable.

She and her father observed a truce. They co-existed, sharing the house-work and shopping, usually taking their simple meals separately, leaving notes for each other when they were going to be late or absent. He was often late. She realised that he was drinking a great deal.

Laura began to pity him and allow that he was also unhappy, though she always knew that his suffering was nothing like hers.

He went away for a few days over the Whitsun holiday. When he came back she noticed that he'd bought himself some new clothes; he was suddenly looking smarter and younger. She found that she was pleased.

'Tell me what you've got against me,' he said the evening he got back. It was as though he wanted to put their relationship on a new footing. 'Just what have you got to complain of? *She* was the wrong 'un, not me. I didn't want her to do what she did. I'd 'ave let her stay, baby an' all. I might 'ave lost my temper a bit when she first told me about the other chap, I might 'ave hit out, what man wouldn't? Where was I to blame. Just tell me that.'

Laura looked hard at him. Pain rose to her throat. 'You weren't to blame,' she said.

Perhaps he wasn't to blame. He'd had a rough upbringing. (Her grandmother's death hadn't blinded her to her defects.) He'd never been encouraged to think; he'd had too few years at school, too many in the army, too much harshness and hardship. Her mother, who'd been afraid to stand up to him, had probably contributed to his insensitivity, his coarseness. How could he have met Annie on any equal terms? What communication could there have been between them, she so large and free, he so restricted and bound?

'You weren't to blame,' she repeated.

Summer. In July Laura sat her examinations and she left school at the end of that term. Her Headmistress had broached the subject of Sixth Form work and university but Laura had refused even to mention it to her father.

She applied for a junior clerical post at the city's Education Office and was chosen for the vacancy out of forty-six candidates. She started work a week after leaving school. The job was boring, mostly filing and carrying messages; at three o'clock in the afternoon she regularly had the feeling that time had stopped, but she'd been assured that there were good prospects of promotion.

The Education Office was near the Central Library; she spent her lunch times there. Her English teacher, Miss Harcourt, had given her the reading list she herself had used at Oxford and Laura lost herself in the maze of other people's lives. For ten days or so she was so much Maggie Tulliver that she was often astonished to find herself walking along the city streets instead of on the verdant banks of the Floss. At the end of the book, weeping at Maggie's death, she realised that she was not only alive, but glad to be so. (In the first weeks after Annie's death she used to look at herself in the mirror before going to bed and think her face looked like the face of someone drowned; under water.)

By this time her father had started courting a widow, a Mrs Mabel Glover who kept a corner shop near his work. He took to mentioning her once or twice every week, said she was keeping him off the drink. He had started going out every evening again, but he was certainly drinking less.

'You'll have to meet her,' he said. 'I've told her about you.'

He was expecting a blank refusal, but Laura agreed that they should meet. Her job had marked her freedom from her father; she told herself that as far as she was concerned he could now go ahead and marry - or not marry - anyone he chose.

One evening towards the end of August, her father told her he was taking Mrs Glover to Weston-super-Mare on the next Saturday, and to her great surprise he asked her to join them, even offering to pay the five shillings for her ticket on the excursion train.

To his great surprise she accepted the invitation.

She made sandwiches and baked some fairy-cakes the night before the trip, and when she went to bed found that she was looking forward to it. She'd never seen the sea.

'This is Mrs Glover. I've told Mrs Glover all about you, how clever you are and how you look down on your poor old Dad.'

'I don't look down on him, Mrs Glover, not all that much.'

Mrs Glover was a dumpling of a woman, about her father's age or a little older. Every time her father took her arm or teased her she blushed like a child. Her eyes were pale blue and very clear, giving the impression that she had nothing to hide; she looked kind and wholesome.

The three were a little shy of one another on the journey down and spent much of the time looking out at the countryside: fields of wheat and barley ready for the harvest, meadows, rivers, orchards and gardens. 'It's a rare treat for me, this is,' Mrs Glover said whenever Laura's father looked towards her, 'stuck in a shop all week.'

They reached Weston-super-Mare at eleven-thirty. The day was warm but unsettled.

The anonymity of a strange town seemed to bring them together; as they walked along the sea-front they began to talk. Laura spoke of her work, of the woman at the next desk who sucked soda-mints all the morning and belched softly into her handkerchief all the afternoon. 'That could be the start of an ulcer, dear,' Mrs Glover said. 'Do tell her to see a doctor.'

'I have a terrible stomach from time to time,' Laura's father said, wanting to claim his share of Mrs Glover's kindly concern. 'Stabbing pains like a knife.'

'Cirrhosis of the liver,' Laura said. 'We did it in biology. The drinker's curse. Fatal, usually.'

'What a tease,' Mrs Glover said comfortably. 'Isn't she a tease, Harry?'

They had a cup of tea in a café and looked at the clouds over the sea. Mrs Glover implored the weather to stay fine. 'This is a rare treat for me,' she said again.

Laura ordered an éclair and tried not to think of Saturday afternoons in the market café with Annie. For a time she withdrew from the conversation.

Her father reclaimed her attention. 'Mabel here's got two lads,' he said. 'I've met 'em both. Fine lads. John's with the Regulars stationed at Aldershot and the younger one, Peter, is apprentice to a jeweller in Brum; he's in lodgings, comes home once a month or so.'

'So you see there'll be plenty of room for you to live with us if you've a mind to,' Mrs Glover said.

'That's very kind of you,' Laura said as smoothly as if she was thoroughly conversant with their plans. 'But my friend Susan Wilkins has already offered me digs in her house. She's got a job as a dentist's receptionist in the city centre; we've got practically the same hours so we'd be going in on the same buses and coming back the same time. We'd be company for each other, we might even . . .'

'We're thinking of getting married in October,' her father said, giving her a chance of getting her breath back. 'There's not much point in hanging about, is there?'

'Not at our age,' Mrs Glover said, blushing again.

'I don't know anything about your age,' her father said. 'But I'm young enough.'

He was in a mellow mood.

Laura enjoyed her day. The weather remained fine. The sea was in. They had a picnic lunch on the beach, watched a Punch and Judy show, listened to the band and finally had a cooked tea: plaice and chips and bread and butter in the Belle View Restaurant.

Mrs Glover seemed to approve of her. Before the end of the afternoon she'd offered to knit her a cardigan for work: they'd even managed to buy the wool and a pattern.

On the way back Laura slept for a while in her corner seat; the compartment was crowded and warm. When she woke she saw that her father and Mrs Glover, sitting opposite, were holding hands and whispering together, so that she quickly closed her eyes again pretending to be still asleep.

Oh, she was pleased that her father was getting married again; Mrs Glover seemed a most suitable wife for him, trivial, it seemed to her, without being stupid, warm without being passionate. Her mother had been too reserved, too superior. Annie . . . Annie . . . had been . . .

'What's the matter, dear?' Mrs Glover asked her, leaning over and touching her hands. 'Whatever's the matter?'

Laura hadn't realised that she was crying. 'I had a bad dream,' she said.

'I'm sorry Mabel broke it to you like that,' her father said when they were back home.

'It's all right. I knew something was up. I'm glad you're getting married.'

'We hadn't really decided where to live. Only it seems daft for her to give up the shop when money's so short. I'll be sorry to leave this house; I've lived here for nearly twenty years. All the same, it hasn't been a lucky house, has it?'

'No. I'll be glad to move.'

'She told you you could come to live with us, didn't she. It won't be no trouble, now you can pay your keep.'

'I'd rather not. You'll feel freer without me.'

They were both silent, he knowing that she was right. They could never really be comfortable together again; she would always remind him of things he'd rather forget.

'*Did* that girl's mother say you could have digs with them, or did you make it up?'

'Her brother's just moved to London, so it may be possible. I'll ask.'

'Are they decent people?'

'Too decent. Chapel people. Susan has to go to chapel

twice every Sunday, and in the week sometimes. Not that they'll get me to go. If I have lodgings with them it will be on my terms.'

'They won't take you on your terms. Who do you think you are? If they give you cheap digs, they'll decide on the terms. You've got strange ideas of your own importance, you have. You're only seventeen. Your friend's mother won't want to be responsible for you if you start talking about your terms.'

'You left home at seventeen.'

'I'm a man. A man is different. A man is grown up at seventeen.'

'I'm grown up. I'm going to get a good job and a good salary and be independent.'

'In a couple of years you'll be wanting to get married.'

'I'm going to night school to study economics and accountancy. I may get married but not until I've got a good job.'

Laura stood up in front of the mirror over the mantlepiece and examined herself. She felt grown up. She was already taller than her father. She had brown, golden-brown hair, greenish-gold eyes, three or four golden freckles on her straight nose. She wasn't too fat or too thin. Her neck was strong and rather beautiful, she thought. She'd do.

Her father looked at her and tried to remember her mother when she was young. He had met her on his first leave from the army; he'd been nearly thirty but she was only nineteen. She had been slighter in build, less aggressive in the way she stood, altogether less forward and pushy.

His heart gave a sudden thump as he realised that it was Annie his daughter resembled.

'You and your bloody independence,' he said harshly. 'A fine lot of good your stupid ideas will do you. You can't change the world. Women get married - when they have the chance - and they have children. They have to, to keep the world going.'

He stamped out of the living room, locked up and went upstairs without further word.

Laura went on staring at herself in the mirror. After a while she started to smile. She'd had her first taste of power.

*

At the beginning of September Laura got the results of her School Certificate examination; she'd gained a distinction in every subject and an exemption from matriculation.

'You should be proud of her,' Mrs Glover told her father when she heard. 'Very proud. You should buy her a gold wrist-watch, that's what you should do, and have her name engraved on the back of it.'

'Would you like that?' her father asked her, rather sheepishly.

'Yes please,' Laura said. Why not? Why shouldn't he give her something?

At work, she had an immediate rise and a letter of congratulations from the deputy director of education.

Mrs Glover came over to the house to decide what furniture she wanted. 'You've got lovely things,' she told Laura and her father. 'I don't like to think of this good furniture being sold. I'll have to try and squeeze as much as I can into our house so they'll be kept for Laura.'

'She's not getting married, she says.'

'That's what she says now. In a year or two it'll be a different story. I can't let that lovely carpet go; there's quality in that.'

'She always had to have the best, did Laura's mother,' her father said mournfully.

'She slipped up with you,' Laura said.

'Tch, tch, tch,' Mrs Glover said, trying to frown. She was plump and glossy, like a cat with cream. Whatever could she want with her father, Laura wondered, but knowing the answer.

The furniture was sold, all except the floral carpet and a walnut china cabinet, and the house cleared.

Chapter Five

Laura packed her clothes and books and took them to Susan Wilkins's house.

Laura and Susan had always had a very close relationship; like sisters they argued, fell out, were reconciled; and finally depended a great deal on each other.

When they had first started school, Susan had been the natural leader; she was bigger and far more spirited. She was six months older than Laura, had a brother already at school and was used to playing on the pavements and in the park. Laura was timid and reserved, she had never played with other children, her only companions having been her mother and an imaginary dog called Paddy who was as big as a house.

For the first few days the six-year-old bullies had given Laura a hard time, shutting her up in the lavatory at playtimes and making her say rude words like knickers and po before they let her out. Susan had stopped them by telling them about Laura's brother who was in the big school. (After a while, Laura had started believing in him herself. A large, sturdy boy with sandy hair and freckles, he took over Paddy's place in her life, accompanying her upstairs in the dark and sleeping in her bedroom.)

In both the Infant and Elementary School, Susan was thought to be the brighter and more amenable of the two girls. Laura wanted to understand the various processes of learning instead of getting on with them, and asked many awkward, unnecessary questions the teachers couldn't answer. She also finished her reading books faster than anyone could supply her with more and day-dreamed in hand-work, instead of getting on with her raffia table-mats and serviette rings.

It took the Headmistress, teacher of the top class, to overlook the inconvenient way she devoured reading books and broke raffia-needles, and recognise that she was quite exceptionally clever.

Both girls eventually won scholarships to the grammar school, but it wasn't until they were in the third year that Laura's superiority at academic subjects became obvious to everyone; except, that is, to Susan, who managed to convince herself that Laura was nothing but a swot, while she had better things to do than bother about getting high marks in stupid tests. Anyway, it was years too late for any measure of role-reversal; Susan continued to treat Laura kindly but firmly, as a middle-class woman might treat the slowest of her servants.

Susan's parents had a green-grocery business, a shop and delivery-round. They had never had a lodger before, but Laura, who had taken to calling at their house occasionally since Annie's death, had impressed them; they thought she would be a steadying influence on Susan who, in their opinion, was getting too flighty by half, wanting to go to the pictures every Saturday night and spending all her wages on cheap clothes and Woolworth's jewellery.

Laura was to share Susan's large room at the back of the house. They had a small table in the window and a couple of chairs, so that they could spend their evenings up there when it wasn't too cold.

When Laura had unpacked, her books filled the little book-case at the side of their bed. 'Where are your books?' she asked Susan.

'I've sold them.'

'Even *Wuthering Heights*?'

'Yes. I got six shillings for them. Would you like me to sell yours? You've got far more than I had. You'd get enough money to buy yourself a new dress. What are you going to wear to the wedding? You should get yourself a decent dress.'

'Mrs Glover, Mabel I mean, is making one for me.'

'And you're going to wear whatever she feels like making? However hideous it is?'

'Why should it be hideous? She's probably quite a good dressmaker. She's bought some peacock-blue material and a lace collar.'

'You'll look a mess. The seams will be lumpy, the skirt will be gathered, it'll be all floppy over the bust and the sleeves will be set in wrong.'

'Wrongly.'

'Have you got a hat for the wedding? Have you got gloves? I'll be ashamed to be with you.'

'Don't come.'

'Don't you want me to come?'

'Not really. It will be very boring. I can't see why you should have to endure it.'

'But Mrs Glover asked me to come. She thought I'd be company for you. Anyway, it may not be boring. Her two sons will be there. They may be very handsome.'

'I doubt it. They'll probably be pink and plump like their mother. Anyway, they're a bit old, aren't they? Twenty-four and twenty-two.'

'Just right. Bags me the oldest.'

'The older.'

'I'll lend you a white hat if you promise to get yourself a decent pair of gloves on Friday when you get your pay.'

'I can't; I need the money. Next week I've got to register at night school.'

'Night school!'

'Yes. Why don't you come? It's time you tried to educate yourself. You needn't give up because you failed at school.'

'You really should have something done to your hair. It's so childish the way it is. You should have it cut off and permed. Your face isn't too bad if you put some powder on, and lipstick.'

'Your father said you weren't to wear lipstick.'

'So did my mother. I've got three: coral, pink pearl and burnt orange. Which do you think is better with my colouring?'

'Best. Pink pearl.'

'You didn't even look.'

'I really think I'm going to get fed up with you, Susan. Oh, if only the YWCA wasn't so expensive.'

Susan was small and dainty with blue eyes, wavy hair that was almost black, a tiny waist and small feet. She spent her evenings manicuring her nails, arranging her hair this way and that, looking into the mirror and dreaming.

'I think it's very romantic, don't you, Mrs Glover and your Dad getting married in the evening of their life.'

'Sharing the fire-side glow,' Laura suggested. 'Walking into the sunset, hand in hand.'

'Do you think they'll, you know, have intimate relations together? Oh, don't gawp at me like that; you know very well what I mean.'

'I don't suppose they realise they're so old,' Laura said, more gently. 'I suppose they'll carry on just as though they were young or middle-aged; a bit of this and a bit of that.'

'Gosh. Do you really think so? Anyway, I'm sure my parents don't... you know.'

'They went to bed very early last night.'

'Oh yes, on Saturday night they always read the Bible together; they prepare for their Sunday school class.'

'Well they'd naturally make some excuse. You wouldn't expect them to say, "Well good-night, Susan, we're turning in early tonight to have intimate relations together," would you?'

'No. Only I can't believe it. It seems such an extraordinary thing. To think of all the married people we know going to bed and doing... you know... that thing.'

'Well, I suppose when we've done it ourselves, it won't seem so extraordinary.'

Laura turned back to her book, Susan, with a little sigh, back to her mirror.

Mrs Glover thought Susan a charming girl, her manner was so natural and friendly; Laura was pleasant enough, but she was too clever, too sharp.

Susan had taken such an interest in her new dove-grey costume, and in her hat and gloves which were in the latest shade called clover. Susan had begged, literally begged her to buy navy-blue handbag and shoes rather than black, 'much more fashionable,' she had said. 'Navy-blue court shoes,' she had whispered, leaning her head forward like a priest granting absolution. Susan had persuaded her to buy a foundation cream and powder, had taken her, on the Saturday afternoon before the wedding, to the big store in the city centre where a qualified beautician, for no extra charge, had advised her on the correct shade and type. Susan would have been a real daughter to her. Laura, though she had looked after the shop very efficiently on the afternoon in question, had shown very little involvement in any of the purchases.

She had tried on the dress which Mrs Glover had, by this time, completed, thanked her very much and said it was fine. Did it need any alteration, Mrs Glover had asked her. No, it was absolutely fine. She was polite enough, but her heart wasn't in it. Susan had spent all her wages on a new dress, rayon-silk with a blue and white geometric pattern; had got it specially for the occasion.

It wasn't that Laura felt above taking an interest in clothes; Annie had loved clothes and had worn them with great panache; it was simply that she was prepared to wait. Other things came first.

The wedding was in the first week of October when Mrs Glover's elder son, who was deputed to give her away, had his annual leave from the army. (To Susan's great disappointment he had proved to be only a private, not at all handsome and rather dull; or at least not susceptible to her efforts at dazzling him.)

The service was at two o'clock. The church was decorated with tawny chrysanthemums and golden asters, 'suitably autumnal,' Laura whispered. She and Susan nudged each other during the service and tried not to giggle.

The reception, which was held in the private rooms of the local pub, was warm and friendly. Mabel had a big family: two brothers, three sisters, several nephews and nieces and in-laws, as well as relatives of her previous husband. The party became more and more noisy as the afternoon wore on.

Susan seemed to be enjoying herself as much as anyone. She had been to several weddings, twice as a bridesmaid, but the receptions had always been in the chapel vestry; this one was different, drinking and merry-making going on all the evening.

The bridal couple were spending a few days in the Lake District, leaving John, the soldier son, in charge of the shop. Before they left to catch their train, her father drew Laura aside to say good-bye to her. 'You'll be all right?' he asked her. 'Of course I will, what about you?' 'Oh, I think so,' he said, 'I think I'm going to be very comfortable ever after.' Laura was surprised at the remark; it revealed a perception she hadn't thought he possessed. For the rest of the evening she felt unusually tolerant of him; perhaps, after all, he had loved Annie more than she'd thought.

Susan's father had arranged to pick the girls up in his van at nine o'clock. Knowing that she wouldn't be allowed to attend a reception at a pub, Susan had told him it was being held at the house.

She sought out Laura. 'Don't forget to be back at the house by a quarter to nine,' she said. 'He's bound to arrive early just to check up on us.'

Susan's father was tall and gaunt with a large melancholy face, rough red hands and bony wrists. Even in the shop he talked very slowly and solemnly as though he were in a pulpit. Susan said he short-changed his customers, as well as giving them rotten fruit and vegetables from the back of the display boxes, but she was naturally prejudiced against him. Laura, for her part, was watching him closely; she didn't feel he could be quite as bad as he looked.

'Yes, I'll be there in plenty of time,' she said. 'Where are you going, anyway? It isn't eight, yet.'

'I'm going for a walk with Peter.'

'I thought you'd settled on John. I thought Peter was for me.'

'No, it's me he fancies. Sorry. I told you you should have done something about yourself. I can't help having more sex-appeal than you, can I?'

Laura went back to talk to Violet and Sylvia, Mabel's nieces, who had only the previous day returned from France.

She'd never before met anyone who'd been abroad except with the army. Violet and Sylvia had eaten exotic foods, drunk a bottle of wine with each meal and, even more daringly, had attended High Mass in a Roman Catholic church. Laura wondered if she'd be able to persuade Susan into going abroad with her sometime; she took down addresses of pensions and restaurants just in case, and felt her father had married into a very adventurous and cultured family.

She left the pub at half past eight – Susan hadn't returned – and made her way back to the house. There was no one there, no sign of Susan, but luckily the side door was unlocked so she went in, put the light on in the front room, drew the curtains and sat down to wait.

At exactly nine o'clock Mr Wilkins arrived. Laura, who'd been listening for his van, rushed out to prevent his coming up to the house and realising that it was empty.

He leaned over and opened the van door for her. As usual his large, unsmiling face made her feel nervous and slightly sick. His dust-coloured hair had been cropped even closer to his scalp than usual so that his head seemed covered with bristles. She could hardly bear to get in to the van. 'I'm afraid Susan isn't here at the moment. She got bored and went for a walk. I know she won't be long.'

He turned his small eyes towards her. He looked so like a pig that she expected him to grunt. 'She won't be long,' she said again. 'She just wanted a breath of air. She'll be back in no time.'

'She should be here. I told her nine o'clock on the dot.' His voice was loud.

'Gosh, is it nine o'clock already? My father and my step-mother will have arrived at Kendal by this time. I hope the weather stays fine for them; I love these crisp autumn days, don't you? Have you ever been to the Lakes, Mr Wilkins?'

He ignored her.

She looked out into the dark, longing to see Susan hurrying towards them. Mr Wilkins stared at the driving wheel as though it were an empty trough.

A minute or two later he looked at his watch again and started up the engine.

'Where are you going?'

'I'm going home young lady. I came here straight from work without even stopping for a cup of tea. I've waited five minutes and I'll not stop a second more.'

'How will Susan get back?'

'That's her problem, that is. It's only two or three miles. She can walk it as far as I'm concerned.'

'Let me wait for her. She won't know the way.'

'You stay where you are.'

'You're always saying it's not safe for her to be out on her own. She won't even know where to get a bus.'

'That's her problem.'

He didn't say another word. Neither did she. She was furious with him.

They arrived back, he parked the van in the yard and she preceded him into the house.

'Where's our Susan?' Mrs Wilkins asked.

Susan's mother was a very nervous woman. She worked hard but said little; she didn't count and she knew it.

'Mr Wilkins will tell you,' Laura said. 'I'm only going to say this; I think he's behaved very unreasonably.'

She went upstairs without further word.

At any rate, she's not on her own, she told herself. Peter Glover seems a reliable type; he'll bring her home.

It was eleven o'clock before Susan came upstairs. She looked very woebegone; her face blotchy and red.

'Whatever happened to you? I tried to get your father to wait for you but he wouldn't. He was in a beastly mood just because you were five minutes late.'

Susan sat on the bed and sniffed. 'It wasn't only that. He stopped at the Queen's Head to ask the way to Mrs Glover's shop and somehow or other they told him about the wedding and how the reception was being held there.'

'Oh.'

'So, you see, I'm a hardened sinner; a liar and a frequenter of wild drunken orgies.'

'As well as unpunctual.'

'Oh Laura, you are lucky not to have parents. At least, you don't have a mother and your father's cast you off. I think there should be a law to make everyone wards of state at sixteen. Everyone should have to leave home and live in a hostel. Oh, wouldn't it be wonderful. Oh God, I think I'll run away to London to live with Arthur.'

'Who's Arthur? I thought it was Peter you were after.'

'Arthur's my bleedin' brother. You know that perfectly well.'

'Well, what's my step-brother like?'

'He's not your step-brother, is he? I suppose he is. Oh, he's not that special. Anyway he's going back to Birmingham tomorrow so I won't see him again.'

'Did he walk you home?'

'He came with me but we didn't walk all the way; we managed to get a bus from the city centre.'

'Did you bring him in?'

'Did I hell. Do you think I'm stupid as well as tight.'

'You're not tight, are you?'

'No, I think I've sobered up by this time.'

'You're just trying to shock me.'

'Perhaps I am.'

'Anyway, why were you late? After warning me to be on time.'

'Why do you think? Use your brains.'

'Is your father still cross with you?'

'Yes. I've got to stay behind after chapel tomorrow morning to have a talk with the minister.'

'How quaint.'

'The Methodist version of the confessional; it's not quaint at all.'

'How much will you confess?'

'Only as far as the waist.'

'Susan, if you get into trouble, don't expect me to help you.'

'Oh, I'm only trying to shock you. Wasn't that what you said?'

'I hope you are.'

'Shall I turn the light off now? Have you finished reading?'

'Why are you so shy all of a sudden? Hey, whatever's happened to you?'

'Haven't you ever had the strap?'

'No. Hell no. Don't cry. Don't cry, Susan. Oh hell, your father's a beast. Let's run away. We can't possibly stay here. Let's go to London. Let's go tomorrow.'

Chapter Six

But they didn't go to London. All they did was have endless discussions on how they could earn more money, enough to afford a bed-sitting room or a double room in a hostel, enough to save the fares to London, enough for a week's lodgings there while they looked for work. Even while they talked and planned they knew that the most modest of the proposals was far out of their reach.

'By the time I'm twenty-five, I might be able to afford a holiday in France,' Laura said one evening, a page full of calculations in front of her, 'only by that time there'll be a war. The war in Spain will engulf the whole of Europe in a year or two; everyone says so. France will . . .'

'Oh, don't start on that stuff,' Susan said, her hands over her ears. 'Just don't. I don't *want* to know the difference between Communists and Fascists. I don't *want* to know about the Maginot Line or Hitler or Mussolini. If the war comes, it comes, and anyway England always wins in the end. Just shut up about it.'

'What a marvellous little statesman you are,' Laura said. 'Just like the rest of them. I'm proud of you.'

'Anyway, I thought we were talking about money. I thought you were trying to work out how I could put by two shillings a week for a winter coat without skipping lunches.'

'Do you realise that if I was a man I'd be earning half a crown more per week,' Laura said. 'Not for doing more responsible work or more arduous work but simply for being a member of the superior sex. Don't you think that's sickening?'

Susan looked at her squarely. 'No, not really,' she said. 'Men have to think about careers and things. We're only marking time, aren't we?'

'You make me sick. I'm not marking time. I'm jolly well going to have a career. What do you think I go to night school for?'

'Because you've got such a dreary little mind that you can't conceive of anything more interesting. I'd rather just stay in and listen to the wireless than go to night school. Anyway, I've got a lot to do every night: washing and ironing and so on. I like to look clean and neat even if I can't be in the latest fashion. In my magazine it says you should never wear a blouse or underwear or stockings more than one day and you should press your skirt every evening. When did you last press that skirt?'

'You never read anything but trash, do you? Come on, when did you last read a proper book? Don't you realise how degrading women's magazines are: how to catch a man, how to pander to him, feed him, cherish him. Is that all you want out of life?'

'Yes.'

'Oh God, you're beyond hope, you really are. Anyway, if you went to night school you might meet a slightly less awful man than you would otherwise.'

'Do you mean, I might find a "clever" man?' (Susan held out the word clever as though it had a bad smell.) 'Are "clever" men any nicer than the others? Perhaps people only go to night school because they've got an inferiority complex; have you thought of that? Because they want to show-off. You're always going on about women being exploited. But what if I'd be perfectly happy ironing shirts and polishing furniture? It's discontented people like you who're always stirring up trouble. I bet most women are perfectly happy to stay at home, looking after the house, shopping, cooking, washing and ironing; they're all perfectly respectable jobs. You want a career; I don't try to stop you. Why should you try to stop me doing what I want?'

'You've been conditioned into wanting marriage and domesticity. I only want you to start thinking for yourself.'

'I *am* thinking for myself. I've suddenly thought that the

reason you're so keen to better yourself is that you don't much like yourself the way you are. Me: I'm quite happy with myself.'

Susan looked at herself in the mirror as she spoke. A tiny smile lifted the corners of her lips, her eyes seemed to hold a lovely secret; there was a glow about her.

Laura thought she looked daft. 'You just see yourself as a contented little housewife,' she said. 'Pretty clothes and softly waved hair, two well-dressed, well-behaved children just like in the magazines. You don't see the other side of the picture: women whose lives have gone sour because their husbands aren't magazine husbands but selfish brutes. And what can they do about it? Susan, they can't even walk out on them. *We're* helpless because we don't earn enough money to leave here. Think how much more helpless a woman is with two or three, or even four or five, children. She can do absolutely nothing, however her husband treats her. The money is his, he earns it, so he can spend it on going out with the lads, or even going out with the girls. And his wife simply has to put up with it. Don't just read pretty magazines, go down to Albert Terrace and Union Street and look about you. God, I'm not trying to tell you not to get married; you will get married, so will I, probably, I only want you to go into it with your eyes open.'

Susan, who had long stopped listening and was busy putting vaseline on her long thick eyelashes, suddenly turned to her and said: 'You've got lovely eyes, too, Laura, but if you read so much you'll ruin them. What if you have to wear glasses? Have you thought of that? Did you ever notice how many of our teachers wore glasses, even the younger ones? I honestly think I'd rather have grey hair than glasses. Are you ready for bed now? There's nothing better for your eyes and skin than plenty of sleep; nine hours every night with the window open. Oh, Laura, why don't you ever listen to me? You'll be sorry one day.'

She put grips in her hair, one at the centre of each wave, cold-cream on her baby-smooth face and neck, and got into bed sighing deeply because Laura seemed determined to keep the light on. In spite of it, she was asleep in five minutes. A couple of hours later, though, when Laura had one of her nightmares about Annie, she was immediately wide awake to comfort her. They were good friends however much they disparaged each other.

A fortnight later, the subject of night school came up again.

Laura had had an economics class that evening. For the first time she had found the work difficult to grasp. Reaching home, she had rushed upstairs without even looking in on Susan who was with her parents in the living room behind the shop, had got out her text-book and read and re-read the relevant chapters trying to get to grips with it.

It suddenly became clear to her, beautifully logical and clear, and she felt the exhilaration she used to feel in school after solving a difficult mathematical problem. She closed her book with a bang, stood up on her toes and stretched herself.

At this point Susan came upstairs, yawning and ready for bed. Laura rushed towards her and swung her off her feet.

'Whatever's happened? Tell me,' Susan said. 'Oh, put me down you fool, you're crushing me.'

'I've had a proposal of marriage,' Laura said, abruptly letting her go, sinking on to the bed and trying to look like one of the Bennett sisters.

'No! How marvellous! Tell me all about it! Aren't you a dark horse! Fancy not saying anything!'

Laura stopped simpering and stood up again, feeling ashamed of herself. 'Of course I haven't, Susan, I was teasing you. I'm sorry. I didn't think you'd fall for it. Who'd be likely to propose to me? Don't be silly.'

Susan was annoyed that she'd allowed herself to be taken in, but also relieved that Laura hadn't stolen a march on her. She was silent for a minute or two, brushing her hair in front of the mirror and trying to compose her face.

'Anyway, something's made you very excited,' she said. 'You've got some secret. Your cheeks are burning.'

'I haven't. Cross my heart. I've just had an enjoyable economics class that's all.'

Susan had had a miserable evening. Her father had bought some sacks of second-grade onions which had turned out to be third-grade. Even the pie factory had rejected them and he'd eventually had to sell them at a loss. 'It won't do,' he'd kept saying. 'You can't trust anybody these days. I'll have to get the money back somehow, but if I put an extra penny on the five-pound bags of spuds the mean devils round here will go to Lumleys. They expect to get even the middling-big oranges at seven for sixpence. The carrots are full of grubs, if I don't get rid of those by seven o'clock Saturday I'll have another loss on my hands. We'll have to sell up if this goes on.' She ought to have been used to his moaning, and she was, but it still annoyed her, like flies buzzing about, and besides she hated seeing her mother upset.

'Hey, I think I might join a night school class,' she said.

'So that you've got an excuse to go out?'

'Exactly.'

'It wouldn't work. Your father checks up on me, asking to see my essays and so forth; what do you think he'd be like with you?'

'What about something like... cookery, for instance?'

'You'd still have to bring back your Toad-in-the-Hole or rissoles every week.'

'But I wouldn't mind going to cookery classes. Are there any?'

'Yes. Plain and Fancy. But the term's almost half over now. You'd probably have to pay your five and six for only half the lessons. And anyway you haven't got five and six, have you?'

'Half the term can't be over already. Hey, how long is it since your father's wedding?'

'Nearly a month. I've promised to go over there every month and I'm going on Sunday. Why?'

'Hey, my period is late.'

'What of it? Mine is often late... Oh no, Susan.'

It was the first time Laura had suspected Susan of keeping anything from her; of having anything to hide. They looked at each other with horror.

Susan fetched the calendar and started counting weeks, her breath coming in little gasps as she did so.

'Laura, I'm over a week late. I'm nine days late. Oh Laura, tell me what I must do. Oh Laura, what can I do? Oh Laura.'

'First of all sit down and stop wailing.'

Laura's fear was almost as great as Susan's. She took the calendar from her. 'Now, let's look at this calmly,' she said.

'I had the curse that Saturday I took Mrs Glover to town. I remember it very well because I had a pimple on my chin and you know I never get a spot except then. And the make-up woman said I should use a special antiseptic lotion but I didn't have any money after buying the dress, so...'

'That was definitely the Saturday before the wedding. I looked after the shop in the afternoon; I've got it marked on the calendar.'

Whichever way they looked at it, Susan's period was nine days late. Laura's period had often been late, though she couldn't absolutely guarantee that it had ever been as much as nine days. Susan, on the other hand, had always been as regular as clockwork. Laura had heard that one could be late as a result of a shock or fright which could surely have been when Susan's father had turned nasty on the night of the wedding. No it couldn't, Susan said; he'd belted her before but she'd never before been late because of it.

They sat together, miserable and hopeless, for what seemed like hours.

'I suppose you messed about with that Peter Glover on the night of the wedding,' Laura said at last. 'I suppose it could be that.'

'I suppose so. I don't remember all that clearly.'

'Oh don't be childish. You did or you didn't.'

'I did... mess about, yes. But I don't think it was, you know, well, going the whole way.'

'You don't think it was sexual intercourse?'

'Oh, do you have to make it sound so common.'

'I'm simply trying to get information from you, that's all. I'm trying to help you. Susan, listen to me, what makes you unsure whether you did or did not have sexual intercourse? Could you tell me that, please?'

'It didn't seem... well, anything very terrific or sensational or anything, that's all.'

Susan was wearing five narrow glass bangles on her wrist and they tinkled together in her agitation.

'Did you have any pain?' Laura asked her.

'Yes. No.'

'I'll try to frame the question differently: Did you...'

'I had a certain amount of discomfort; he was very heavy lying on me, but no pain, not as far as I remember.'

'I'm sorry, but I don't know any way of asking this politely: Did he... penetrate you?'

'Oh God, I'm not sure. He moved about on top of me and he made me sticky, that's all I remember.'

Susan's voice was so low that Laura could hardly hear her. 'I'm scared,' she said.

'Listen, Susan, love; what you're describing is certainly messing about but I honestly don't think it was intercourse. If it was proper intercourse, the stickiness would have been inside you, wouldn't it? Did you have your knickers on?'

'I did to start with.'

'Oh yes, Susan, I know that. Nearly everybody does to start with. Did you have your knickers on when he was moving about on top of you?'

'I don't remember. I think I was drunk. I had two glasses of port and lemon first of all and then two, or was it three, glasses of gin and orange, and I'd never had anything to drink before.'

'Well, in my opinion, you just messed about and that was enough to unsettle your monthly cycle, but I don't think you can possibly be pregnant. Honestly.'

'You could be wrong though, couldn't you? You don't know everything, do you? How soon will I know for certain?'

'You'll know definitely in a fortnight's time, a fortnight on Saturday.'

'How?'

'If you miss your second period then you'll know that you're pregnant. All the same, I'm sure you're not.'

'But how can I bear to be in this state for another fortnight?'

Susan's glass bangles began to tinkle again; Laura could hardly bear it. 'You may not have to,' she said. 'It may come tonight. Or tomorrow or the next day.'

'But I can't bear this for another hour. How can I? Feel my heart.' She clutched Laura's hand. 'My father'll kill me if I'm pregnant.'

'Pull yourself together, love, please. Tell yourself that you won't worry until you know definitely. Try to be philosophical about it.'

'How can I be philosophical when I've got this terrible thumping in my chest? Oh, I'll have to tell my mother. To see what she thinks about it. I'll have to.'

'Oh please don't, Susan. It will only pass the worry on to her. What good would it do?'

'She'd pray for me.'

'I'll pray for you. Please God send this girl some sense. Oh Susan, do you honestly think your Heavenly Father is going to concern himself with your menstrual cycle? Anyway if he is a Creator, wouldn't it be blasphemy to ask him to uncreate something? I mean, if it is created, which I doubt.'

'Laura, would you mind if I went on my knees to pray?'

'Yes, it would embarrass me horribly. Do it when I'm asleep if you have to.'

'Oh, please don't go to sleep.'

'Susan, love, we can't keep awake for fifteen days.'

'I can't bear this anxiety. I can't bear it. I can't bear it.'

But of course, she had to bear it. If she had known Peter Glover's address she might have told him about it so that he should worry too. Though as far as he was concerned it would have been a far more objective worry. For her, the worry was a physical pain; it was inside her body.

By the end of the week Susan had made herself pale and plain.

'Do you think we might be able to find someone who performs abortions?' she asked Laura very quietly one night between two o'clock and three.

Laura had been expecting the question. 'No we certainly couldn't. They're terribly dangerous and they cost the earth. If you're really pregnant we'll steal the week's takings from your father's strong-box – I've found out where he keeps the key – we'll take every penny he's got and go on the night train to London and we'll get work there in a factory.'

'He'll set the police on us. They'll find us.'

'No they won't. Go to sleep now. Your big friend will look after you.'

*

When the alarm went off at seven the next morning, Laura dragging herself out of bed, cold and stupid from lack of sleep, saw a dark stain on the sheet between them.

'Oh Susan,' she said, 'one of us is bleeding and it's certainly not my turn.'

Susan threw off the bedclothes. 'Oh Laura,' she said, 'God has answered my prayers.'

Chapter Seven

Laura's step-mother liked Laura and her father to go for a walk together while she was preparing the Sunday dinner. She saw this as a way of healing the mysterious breach between them.

'No, my dear,' she would tell her husband, 'it's no use saying she'll come around in her own good time, that won't do for me. I don't like bad feelings in a family. You must have a little talk with her and find out why she's so sharp towards you: you must have offended her in some way and you must put it right. Perhaps she thinks you've slighted her own mummy by marrying me. You must get her to tell you just how she feels, then you'll know how to comfort her and put things right. A girl will never trust any man, dear, unless she trusts her own father, so you see how important it is; you've got her whole future in your hands.'

Harry Brown was bemused by his wife. He'd married her thinking she was a pretty little widow with a kind smile and her own business. He'd found out that she was a powerful matriarchal figure whom he kept having to live up to and please. He'd always lived his own life before, now he was living hers; and trying to earn good marks at it as well.

Who'd have believed, he said to himself, that instead of relaxing in a cosy, smoke-filled pub with a pint or two, he'd be spending the best hour of the whole weekend walking about the dirty lanes behind the shop, trying to make conversation with his stuck-up daughter.

He'd tried the weather, 'Horrible day, in't it,' and her job, 'It's pretty boring, I suppose, office work, but there you are, it was your own choice. I hope the money's not too bad' and had then, in some desperation, come out with 'Your mother would like it round here. She came from the country, she did. Do you ever think of her, at all?'

Laura, looking at him coolly and realising that he wasn't anything like as nasty as Susan's father, had swallowed her initial response, Do *you* ever think of her at all? Did you *ever* think of her, at all? and only said 'Oh yes. From time to time.'

Poor, benighted man, she'd thought, does he really think this is the country, this filthy urban wasteland?

'I remember her talking about the village she'd come from,' she said. 'I'd like to go there sometime.'

'There's no one there now, not since your grandma died.'

'I remember Grandma Wells; just about. How old was I when she died?'

'Let's see. Had you started school, I wonder? These things don't stick with me. Must be ten, twelve years since she went, I suppose.'

It was the second week in December. There was a cold east wind. Dead leaves and scraps of old newspapers swirled around their ankles. The skin on Laura's face seemed to be clinging to her bones. 'Can we go back now?' she asked. 'Have we walked far enough?'

'We'll go as far as that gate. A walk does you good, gives you appetite. Beer . . . beer just fills you up.'

They walked on. The sky was a yellowish-white like a sick face. The path was muddy.

'There was Auntie Kitty as well, wasn't there? I remember Grandma Wells talking about Auntie Kitty. What became of her?'

'I don't know. We lost touch with her. She was one of these spinsters. She went to London to work.'

'To London? Gosh. Was she older than Mum or younger?'

'Older. Quite a lot older.'

'How could I get her address? Perhaps I could go and stay with her sometime. I'd love to go to London.'

'She was a very prickly sort of a woman, very high and mighty. She never wanted anything to do with us. She never even came to your mother's funeral.'

'Did you write to her?'

'I think I did. Yes, I'm pretty sure I found her address on the back of an old Christmas card.'

'How could I get hold of her?'

Her father whistled through his teeth. 'That's a tough one,' he said. 'I don't think I can help you, there. We lost touch years ago and everybody's dead now.'

It came to rain heavily. They reached the gate, then hurried back through the squelching mud.

'Well, my dears, you look ever so much better for your walk,' Mabel said when they got to the house. 'The fresh air's put the roses back in your cheeks. Give me your coats now and come to the table.'

They had roast pork, apple sauce, potatoes and cauliflower. She piled their plates high but took little herself, seeming to be happier watching them eat.

'He's a handsome man, isn't he?' she said when her husband had cleared his plate. 'A good-looking man with a good job and no dependants. People think I've done very well for myself.'

'There's plenty worse,' Laura said. It was a new thought.

She insisted on doing the washing-up and then wondered how soon she could leave; there were aunts and uncles coming to tea. She dried her hands and took her place in front of the fire with a glass of home-made wine.

'Now Mabel, you're a business woman with a head on your shoulders,' she heard her father say, 'and Laura here's got a problem: How can she get in touch with her Auntie Kitty, last heard of living in London about twelve years ago?'

'Easy, my dear. She can write to the "Missing Persons" column on the *Sunday World*. She can do it now, this very afternoon. I've got paper, envelope and a stamp. It's wrong to lose touch with family; you never know when you might need them.'

She stood over Laura while she wrote, and read out the finished message: 'Would Miss Kathleen Wells, formerly of Lower Batswood, Warwickshire and now believed to be living in London, please get in touch with her sister's daughter, Laura Brown.'

'Very nice, dear, though "residing in London" sounds better than "living in London" and "get into communication with" is more stylish than "get in touch". But never mind. Now put your address on the bottom – capital letters – and send a stamped addressed envelope as well, and I'll bet you five shillings that you get an answer before the end of the year.'

'She may be rich,' her father said. 'She certainly thought she was somebody.'

'Or she may be destitute and I'll have to look after her for the rest of her life.'

'It's very exciting anyway,' Mabel said. 'And you're doing the right thing. An auntie is worth a lot of trouble to anyone. And now, my dear, there's something you can help me with, and it's about our Peter.'

Laura's heart beat faster.

'Peter came home last weekend and he wants me to invite your friend, Susan, here for Christmas. He's only met her once but he seems very taken with her.'

'Her parents are terribly strict,' Laura said. 'I think they'd be dead set against her having Peter for a boyfriend. When her father found out she'd been to a wedding reception at a pub, he was absolutely horrible to her – I can't tell you how horrible. She wanted to come over here with me today – and last time – but he wouldn't hear of it. I'm afraid he thinks you're people of very loose morals. If he saw me sitting here drinking this cowslip wine he probably wouldn't have me in the house again.'

'Well,' her step-mother said comfortably, 'he must be very silly.'

'These chapel people are all alike,' her father said.

'Susan's mother is all right. She's tolerant of other people's opinions; it hasn't gone to her head. If she didn't let that man bully her she'd be really nice. She'd probably like Susan to have a normal life but she's too frightened to stick up for herself.'

'Has Susan got a boyfriend? That's what I really wanted to know. I'm not all that concerned about her parents.'

'No. Boys are always asking her out but she's not allowed to leave the house on her own. When we go to the pictures on a Saturday night, her father always comes to fetch us. He's always there waiting for us however early it finishes.'

'He wouldn't object to a decent chap from a good background,' her father said.

'He wouldn't think my son was a decent chap,' Mabel said, unable, though, to give serious consideration to such an idea.

'Unless he signed the pledge,' Laura said.

'He'd sign anything the way he was last Sunday. But I must say, I don't blame him. Susan is very nice and very pretty too. How old is she?'

'Eighteen last August.'

'Eighteen? That's old enough for a sweetheart surely. I was married at eighteen.'

'I wish I'd seen you first, lass,' her father said, leaning towards her and putting his hand on her plump knee.

'I'd better be off,' Laura said. 'I have to get in before dark. I won't forget to post the letter.'

'He wants to see you again, that's all. Why are you so excited? You know they won't let you go there.'

'Oh Laura, Arthur'll be home for Christmas, I'll say I'm going out with Arthur. He's a good sort, he'll take me over, find something to do in town, and come and fetch me later. It'll be all right. They'll let me go out with our Arthur.'

'But do you really want to see him again?'

'Oh, yes.'

'You said he was nothing special.'

'But he likes me, that makes him special, doesn't it? It's two months since the wedding. I thought he'd forgotten me. Why are you cross? Are you jealous?'

'Of course I'm not jealous. It's just that he seduced you, that's all. He got you tight and took advantage of you.'

'He took advantage of me, yes, but we don't really know whether he seduced me, do we? Not all the way.'

'Well, he certainly bounced up and down on top of you, you do remember that much, and on his own mother's bed, too.'

'I'll be more careful in future. I won't ever get drunk again. I expect he was drunk too, you know.'

'Listen, if you do get into any sort of trouble again, don't count on me will you. Because I shall simply leave you and go to the YWCA. It will mean I have about ninepence a week left over, but it will be worth it.'

'I think you are jealous, Laura. Look, I can't help having more sex-appeal than you, can I? If you had a perm and didn't talk about politics all the time, you'd get a boyfriend too. Oh Laura, he's very good-looking, isn't he? Didn't you think so? Didn't you think he was gorgeous? Oh, I can't wait for Christmas. I'm going to buy some lily-of-the-valley scent and an angora-wool cardigan to wear over that dress I had for the wedding; pink I think, or a very pale blue. Oh, Laura, I'm so excited.'

In the event, Peter Glover, as Laura's step-brother, was invited to the Wilkins's house on Boxing Day.

A fire was lit in the seldom-used parlour after dinner that day, and Peter, Arthur, Laura and Susan were actually allowed to be there on their own, with Arthur's portable gramophone which he'd brought with him from London, and some borrowed records.

Arthur had proved a pleasant surprise. Though he looked rather like his father, he was cheerful instead of morose and seemed relatively intelligent. He admitted to going to church every Sunday, morning and evening, but at least he went to the theatre as well; he'd been to several of the plays Laura had been longing to see and talked about them with great enthusiasm. His job with a large engineering firm sounded boring, but his union activities more than made up for it. He and Laura had talked animatedly all the morning, but in the parlour, that afternoon, Susan forbade them to talk on serious subjects.

'Quite right,' Peter said, 'after all it is Christmas. We should play party games. Or dance.'

'I don't think we'd be allowed to dance,' Susan said. ('I hope there's no music-hall songs there,' her father had said earlier, viewing the pile of records as though they were writhing snakes. 'I hope we all remember that this is a religious festival and behave accordingly.')

'We'll have to fall back on small-talk,' Arthur said. 'Did

you get any nice Christmas presents, Laura?'

'Talcum-powder from Susan and soap from Mrs Wilkins. I don't know what they're trying to tell me.'

'I had a really ghastly tie from my mother,' Peter said. 'She always gets me ties, each one ghastlier than the last. Did you get any ties, Susan?'

Arthur was probably the more intelligent and interesting of the two men, Laura thought, but to her chagrin she couldn't help her thoughts turning towards Peter, the seducer. She couldn't help admitting that she found him very attractive. His eyes were dark and restless, his body, very still, was somehow like an athlete's at the starting-line.

She forced herself to turn her attention to Arthur. 'What about the Blackshirts?' she asked him. 'Do you see anything of them in London?'

It was such a sudden switch from talcum-powder and ties that they all laughed.

'Honestly,' Susan said, 'you've no idea what I have to put up with from this girl. She goes to night school twice a week and she comes home and lectures me about unemployment and somebody called Keynes; she won't believe I'm not interested. She gets so excited and worked up about everything: the hunger marches and Spain and the Labour Party. Honestly, she's impossible.'

Peter gave Laura a quick, swooping glance and then re-focussed his attention on Susan. 'What are your interests?' he asked her. His voice had softened.

'Oh, I don't know,' Susan said. Laura noticed how pretty the line of her cheek was as she looked down at her hands as if suddenly shy. 'I like... window-shopping and meeting people; young people. I don't like old people much. I'm quite a frivolous person, I suppose.'

Laura was taken aback at the shy, serious way she was answering Peter's question. For the first time she wondered if she could be in love with him. She longed to ask her.

'We're living in very exciting times,' Arthur said. 'Everything's happening, do you feel that? There's so much talk of war, yet the British people, the ordinary working people have never been so determined on peace. We've been collecting signatures at work; signatures for peace.'

'I've heard all about that,' Peter said, 'but, honestly, what good are signatures? When Hitler's building up the greatest army Europe has ever known.'

'Now Arthur is going to tell us about the power of prayer,' Susan said in a pulpit voice.

'Don't you ever pray?' Laura said, drily.

'Does she?' Arthur said. 'I wouldn't have thought so.'

'You'd be surprised.'

'What do you pray for?' Peter asked her. His voice was serious, almost as though he'd suddenly had an inkling of the trouble she'd been in. She didn't answer him. 'Laura likes to tease me,' she said. 'She's so clever she can turn me inside out.'

There were tears in her eyes.

Peter turned to Laura as though for enlightenment. She only noticed his handsome shoulders, his eyes gone cloudy. She held his gaze as long as she dared.

'I was surprised when you said you weren't eighteen yet,' Arthur said, breaking the silence. 'I thought you'd be older than our Susan. I'm sure you look older.'

'She's old before her time,' Susan said. 'Sometimes she seems about a hundred.' She sounded very upset.

Arthur put a record on his gramophone and wound it up. The music, a sad Irish folk song, seemed to soothe them all.

After a minute or two Peter took Susan's hand and she was immediately happy again.

Laura and Arthur started whispering together about the troubles between Blackshirts and Jews in the East End.

At five o'clock they were called in to tea: turkey salad and Christmas cake, jelly and blancmange.

Peter talked to Mr and Mrs Wilkins about his apprenticeship which had still a year to run.

Laura thought designing jewellery an exotic job but possibly rather degrading; was jewellery a luxury product, she wondered, or an art-form?

'There's money in it, no doubt,' Mr Wilkins said.

'We sell pieces for hundreds of pounds.'

'When I want a tiara, I'll know where to come,' Laura said. 'It's useful having contacts.'

'I made my mother's wedding ring,' Peter said. 'It was twenty-two carat but she got it cost.'

'You mean my father got it cost,' Laura said. 'At least, I hope he paid for it.'

Everyone laughed. Laura noticed how small and pretty Susan's hands were, fluttering about the table like little birds. Her eyes, blue and short-sighted, made her look very vulnerable, like people who've just taken off their glasses. (Not that Susan would ever wear glasses. 'I'd rather go blind,' Laura could hear her say. 'What do I want to read for?')

Mr Wilkins asked Peter when he was returning to Birmingham. He was catching the first train in the morning. They talked about Birmingham; Mr Wilkins went there for his fruit and veg. Mrs Wilkins wanted to know where his digs were, whether he could walk to work. Or did he ride a bicycle she wondered. Did he ever go to the Central Hall, Mr Wilkins asked him. He thought it was a fine church. So did Mrs Wilkins.

Susan, realising how time was passing, was getting bored and fidgety.

'Have you got a sweetheart in London, Arthur?' she asked. 'I'm sure you have.'

'I'm sure I haven't,' Arthur said. 'I haven't the time or money to spend on sweethearts.'

'Quite right, son,' his father said. 'You finish your training first. One thing at a time. A young chap can lose everything by wanting too much too soon.'

The words fell on Susan like a doom.

'I agree he can't get married till he's finished his training,' Peter said, 'but having a sweetheart can steady a man, surely. I had a mate would drink all his wages away on a Friday night till he met this girl . . . and after that he went on the wagon, pretty near.'

'I don't think our Arthur takes a drink,' Mrs Wilkins murmured complacently.

'No,' Mr Wilkins said. 'No, I don't think Arthur needs a sweetheart yet, not to keep him off the drink anyway.' He and his wife smiled at each other.

If they had understood Peter's appeal, they were determined to ignore it.

Yet even Mr Wilkins was quite civil towards him.

At about eight o'clock Arthur suggested that he and the two girls should take Peter as far as his bus stop.'

'We may even walk as far as the city centre,' he told his parents. 'It'll do us good; we've been sitting about all day.'

Susan and Laura got themselves ready at once; before Mr Wilkins should find an excuse to keep them in.

'How lovely to be out,' Susan said. She hated the cold and hated walking. 'Look at the stars, isn't that Orion with his sword?'

'You two go on in front,' Arthur said. 'Laura and I will walk behind and keep an eye on you.'

'They met at my father's wedding,' Laura said, before Arthur should start to question her. 'My step-mother is very fond of her; she thinks Peter's made a very good choice.'

'A choice? Good heavens, you can't mean that Peter is serious about her?'

'My step-mother seems to think so.'

'I *am* surprised. He seems too quiet for Susan. I imagined her attracting all the wrong types; she certainly used to. I'll have a word with my father tonight.'

'Oh don't. He won't be at all pleased. You see, the wedding reception was held in a pub, and Susan kept it from him and he was furious.'

'That wasn't Peter's fault.'

'They're too strict with her, that's the trouble.'

'Yes, but Susan isn't a sensible girl like you.'

They walked in silence for a while, Laura wondering why she was feeling so depressed.

'Now I won't see him till Easter at the earliest,' Susan said the next morning when they were getting up for work. 'I might as well be dead.'

'Arthur said he was going to have a word with your father.'

'What about?'

'He thinks Peter is better than the riff-raff you usually attract; all those delivery boys who whistle after you.'

'Arthur's a decent sort, isn't he? Did you like him?'

'Very much.'

'I mean, is he your type?'

'I don't know what my type is.' (Laura had dreamed about Peter.)

'Because I know he likes you. He's going to write to you. He hopes you'll write to him.'

'Oh, I will. I've never had anyone to write to before.'

Susan's father agreed to recognise Peter as Susan's sweetheart in exchange for a promise from her that she never meet him except in the presence of a third party, a hard bargain in Laura's opinion, especially for the third party.

At the beginning of February it was Laura's eighteenth birthday. She spent her birthday money (a pound from her step-mother, half a crown from her father, half a crown from Mrs Wilkins) on a complete set of Dickens, illustrated and quarter-bound, at which Susan refused to talk to her for almost a week.

Chapter Eight

It was a hot Saturday in July 1937. A Miss Edith Simpson was unpacking some groceries when she caught sight of a riveting paragraph in the newspaper wrapped round her packet of soap flakes.

She took it to the window. It was a yellowing copy of the *Sunday World,* a newspaper she was ashamed to buy but always read avidly whenever it came her way.

How strange, she thought, how intriguing.

Leaving the groceries just where they were on the kitchen table - her cat, Peter, was to discover and disorder the small packet of cooked ham later in the afternoon - she telephoned her friend and colleague, Kathleen Wells.

'Kathleen,' she said, 'what was the name of that village you came from?'

'Lower Batsford,' Kathleen Wells answered. 'Lower Batsford, Warwickshire. Why?'

'Never mind,' Edith said. 'I'm coming round.'

Kathleen Wells worked in Whitehall as a senior civil servant. She was fifty-seven years old; young for her age. Her hair was thick and still brown, she was slim and her back was straight.

For the last ten years she had lived in a modern block of flats in Camberwell.

Her flat, on the first floor, overlooked the park from the front and the sports ground from the back. It was both comfortable and convenient; her sitting room was decorated in bright colours, blue, green and violet, her kitchen was all-electric, her bathroom tiled to the ceiling and her two bedrooms were light and airy.

She led a healthy, energetic life, still playing tennis or squash on two evenings a week. She went hiking on fine weekends and abroad for a fortnight every year. She boasted that she worked hard and played hard and knew how to enjoy herself. Worries she certainly had, what thinking person hadn't, but for the most part they were the lofty, world-scale ones. Of small, personal worries, the soul-shrivelling ones, she'd had remarkably few for many years; it was a case, she said, of knowing how to avoid trouble; you could be involved in mankind, she maintained, without having it breathing all over you.

And meanwhile her friend Edith Simpson was driving along in her Morris Eight, a page of a six months old newspaper in her handbag.

'I'll tell you this, Edith,' Kathleen said, when they were sitting down later in the afternoon, having tea and buns, 'I'm filled with alarm, foreboding and despondency.'

'But you must be excited as well; you must be.'

'I've never enjoyed excitement. As a child it brought me out in a rash. Latterly it's been giving me diarrhoea.'

'Well run along, dear. Don't mind me.'

'Shall you ask her to come here to visit, dear, or shall you go to find her?' Edith refused to allow Kathleen to shelve the problem.

'She's going to be such a responsibility. I don't feel I can face it. Her father must have died, I suppose. That must be the only reason she'd contact me like this.'

She took another sip of tea. 'The *Sunday World,*' she moaned. 'An orphan,' she moaned. 'And probably in some trouble.'

'How old is she? Really, Kathleen, it seems strange that you know so little about your only sister's only child. You'd have thought she'd have been your goddaughter, here for every holiday; pantomime at Christmas, the zoo at Easter and a week by the sea in August. Only think of the money you owe her; all her birthdays, the ivory-backed Bible and the gold cross for her confirmation. How old is she?'

'She must be sixteen or so. P'raps seventeen.'

'I'm not saying it's an easy age, dear, but, Heavens above,

she could have been left to you in nappies.'

Kathleen shuddered.

'What was your sister's name?'

'Molly.'

'Kathleen, why are you making me drag everything out of you? What caused the rift between you?'

'I'm not sure there was a rift, not exactly. I was a lot older than she was. We were never close. She was only about six when I left home and I never went back much; I couldn't afford it.'

'I see.'

Edith patted her mouth with her napkin and sat back in her chair.

'You sound disappointed,' Kathleen said. 'You were hoping for a huge family scandal, weren't you?'

'I thought she might have stolen your sweetheart, something like that.' Edith tried to sound facetious.

'No . . . Oh yes, damn you. Not that of course. But there was . . . unpleasantness.'

'What sort of unpleasantness? Oh come on, it will do you good to tell me.'

'And you're dying to hear the sordid details, aren't you?'

'Of course I am.' Edith leaned forward again, her plump, well-corseted body eager and responsive.

'I should have helped her,' Kathleen said.

Her voice had become thick; for a dreadful moment Edith thought she was going to cry.

'That's all, really.' She became brisk again, throwing her shoulders back. 'I should have helped her. You see, I'd had my chance; four years at the County Grammar School. By the time she was eleven, my father was dead and my mother couldn't afford to let her go.'

'Well really, Kathleen, how could you have helped her? On your pittance. You were far too young. I was still at the receiving end of financial help until I was almost thirty.'

'I suppose I could have done something if I was the right sort of sister. Anyway I wasn't, and I didn't. Neither did I raise a finger to help when she went into service at fourteen or fifteen. I just rather despised her for not fighting against it. When she was about twenty she got engaged to a newly demobbed soldier who was... well, handsome enough, I suppose, but...'

'Common?'

'Don't put words into my mouth. I was going to say "rough".'

'A rough diamond?'

'Just rough. She was a lady's maid by this time, very pretty and presentable. By now, I was earning considerably more and did offer my help. I got her an interview at a very nice private hotel in Knightsbridge; they wanted a receptionist cum general help. I said she could live with me and save her wages; I had a couple of rooms nearby. Of course I was hoping she'd meet someone else. But it was too late.'

'She wasn't tempted?'

'Not by the job. She was tempted by the soldier, succumbed and became pregnant.'

'And that was little Laura?'

'No. After the wedding she had a miscarriage; a nice irony, that. Laura was born three or four years later. In respectable wedlock. That is, if wedlock is ever respectable.'

'That's a very old-maidish thing to say.'

'I may be old, Edith, but I'm certainly no maid.'

'I know all about you, dear. Let's stick to Laura, shall we?'

'I sent her a christening present, I remember that; a beautiful little embroidered dress I'd got in Portugal.'

'I used to get those for Dolly's girls. Dirt cheap, weren't they?'

'I don't think I ever saw her. Yes, I did. She was staying with my mother, once, when I went down there on my annual visit. I think Molly was ill.'

'You didn't see your sister?'

'Not after the wedding. I went to her wedding.'

'Did you go to her funeral?'

'How cruel you are. No, I didn't go to her funeral, but only because my brother-in-law's letter arrived too late. He'd sent it to my last address but one. I wrote a letter and sent a cheque in lieu of a wreath.'

'Very proper and worthy. When people do things "in lieu" you can be quite certain that their motives are of the highest. But you didn't go to visit the motherless child?'

'I didn't know her, did I? I assumed my brother-in-law would soon marry again; that type of person does.'

'That "rough" type of person?'

'Mock me as much as you like. It's easy for someone like you - so safe on your middle-class perch - to swoop down and be charming now and again. I was afraid of becoming too involved: I stayed away.'

Edith opened her handbag and searched inside as though trying to find something to say. After a moment or two, and still silent, she snapped it shut.

'Oh Edith, I feel as though I'm being weighed in the balance and found wanting. I feel I'm being made to pay for all my years of self-indulgence.'

'I look upon it as a wonderful opportunity,' Edith said. 'An exciting chance to play fairy godmother.'

This time it was Kathleen who failed to reply. She stood up and started to clear the table. Without even excusing herself, she took the dishes to the kitchen and washed up. She cleaned a saucepan, which had been in soak since lunchtime, and then the sink which was already clean.

'I think you'd better go, Edith,' she said when she got back to the sitting room. 'I'm much too overwrought to ask you to stay to supper. I shall just heat myself a tin of beans and go to bed.'

'I suppose you'll be setting off quite early tomorrow? I suppose you wouldn't want my company...? All right, I'm going, dear. Don't trouble to see me out. I'll leave the address here.'

Kathleen Wells (who hadn't been called Kitty for years) arrived outside the Wilkins's shop on Sunday morning at precisely the minute Laura was closing the back door behind her, on her way to visit her father and step-mother.

They met on the pavement.

Kathleen recognised Laura immediately, not from the shaggy-haired little five-year-old she'd once seen at her mother's, but from old snapshots of herself. Seeing Laura was like stepping back in time.

'You must be Laura Brown,' she said. 'I'm your aunt, Kathleen Wells.'

'I've been expecting you,' Laura said.

They shook hands.

'Won't you come in? I was going to my father's house, but it doesn't matter.'

'You were going to church?' Kathleen asked nervously.

Laura smiled. 'No. To my Dad's house. My earthly father's earthly house.'

'Then you're not an orphan?'

'Oh no.'

All the worries Kathleen had had about Laura were groundless. She wasn't small and thin with a runny nose, nor dressed in workhouse calico and big boots. Neither did she sound at all like Wendy Hiller in the first act of *Pygmalion*. 'I've been let off the hook,' Kathleen told herself. 'I can slip back into that stagnant pond I came from as soon as I like.'

'I *am* glad,' she said.

'I'm sorry if I worried you.'

'I have been a little worried, yes.'

'I don't live with my father, that's all. He remarried. We don't get on very well, at least not when we're together.'

'Then it's very sensible to live apart. Have you got good digs here?'

'Not very. But next year I may be able to afford the YWCA.'

'I stayed in a hostel when I first went to London but I didn't like it much. I think perhaps they've improved now.'

'Are you sure you won't come in? I could take you to the parlour; nobody's ever in the parlour.'

'I think I'd rather go for a walk. I've been sitting too long.'

'We'll go to the park. It's not far.'

They set off together down Albert Road.

'It was my step-mother who suggested advertising for you,' Laura said. 'Thinking of it in cold blood, it seems rather a cheek.'

'Not at all,' Kathleen said. 'No one's ever advertised for me before.'

'You see, you're my only living relative. Unless you count my father . . . my earthly father.'

'I hope I'm not too much of a disappointment to you.'

'Oh no.'

They looked each other over with mutual satisfaction.

The park with its high railings, gravel paths and overgrown shrubs was a cheerless place even on a July morning; there were no flowers, not even weeds, and the birds shuffled about under the dusty laurel bushes instead of singing.

Kathleen and Laura sat on a bench studying each other.

'How well do you remember your mother?' Kathleen asked.

'I remember that she was very nice, very gentle, that's about all. Am I like her? I mean, in appearance.'

'No,' her aunt said. 'No, not really.' She felt suddenly shy, too shy to claim Laura for herself. 'You take after your grandfather,' she said. 'Big Ben they called him in the village.'

Laura thought of Westminster, the Houses of Parliament and the Abbey. 'It was because you lived in London that I wanted to find you,' she said.

'Oh.' Kathleen tried not to sound hurt.

'You see, I've always wanted to spend a holiday in London. It's always been a dream of mine.'

'You must come to stay whenever you'd like to. When do you have your next holiday? Are you still at school?'

'Heavens no. I left school last summer. I've got a job at the Education Office. And my annual holiday is at the end of next month.'

'Good. August isn't the best time to be in London but perhaps you can come again for Christmas. What did you particularly want to do?'

'Everything.'

'Well, we'll see what we can manage.'

Kathleen gave Laura her address and telephone number and they made plans, discussing dates and train times. They sat still and silent then, for several minutes, Kathleen feeling more tired than she'd ever felt in her life. Becoming an aunt was certainly an emotional business, she told herself.

Laura was thinking of London: of theatres and concerts and art galleries.

The Salvation Army Band passed by outside the park and

roused them. As soon as they could talk normally, Kathleen invited Laura to have lunch with her, but was relieved when she said her step-mother was expecting her.

'I'll drive you there,' she said.

'That would be marvellous. Thank you.'

They walked back to the car trying not to keep in step with the brass band. 'Why does everyone have to make such a noise on a Sunday?' Kathleen grumbled.

'Yes. Church bells for instance. Why do they have to start up on the one day you can sleep in?'

Laura directed her aunt through the small streets to the city centre and then out again on the other side.

Kathleen declined to meet her brother-in-law and his new wife. 'Not this time,' she said. 'I must admit that I feel drained; rather like used tea-leaves.'

As Laura got out of the car, Kathleen leaned over and kissed her. It was a shy, awkward kiss, but both felt a sense of promise in it; something understood.

'Who brought you over?' Mabel asked as Laura went in. She'd been standing by the window and had glimpsed the car.

'You'll never guess.'

'I've got the feeling it was your Auntie Kitty.'

'You are a one,' Laura said. 'Dad's right about you. You really are a one.'

She hugged her plump little step-mother until she squeaked.

Susan was getting engaged on her nineteenth birthday on August the twelfth and getting married on Boxing Day. Peter was designing and making her engagement and wedding rings; Susan was saving hard for her wedding dress, which on Laura's insistence was to be in the shade known as off-white. Everything was going swimmingly.

All the same, Susan didn't take the news of Laura's good fortune without a great deal of envy.

'Honestly, I wouldn't lower myself to covet your ox and your ass,' she said, 'but an auntie with a motorcar who can take you shopping in Regent Street and Oxford Street, oh,

Laura, you are lucky. Swan and Edgar. I think those are the loveliest words in the language. I wonder if you can call a girl Swan? I'd love to have twins called Swan and Edgar. Do you think Peter and I could stay with your auntie on our honeymoon? Would you have the nerve to suggest it? We could afford the train fare if we had somewhere to stay. It costs fifteen shillings *per night* at the Regent Palace Hotel.'

Susan and Peter were now confining their love-making to a relatively safe measure of kisses and scramblings in the back row of the cinema on the occasional Saturday night they could be together; Laura, who was deputed to chaperone them, leaving them at the ticket office on the way in and meeting them at the cigarette kiosk at the end. Susan's greatest fear was that the film might be a Western, during which Peter had a nasty habit of trying to keep at least one eye on the screen. Her favourite film had been *The Travels of Marco Polo,* which had been so boring that neither of them had seen anything but the last reel, when the music, drawing to a huge crescendo of sound, had warned them to sit up, and, in a distinctly heady state, their shortage of oxygen probably as great as that of the Himalayan climbers, they'd seen a breathtaking vista of mountain tops stretching out mile after mile to the far horizon. 'And what is that country beyond the mountains?' a small man, presumably Marco, was asking his small companion, perhaps his guide. 'Sir, it is called Cathay,' was the answer; and the end of the film. Susan, though not usually of a poetic nature, often declaimed that line with great feeling. 'What *is* the girl on about?' her mother would ask.

Laura had no sweetheart. She tried to interest herself in a fellow student at one of the evening classes she went to; they sat at the same table for their interval coffee and walked part of the way home together afterwards. He was twenty-one, intelligent, earnest and ambitious, the sort of man she wanted as a friend. If he had tried to hold her hand, though, when they walked home, she would have been embarrassed and upset. Luckily it seemed as far from his mind as from hers.

Since the Christmas holiday, she had been receiving a long

weekly letter from Arthur in which he discussed politics and world affairs, religion, including Buddhism, his work, his place in society and in the scheme of things, and always remained her sincere friend. She answered them seriously and sincerely.

Sometimes Susan teased her about Arthur. 'Here's a letter from your boyfriend,' she'd say, dancing about in front of her with the letter in her hand. Laura used to get more annoyed at these times than the occasion warranted. The truth was that she wanted a boyfriend; but she wanted Peter.

For all that she pretended to dismiss him as 'your little jeweller,' she could never be comfortable with him. Whenever he was in the same room, she was aware of her racing pulse and her faster breathing.

One Saturday, because Mrs Wilkins's mother and sister were coming for a weekend and they were short of beds, it had been arranged that Laura would stay at her stepmother's. It happened to be a Saturday when Peter was home, so the outcome was that Peter and Laura, after taking Susan back from the cinema, had set out together to his home. (Except for her duties as chaperone Laura would have gone over in the afternoon to avoid the embarrassment of being alone with him.)

Peter, she told herself afterwards, had obviously been roused to fever-pitch by the three-hour kissing and petting at the cinema.

When they were about two hundred yards from the bus stop, he had suddenly grabbed her hand. 'Let's run, the bus is coming.'

There was no bus in sight but she started running with him, he pulling her along at a great speed, the night streaming past them, a cool breeze in their faces.

It was marvellous: the excitement, his strength, his hard grip on her hand. They sped past the bus stop. 'We'll go on to the next,' he said.

'I can't,' she said, after another hundred yards, 'I can't go further.' Her breath was coming cold and hard, her heart thumping against her ribs. 'Yes, you can. Don't stop,' he commanded her. 'We're nearly there. Don't stop.'

But a bus came past and she threw out her hand to stop it and it slowed down for them in between stops.

She stumbled on to the platform. 'Spoilsport,' he said. 'We could have run all the way.'

She dropped like a stone into the nearest empty seat and he smiled down at her. He laughed at the way she was struggling for breath.

They had to change buses at the city centre. The bus they needed was already in and almost empty. They sat down together and again he took her hand. 'What now?' Laura said, in a tone which was half protest, half submission. 'What indeed,' he said, kissing her hand and then releasing it.

He was silent during the ten-minute journey; so was she. They walked in silence to the house.

When they arrived, she sat down to have a cup of tea with her step-mother, but he went straight upstairs.

She couldn't sleep. She wanted him to come to her. Her body wanted him. She could almost feel his lips crushing hers, his body heavy on hers. 'What a fool I am,' she told herself, 'what a stupid fool.'

He went back to Birmingham on the first train the next morning. She wasn't up.

'How did you sleep last night?' her step-mother asked her over breakfast. 'Peter said he didn't sleep a wink; he was burning all night, he said. I hope he isn't coming down with anything.'

Why should he tease her? She was angry with him, angry with herself, and angry with Susan, too, for being such a simpleton. She knew there was something in Peter that Susan couldn't satisfy for long. She knew it, but could do nothing about it but be hurt and miserable in turns.

So while Susan envied Laura her holiday in London, Laura was suffering more deeply. 'I'll get over it,' she told herself. 'I've got to bloody get over it.'

Soon after their meeting, Kathleen had sent her a five-pound note to buy what she needed for her holiday. After getting the return fare to Euston, a cardboard suitcase and a lightweight dressing-gown, she had two pounds left.

She gave one of them to Susan for her trousseau. She felt that it squared up something.

Chapter Nine

Laura's step-mother had insisted that only a black suit was smart enough for London, and as good luck would have it, had the very thing in her wardrobe.

'It'll fit you a treat,' she'd said. 'It's ten years old and I was slimmer in those days.'

She'd fetched it. 'I had it for Joe,' she'd said, her voice trailing a little, 'for Joe's funeral. And of course I had to have the best. It's a beautiful material, so soft, look, it's got a bloom on it. No, not another word, I'm going to do it over for you. I wanted to give you something for London.'

Laura's step-mother was short and plump, Laura tall and slender. At first sight a reconciliation seemed improbable, but measurements were taken, the sewing machine and a box of pins brought out and the suit unpicked and altered. Later in the day, Laura was sent upstairs to try it on.

When she came down she was rather subdued. Her fashion-sense was not particularly well developed but a glance in her step-mother's mirror had given her a very definite inkling that all was not quite as it should be.

Her step-mother, though, had been thoroughly satisfied. 'Beautiful,' she'd said in a breathy voice, 'the skirt is just right, they're shorter again this year, and the jacket, well, all the jacket needs is two tucks here and the buttons moved here and here. Harry, put the paper down and come and see your little girl. Now then. Isn't this beautiful material? Anybody who recognises quality will appreciate this, I can tell you. What you need now is a new white blouse with a jabot, then you'll look perfect, the perfect lady.'

'She looks... different,' her father had said, 'but I'm not saying it's not good quality; I can tell it is.'

Susan, torn between loyalty towards her future mother-in-law and a frank desire to tell Laura that it made her look a frump, compromised by saying 'Don't bother about a white blouse, what that suit needs is a really eye-catching hat; a large poppy-coloured straw for instance.'

'I couldn't possibly wear a big red hat,' Laura had said. 'Don't be an idiot. I haven't worn a hat since I was at school.'

'People wear hats in London,' Mrs Wilkins had said. 'Oh yes. And your auntie will want you to look right. You owe her that.'

So Susan had met Laura at lunchtime the next day and taken her off to C and A's. ('Do you know what C and A stands for? Coats and 'Ats,' Susan had said.)

For a few minutes they'd fooled around, trying on velvet turbans, pill-boxes with spotted veils, dowagers' black hats and brides' mothers' pastels. Then Susan had caught sight of the large straws, and, failing to find the scarlet she'd hoped for - it was that season's colour and sold out - had talked Laura into buying the cerise. 'It's a lovely shade,' Susan had said. 'It makes me think of...' 'Beetroot,' Laura had said. 'And God knows why I should spend my hard-earned money on the wretched thing.'

'Gosh,' Mrs Wilkins had said, seeing hat and suit together on the morning of Laura's departure. In the mouth of that mild woman it was a daring expostulation.

Mr Wilkins had driven Laura to the station in his van and left her on the platform with three oranges, only slightly bruised, and a warning that she should travel in a ladies-only compartment, talk to no one and not let her suitcase out of her hand until she reached her auntie's.

'Thank you, Mr Wilkins.'

Hating Mr Wilkins as she did, Laura would have felt compromised to accept his advice on anything, so the moment he'd left, she'd followed a good-looking, middle-aged man on to the train, smiled pleasantly at him, 'Will you look after my suitcase for a minute? A beastly greengrocer's just palmed off some rotten fruit on me.'

After running up the platform and tipping the oranges into a litter-bin, she'd returned to find the compartment filled. Luckily, the man left in charge of her suitcase had kept a corner seat for her opposite his own.

Naturally, they began to talk. The good-looking, middle-aged man thought her eccentric and dowdy but nevertheless found her friendliness refreshing. Talking to her would certainly help pass the time; he hadn't even managed to get himself a newspaper that morning.

As the sun got hotter Laura took off both her hat and her jacket and her companion noticed how attractive she was, her plain white blouse, one left over from school, fitting tightly over her large round breasts. He asked her where she was staying in London; she'd already told him that she was going there for a fortnight's holiday; she told him.

He talked knowledgeably of London. He'd lived there, he said, for over fifteen years.

She told him that she hoped to visit the art galleries and the British Museum. He admitted to knowing very little about art, but said he knew the Museum well. He seemed to, calling it the BM, talking at some length about the richness of the foreign collections and advising her which to see first. He told her how to get there from Camberwell. He drew her a map.

At Reading he insisted on getting her some orangeade and a bun from the Refreshment Rooms though he had nothing himself.

For a time he sat and watched her eating and drinking.

'I shall stay and have a word with your aunt,' he told her as they were approaching Euston. (He hoped the aunt would prove as unconventional as the niece.) 'Since she isn't able to have time off work, she may allow me to take you sight-seeing.'

'That would be lovely,' Laura said. 'Unfortunately, though, she isn't able to meet me. She wrote earlier in the week telling me I'd have to take a taxi but that she'd be home by the time I got there.'

'My dear young lady, you mustn't dream of getting a taxi.

My car is at your disposal. My flat is only three or four minutes walk from the station and it would give me the greatest pleasure to drive you to Camberwell. London taxis are damnably expensive.'

Laura had been warned often enough about the advances made to young girls by strange men, but after the three-hour journey he didn't seem at all like a strange man. Also, he was old in her eyes, almost as old as her father, and quite obviously respectable and well-educated. She felt totally at ease with him.

He lifted down her suitcase from the rack and carried it for her.

It was very hot in London; hot and sultry. It was certainly more than three or even four minutes' walk to her new friend's house, but he was a wonderful companion, pointing out everything of interest as they walked along.

His flat was in the basement of a handsome but delapidated terraced house. 'Come in a moment while I pick up the keys,' he said, leading her down a side entrance and stepping aside to let her in.

At that point, he made a small mistake. He locked the door after him and glanced at her to see whether she'd noticed it.

She pretended she hadn't.

When she turned towards him in the sitting room he had a great surprise. She wasn't, as he'd supposed, a foolish innocent, but an experienced girl who knew well what she was doing; she stood facing him with a mocking, combative smile on her face.

He put down the suitcase, laid the key on the table and took a small step towards her. 'Your aunt won't mind your being a little late,' he said, his voice low and not entirely steady.

She kicked him hard in the shin and as he doubled up with pain and shock, she clapped the large cerise hat over his face, picked up the key and the suitcase and let herself out. She had no idea where she was but she walked along swiftly in the direction she had come.

A minute or two's walk led her to a main street where she was soon able to hail a taxi.

*

'I think you dealt superbly with the situation,' her aunt said over tea. 'Anyway, it seems exactly the thing to have done with the hat. I'm afraid I can't agree with your friend about that black suit, it isn't a large straw hat it needs as much as an elderly occupant. If you'd like to take it off now I'll parcel it up for my friend's charwoman.'

'I hope I didn't break his ankle,' Laura said, 'he was such a nice man.'

She had a wonderful two weeks in London with no more startling adventures. She found her way about very easily and, with no one to consider but herself, managed to see and do at least a quarter of the things on her list. Her aunt took her to the theatre twice; on the other evenings she went to concerts on her own.

Edith Simpson, whose grocery order had brought aunt and niece together, had been busy imagining a plump, round-faced orphan, docile but rather backward. A well-grown girl, tidily dressed, with penetrating eyes and a humorous expression seemed rather a disappointment.

'She seems so old for her age, dear,' she told her friend. 'I suppose it must be her deprived childhood. Dolly's girls are so jolly, so full of fun. Is it normal for a girl of eighteen to like opera? Do you know that she went to a lecture at the National Gallery this afternoon. On El Greco. Oh, I know there's nothing wrong with it, dear, only it seems . . . sad. I rather hoped she'd want me to take her to the zoo tomorrow but she says she doesn't care for caged animals so we're going to the Victoria and Albert instead. Well, some of the museums do very good afternoon teas. All the same, Dolly's girls loved the zoo. Oh Kathleen, I'm afraid she's going to become another dry-as-dust spinster just like you and me.'

Kathleen found her niece's company exhilarating. Laura was excited and enthusiastic about things she had long taken for granted. They talked until late every night.

On the second Sunday of Laura's stay, Arthur came to have tea with them.

Kathleen, who had feared a too-early romantic attachment, was relieved to find only a perfect casual friendship.

'He's much more intelligent than he seemed this afternoon,' Laura said. 'His letters are very interesting. It's wonderful to find someone else who's as ambitious as I am. Susan's so different. Susan's my best friend but I despair of her, I really do. It's as though she's shut up her mind and marked it "not wanted on voyage". And she used to be so bright.'

'Lots of girls are like that. When's she's married and settled, she'll begin to develop again. Is she very much in love?'

'I suppose so. She's got a boring job as a dentist's receptionist. She's never had much to do all day but day-dream; now her dream's come true. She's certainly very happy at the moment. She loves meeting Peter, introducing him as her fiancé; she even loves parting from him.'

'She loves courting,' Kathleen said. 'Why ever can't she put off the wedding for seven years or so? That's what she should do.'

'Because Peter's too impatient, I suppose. I suppose he's not satisfied with courting. And when they're married, neither of them will be satisfied for long. Susan expects far too much; a different world. She might be happy for a bit longer if Peter was rich, but he's not. They'll be poor for a long time. They'll probably have a baby quite soon. Susan will be old by the time she's twenty-five.'

'You're very cynical for someone so young.'

'I suppose I am.'

Kathleen stared at Laura's worried face and felt very close to her.

'I shouldn't worry too much about Susan if I were you. Even if her marriage is unhappy, she'll be prepared to suffer; she'll still think her state far superior to being unmarried. For her, marriage is a matter of prestige; she's won the prize.'

'You talk as if you knew her,' Laura said.

'I've known many girls like her: she'll be all right.'

Laura heard a note of bitterness tightening Kathleen's voice.

'Do you ever regret staying single?' she asked her.

Kathleen was silent for some moments. 'I suppose I do,' she said. 'I'd have liked children . . . I think.'

Then she told Laura about her long love-affair with a married man. He'd been her boss, forty-one or two when it had begun, she'd been twenty-six. At first he'd talked of leaving his wife; sometimes she'd half believed him. He hadn't, of course. All the same, it had gone on; the affair.

At the beginning she had occasionally tried to end it; later she'd become used to being a mistress, to eating out in strange, out-of-the-way restaurants, used to avoiding people, used to spending weekends and holidays alone.

'I was often happy,' she'd said. 'It lasted about twelve years.'

'How did it end?' Laura asked. She didn't really want to know but the question seemed to have been planted for her.

'He fell in love with another twenty-six-year-old, another ambitious career woman who was flattered by his attention – he was Head of Department by this time – and he took up with her. He had to endure one very trying evening when I shouted at him and threw things. Apart from that it was all plain sailing; his wife was probably not even aware of any change. He's Sir Desmond now. I see him from time to time but we don't speak.'

'How do you feel towards him now?' Laura asked.

'Only a mild sort of hatred. Love and hate are very close; at least they were in my case.'

'Oh God,' Laura said. 'I've bitten off a perfectly good nail... I may as well start on the others now,' she added morosely.

'Sir Desmond Hartley,' Kathleen said. 'I haven't spoken of him for years. I think I'll have a whisky. Would you like some? Or would you prefer some wine? I've got some rather nice white wine?'

For a time they drank together in silence.

They heard midnight strike. 'Another glass won't hurt you,' Kathleen said.

On the last morning of her stay, when Laura was busy with her packing, her aunt came into her bedroom wearing her tortoiseshell reading spectacles and carrying a sheaf of papers.

'I think we should get you into university, Laura,' she

said. 'I've been up all night planning it. I'm sorry it's all going to be a bit of a rush but I think it's the right thing, don't you? If you start this October, you'll have almost finished by the time I'm due to retire, so it will work out very well.'

'It does sound a good idea,' Laura said, sitting down heavily on her bed.

'Good,' her aunt said. 'And Edith thinks so too.'

Chapter Ten

'That's a lovely stone, that is,' Mr Wilkins said. 'That stone will keep its value. I don't like these chippings.'

'I'm going to university,' Laura told herself, putting up the five syllables of that glittering word like a shield against her envy of Susan.

Peter had been staring at her for the last half-hour; she felt confused again. 'Un-i-ver-sit-y. An educational institution for the instruction of students in every branch of learning.'

She had arrived back from London just in time for the engagement party, her head still aching from the excitement of the morning; she had expected to feel nothing but a mild irritation at being back.

'It's not a stone, it's a diamond,' Susan said in a child's voice, everyone except Laura smiling indulgently at her.

'From the Latin universitas: whole,' Laura continued, trying not to grind her teeth.

Susan was almost beautiful that day, dressed in baby-blue, her baby-blue eyes dizzy with triumph and happiness. The white heart-shaped box which had held the engagement ring was in front of her on the table. From time to time she'd put out her hand and stroke it as though it was a small animal.

'It's a gorgeous ring,' Peter's mother said. 'He spent hours and hours making that, I'm sure.' She was in her dove-grey wedding dress, pearls at the neck.

Mr Wilkins, who had obviously decided that it was necessary to overlook the rowdy wedding reception held at the Queen's Head the previous year, was behaving very graciously towards Peter's mother, continually pushing things at her: the plate of ham, the cucumber - sliced thinly and soaked in vinegar - the bowl of salad - best English tomatoes, hard-boiled eggs, spring onions, finely chopped lettuce, the bottle of salad cream.

'A beautiful ring,' he agreed, inclining his head towards her and smiling, his false teeth, large and yellow, slipping a little as he did so. 'A very good investment.'

Having, at length, exhausted the subject of the engagement ring, Mr Wilkins started asking Peter's mother about her shop; how much patent medicine she sold and whether she stocked things like mop-heads and hair-nets and babies' dummies. A good corner shop could be a little gold mine in his opinion.

'Mrs Brown hasn't come here to talk about business,' Mrs Wilkins said in her slow mild voice. 'We want to plan the wedding, dear, don't we?'

'Wedding, wedding, what wedding?' Mr Wilkins asked in a ponderous effort to recover his party manners.

'Oh Dad,' Susan said, rising to the bait like a dutiful little fish. 'Oh Laura, isn't he awful?'

'Yes, he is,' Laura said grimly.

Peter was still staring at her. She tried to hold on to the picture of herself in academic gown crossing a wide quadrangle.

The wedding was to be held in Mason's Lane Chapel, where Susan and Arthur had been christened and confirmed, the reception in the Vestry. John, who was having a few days' leave over Christmas, was to be the best man and Laura the bridesmaid.

Laura, on hearing her name, started up and spilt some of her tea on the best lace cloth.

'Oh Laura,' her step-mother said, dabbing at it with her handkerchief. 'What a dreamer you are.'

'She's still thinking about London, I suppose,' she told the others. 'She's hardly said a word to me yet, though it was me, you know, who thought of advertising for her auntie in the first place.'

'Perhaps she's dreaming of Arthur,' Susan said. 'Arthur

wrote to tell us he'd met her in London.'

Laura looked about her wildly.

'My, but haven't you got brown in London, Laura,' Mrs Wilkins said, trying to calm her. 'Anybody'd think you'd been to the seaside.'

'It's her gypsy blood,' Mr Wilkins said. 'Ha, ha, ha.'

'It's fashionable, anyway,' her step-mother said. 'A tan is very fashionable nowadays. And it sets off her eyes lovely.'

Laura's eyes, which were usually greenish, seemed acorn-coloured that evening.

'My boss has been making a topaz necklace this week,' Peter said. 'Eighteen carat-gold and stones big as my thumbnail.'

'That would be worth a fair bit,' Mr Wilkins said. He always enjoyed a conversation weighted down with really large sums of money.

'Was it a commissioned piece?' his mother asked. Mabel loved hearing about the aristocracy: Lady So-and-So and the Honourable Mrs Such-and-Such.

'It would suit Laura,' Peter said.

'Lay not up for yourselves treasures upon earth, where moth and rust doth corrupt,' Laura managed to say. No one else seemed to be noticing the way Peter was staring at her. What a rotter he was.

As soon as she could, she got up to help Mrs Wilkins clear away the plates. In the scullery, she laid a cold dish to her burning cheeks. 'What's the matter, dear?' Mrs Wilkins asked. 'Can't you tell me? I know there's something.'

'Shall I take in the trifle?'

'I'll carry that, you bring the glass bowls. I know there's something on your mind, dear. Is it anything to do with our Arthur?'

Laura smiled at the idea of Arthur being capable of agitating anyone.

So that's how things are, Mrs Wilkins thought. Well, he certainly could do worse.

When Laura told Susan about her aunt's plans for her, she seemed quite pleased. 'It's what you wanted, isn't it,' she'd said, giving her an affectionate hug.

But when she realised a few days later that Laura would be starting her new life at the beginning of October, she became almost hysterical.

'But you can't possibly go until I get married. How can you? I'll have so much to do; I'll need you. I won't enjoy any of the preparation unless you're here. We've always done everything together, haven't we? Oh, why can't you start after Christmas when I'll be living in Birmingham? I'm sure they wouldn't mind; not if you explained things to them.'

To calm her, Laura had to make several more concessions than she'd intended. 'I'll come back here as soon as term's over,' she promised. 'I think it finishes about the tenth of December, so I'll have heaps of time to help you. And you can come up to spend a few days with me at half-term; Kathleen said I could invite you. I'll take you round Oxford Street. We'll have a lovely time. Come on, cheer up. Anyway nothing's fixed yet. I don't even know whether I'll be accepted. They like people to have got 'Higher'; the Higher School Certificate. It's quite likely they'll turn me down.'

'When will you know? Oh Laura, I do hope they will. And it's not just for my sake but for yours. Everybody's worried about you going to university. Peter says you'll lose your femininity; he says girls who've been to university get very hard and spiteful. And my father's afraid you'll get into trouble. He thinks you're very wilful. Oh, I know this isn't true, Laura, but he thinks I've been a good influence on you. And my mother's afraid you'll be lonely on your own. Well, you don't really make friends, do you? I mean, what friends have you got but me? And you're part of a family here, aren't you, Laura? Even when I go to live in Birmingham, you'd still have my Mum and Dad, wouldn't you, and they feel a responsibility for you . . . Oh, what I hope is they'll turn you down for this year and accept you for next. After all, you're awfully young for your age . . . Oh God, Laura, how will I manage without you? You know I'm always broke by Wednesday. They probably won't even let me go out with Peter when you've gone; you know my Dad's always insisted that you come everywhere with us.'

'But now that you're engaged he'll surely trust you on your own. Anyway, I'll only be away about ten weeks; they'll soon pass. And when I get back we'll have all the last minute things to do together. It'll be fun.'

'Oh, Laura, I hope they turn you down.'

At the beginning of September, though, Laura heard that she'd been accepted at University College and was to start in a month's time.

She gave in her notice at work and immediately started making preparations for her new life.

Susan was rather quiet when she first heard the news, but soon Laura heard her boasting about her to one of her father's customers. 'Yes, they made a special ruling for her. You wouldn't think she was clever, would you?'

'Will she miss us, Harry?' her step-mother asked her husband a few days before Laura was due to leave.

'Not a bit, lass,' her father said. 'She's always been too independent by half.'

'Oh Harry, but you can understand it, can't you? When her Mummy died she had to be independent, didn't she? All those years without a mother's love. If only you and I had met earlier! There was your little girl without a mummy and my two lads without a daddy, why didn't we have the good fortune to meet before?'

Laura and her father looked at each other reflectively.

'Of course I'll miss you,' Laura said. 'I'll write every week, I promise.'

'Do you know what Peter told us this week,' her step-mother said, when they were sitting in the parlour after dinner. 'He wants to put off the wedding until Easter. He's got a chance to have a week in Amsterdam over Christmas. The Birmingham Jewellers' Association send two promising apprentices to the diamond centre every year and this year he's been chosen.'

'Oh gosh,' Laura said.

'Well, that's what I thought. Susan would never put up with it, would she? "You must choose," I told him in my letter yesterday. "Perhaps it would be a wonderful opportunity for you, son, but I'm not at all sure that Susan wouldn't call off the wedding if you went."'

'Perhaps she'd be sensible,' Laura said. 'After all, she'd benefit in the long run, wouldn't she?'

'But I don't think Susan would be ready to consider the long run, do you? She's a very nice girl and I'm very fond of her, but for all that, I don't think she'd want the wedding put off; she's already counting the weeks. What do you think, Harry?'

'I've told you what I think. He should go, that's what I think. It's a big chance for him.'

'Couldn't he do both? Get married and take her with him to Amsterdam?'

'Where would he get that sort of money from, dear?'

'Well, I wish you hadn't told me about it; I'll be on tenterhooks from now on. I'll never get away to London if there's any sort of trouble between Peter and Susan.'

'You mustn't let Susan boss you around,' her step-mother said. 'It's not good for either of you. I say the same thing to Peter.'

'She's the only friend I've got,' Laura said. 'I must put up with her, I suppose.'

That evening, when she was getting ready to leave, her father surprised her by announcing his intention of walking with her as far as the bus stop.

Her step-mother blushed and twinkled. 'He's going to tell you about the birds and the bees, dear,' she said. 'Anyway, here's a little something from me to be getting on with. Good advice is all very well but you can get a lot more cups of tea with a ten-shilling note. And I'll be sending you another when I can.'

For twenty yards or so, Laura and her father walked along in silence. The street was deserted. It had been raining heavily during the afternoon, the sky was still leaden. Laura shivered in her light coat. Autumn was in the air; autumn and the smell of rain.

'You're always on the wrong side, you are,' her father suddenly burst out. 'And you always were. But this time, have a care. He's her son, that's what I want you to remember.'

'What are you talking about?' Laura asked. 'What are you asking me to do?'

'Your Susan's not right for her lad. You know that.'

'It's not true. Why do you say that?'

'Any husband would do for your Susan. If Peter broke with her next week, she'd have another chap in three months. She's that sort of a girl.'

'I don't think you're right. Anyway, what can I do about it? I can't do anything. Susan's my friend; she always has been.'

'You could write to her Peter and tell him to go to Amsterdam. He won't get another chance like that. Tell him she'd wait for him if she was any good for him; if she was the right sort of a girl.'

'I couldn't do that,' Laura said.

'No, I knew you wouldn't,' her father said savagely. 'Why did I bother to ask you? I knew you wouldn't do it.'

She got hold of her father's arm and shook it. 'I can't do anything,' she said. 'Not because I can't be bothered but because I'm involved. I'm in love with Peter myself if you have to know; half in love with him anyway. Now do you understand why I can't do anything?'

'*In love,*' he said, mocking her. 'Here's another one *in love.*'

But his anger had left him; he seemed tired, nothing more; he dragged his feet as he walked along beside her.

Laura was appalled that she had let her father into the secret she had hardly admitted even to herself. 'What a mess,' she said when they reached the bus stop. 'What a mess everything is.'

The bus came round the corner towards them.

'You try to forget all about it,' her father said. 'You just get on with your work, like poor Annie used to tell you.'

It was the first time Annie had ever been mentioned between them. She wanted to fling her arms round her father and kiss him, but the bus had stopped and the conductor was at the door; she only managed a quick little smile.

All the way across the city, her heart felt small and helpless.

Dear Peter, she wanted to write. I think you love me. I think I love you. We'd suit each other, I think. There would be hell to pay from Susan but I think I could bear it if you could. Couldn't we at least meet and talk it over?

She knew she would never write it. How could she?

When she got in, Susan was in the highest spirits.

Knowing how she was going to miss Laura, her father had promised to take her to Birmingham, 'her future home', on the following Saturday.

'Don't get too worked up,' Laura said, like a mother concerned that too much excitement would lead to tears. 'Oh dear, are you sure you're going to like Birmingham so much? I thought it very big and ugly that time Miss Allard took us to the museum. Don't expect too much will you; it's not heaven on earth or anything like that.'

'Oh Laura, it's got Lewis's,' Susan said.

Chapter Eleven

At first, Laura's new life proved exhausting and bewildering; she was often tempted to give it all up. (She was also very home-sick. Kathleen provided her with intelligent companionship and every comfort, but she missed Susan's empty-headed chatter and the clutter of their shared room more than she'd have believed.)

She was behind with her work.

At evening school the previous year, she'd studied economics and political history, because they'd seemed more relevant to a career in social administration. Kathleen, though, had persuaded her to read at university what she'd most enjoy, so that she'd opted for English, her favourite and best subject at school.

She'd read widely but rather haphazardly and was therefore far behind the rest of her class, who'd had two years of disciplined study in a Sixth Form; she had a formidable amount of catching-up to do.

She was also finding linguistics and Old English very difficult.

To make matters worse, she wasn't able to concentrate all her attention on getting to grips with her work because it had been impressed on her that the social life of the college was a necessary and important side of the curriculum; for the first half of the first term she'd attended the meetings of various clubs and societies as though they were a compulsory part of her hard labour.

'At least I'm not having time to moon over Peter,' she used to tell herself as she crawled into bed every night. 'Oh, Peter, why couldn't you have fallen in love with me instead of Susan, and saved me from this.'

She'd expected to become a different person in London, a cool and mature undergraduate, but she hadn't changed. She felt like someone transformed by a wardrobe of expensive new clothes who undressing is dismayed to find the same old flesh and bones underneath.

She was often tempted to tell Kathleen about her feelings for Peter, but something always stopped her. 'Perhaps I'm only infatuated with him,' she used to tell herself, 'perhaps only jealous of Susan.' All the same it certainly seemed something else.

Six weeks after the beginning of term she got a letter from Susan.

> Guess what? I'm pregnant. (You shouldn't have left me on my own, should you?) Anyway, I'm not frantic this time. I'm not even going to tell anyone but you. In a way it's been quite lucky because Peter was offered some silly trip to Holland and wanted to put off the wedding till Easter, but in the end he didn't have any choice, did he? (Don't tell his Mum about that, she doesn't know.) I hope I don't get fat for a while because my wedding dress is already a teeny bit tight. I won't be able to have any Christmas dinner. I'm dying to buy baby dresses (cross your fingers it's a girl!) but I dare not because if my Dad saw them he'd kill me. Oh, I'm longing to be married. Please burn this letter. Don't forget. *Do it now.* Your ever loving and devoted Susan.
> PS. Have you done it? X X X

Laura tried to burn the letter but failed: she found it very moving. She cried for Susan, for Peter and for herself. She couldn't decide whom she pitied most.

In the middle of November, a week or two after the letter, Susan came up for the weekend.

Laura spent the entire Friday afternoon walking round Oxford Street and Regent Street with her. Neither of them had much money, but they bought each other small presents and looked at prams.

Kathleen had borrowed a camp-bed for Susan, but she and Laura slept together as they always had, and talked and giggled for half the night. Laura couldn't believe that Susan would accept her new role as expectant mother with such apparent ease. 'Well it's natural, isn't it?' Susan said. 'It's you that's unnatural.'

On Saturday morning, Kathleen took the two girls to Kensington High Street where she bought seven yards of material for Laura's bridesmaid's dress. (The task having been allotted to her when she was five-and-a-half, Laura hadn't even tried to get out of being Susan's bridesmaid.)

Kathleen and Laura had both favoured an almond-green watered silk, but Susan had insisted that any green was unlucky. Laura had then refused all the pastel shades, pink, mauve and lemon, which Susan had wanted, so that they'd finally had to compromise on a golden-brown satin. 'You'll look like a sofa,' Susan had said, kicking her ankles.

Afterwards they'd had lunch in Derry and Tom's and had gone to see a Noel Coward play in the afternoon.

'I like her,' Kathleen had said after they'd put her on the six o'clock train that evening. 'I didn't think I would, but I do. She's a dear.'

The remainder of Laura's first term passed quickly and successfully. She felt that she'd got into her stride; she managed to get good marks in all her essays and even ventured to speak once or twice in class discussions; at last she knew she was going to be all right. Girls she'd thought haughty began to be friendly, even cordial. She started to enjoy herself.

Kathleen, who had worried a great deal about the change she was making in her life, was also beginning to feel more optimistic. With the extra work and responsibility she'd taken on, she'd expected to feel tired and older; to her surprise she was feeling tired but younger. Laura had involved her in so much that she was almost having a second fling.

*

A few days after the end of term, Laura returned home.

On the train she felt as though she was becoming another person, shrinking to fit an old mould; the maturity and the confidence she'd struggled so hard to achieve were slipping away from her. She'd recently found her true self, it seemed to her, but what if her true self was the old self: Harry Brown's daughter, Mabel's step-daughter, Susan's friend and protagonist, the Wilkins's lodger? It was four o'clock and already almost dark. The train sliced through vivid blue countryside like dream landscape. Why did she feel so insubstantial? What was real?

She didn't want to go back, she knew that much. She wasn't looking forward to Christmas, she was dreading the wedding, sick with fear at the thought of seeing Peter again.

The only thing she was looking forward to was giving Susan the present she had for her in her suitcase: a tea-set decorated with exotic birds and flowers. Susan had admired it in a display case in one of the Oxford Street shops and Kathleen had given her the money to buy it. She tried to keep it in the forefront of her mind; birds of paradise and plum blossom flashed on the darkening windows of the compartment as the train sped across small towns and farmland to the Midlands.

Mr Wilkins and Susan met her at the station. Susan hugged her but said very little. Mr Wilkins carried her cases to the van and grumbled about the rush hour traffic.

Mrs Wilkins was hovering about in the passage waiting for them. 'You're just in time for supper,' she said. 'Arthur says you're working much too hard, but you're looking well; I think you've grown again.' She took her coat, as though she was a visitor. She felt like a visitor. The house seemed to be smaller and darker than she remembered.

It was cottage pie and sprouts for supper.

'What are your vegs like in London?' Mr Wilkins asked her. 'I'm sure you haven't tasted sprouts like this since you've been away. Ah, but these are grown locally, aren't they, that's the difference. We have the pick of the Evesham crops here at six o'clock every morning. These sprouts were out in a field yesterday. Well, they could be days in Covent Garden before they ever get to the London suburbs. Same with savoy. What do you pay for savoy in London?'

Had supper-time conversation always been like this, Laura wondered. Or was something the matter? The main difference seemed to be that Susan was being most unnaturally silent. 'Oh, Dad, we don't want to hear about sprouts,' would have been her normal rejoinder. 'Hey, we had a man in today who'd left his false teeth in a bus. Guess who I saw in Woolworth's lunch time?' What was the matter with Susan? She wasn't saying a word, she was looking attentively and affectionately at her father; there was something seriously wrong: Laura felt sick with apprehension.

'Eat up, love,' Mrs Wilkins said gently. 'There's tinned pears for afters.'

'Oh Laura,' Susan said, the moment they were alone. 'Oh, Laura, my wedding dress is too small for me. The buttons won't close. I can't wear it.'

Laura looked her up and down crossly. 'Oh, don't be silly,' she said. 'You don't look any different; not a bit.'

'That's because I've got this awful navy-blue thing on. I daren't wear anything but this. I've got a terrible bulge. I'll show you.'

She got a cardboard box down from the top of the wardrobe and lifted the wedding-dress out from its layers of tissue paper.

'It's lovely,' Laura said dutifully.

'It was four pound nineteen and elevenpence - all my savings - and now I can't wear it and I haven't any more money; even next week's is already spent. What can I do?'

'Try it on. Let me see it on. There must be something to let out.'

It was a plain, long-sleeved dress in figured satin. The tight-fitting bodice was closed by about thirty tiny buttons. Susan lowered it carefully over her head and breathed in.

'You see,' she said sorrowfully. 'It's a whole size too small.'

Apart from three or four at the neck, the buttons didn't come near to meeting the tiny buttonholes.

'Take it off,' Laura said. 'Let's have a look at the seams.'

'There's nothing to let out. I've already looked. What can I do?'

Susan took off the dress and her petticoat. She turned slowly to show Laura her thickening belly. Her breasts were larger, too, the nipples darker, the veins bluer. 'For God's sake don't catch cold,' Laura said.

She was distressed by the signs of her friend's pregnancy. She shut her eyes to recall her former shape: firm stomach small firm breasts with pale pink nipples. Her own breasts were large and long, the nipples brown: whoever said all girls were the same underneath hadn't seen her and Susan.

'I haven't got any money either,' she said miserably. 'I've already spent this month's allowance on Christmas presents.'

'And I daren't ask my Dad for any more because he keeps complaining about how much the reception is going to cost, and the cars.'

'You could wear my dress,' Laura said at last. 'Kathleen got a proper dressmaker to make it. It's very . . .'

'I couldn't wear a *brown* dress, Laura! No one but you would suggest that I could wear a *brown* dress for my wedding.'

'It's not brown, it's a sort of golden colour like china tea. Would you like to see it?'

'No, I would *not* like to see it. I've always dreamed of having a white wedding, you know I have. How can you be so cruel to me.'

They got ready for bed. Neither of them could sleep.

'Laura.' Susan's voice wormed up from the darkness. 'Laura, do you think you could try to change the dress for me? I mean, take it back to the shop and ask for a bigger size.'

'Why can't you? I should think it would be much better if you did it.'

'How could I? I'd be much too embarrassed. It was a very posh shop. They'd notice I was pregnant.'

'I didn't notice anything. People can put on weight without being pregnant.'

'They'd guess. They'd know. I wouldn't have the nerve to

do it . . . wouldn't you do it for me?'

Laura sighed. 'If I have to,' she said crossly.

'Oh Laura, you're such a good friend. I knew I could depend on you. Do you think you could go tomorrow? Peter will meet you and show you the shop where I got it.'

'You bought it in Birmingham?'

'Oh yes. Where else?'

'Anyway, Peter needn't meet me. I can find my own way if you've got the address.'

'But he wants to help. He knows how frantic I've been. He'll meet the eleven o'clock train. He can get an hour off work. We've arranged it now.'

The darkness seemed to be breathing and expectant.

'You're pretty sure of me, aren't you?'

'You always stand by me. I trust you: you know that.'

'All right, I'll go. Go to sleep now.'

Having handed over her problems to Laura, Susan slept at once.

But Laura was awake for hours. Why ever had she come back? Kathleen had invited her to spend Christmas with her. 'Just go down for the wedding,' she'd said. She'd been so safe in Kathleen's flat in Camberwell with her lovely books.

Peter's face was suddenly vividly before her, his dark eyes destroying her composure.

Peter was meeting her off the train. He looked less handsome than she'd remembered, his overcoat which was shabby and too large for him, hiding the lines of his body. His face was almost plain that day; a work-a-day face.

'You needn't have bothered to meet me,' she said. 'I could have managed on my own.'

'I thought you might like my company,' he said. He sounded hurt and not at all dangerous. 'I knew you could have managed.' He took the large cardboard box from her and they walked swiftly through the crowded station.

'Would you like a coffee, first?'

'No, I'd rather get this over first.'

'It's a hateful thing to have to do; I hate taking things back to shops. I'm really upset you've got to do it.'

She was surprised and grateful for his sympathy. He was walking half a step in front of her, she could glance at his face; he looked stern.

'It was a pity you had to turn down Amsterdam,' she said.

'It's all been pitiful, one way or another.'

She pretended not to have heard him.

'How is Susan?' he asked at last.

'She's fine. Very excited.'

'She didn't seem excited when I saw her last. She seemed rather... regretful.'

'Not a bit. As soon as she gets this dress changed she'll be in top spirits again. She's very...'

'Very what?'

'Oh dear, I was going to say very brave, but it seems an insult.'

He smiled. She'd forgotten how lovely his smile was; how it softened his face.

'Have you managed to find a place to live yet?' she asked him, making an effort to keep her voice steady.

'I've got two or three to look at; all pretty awful.'

They walked on; in silence for the most part. He asked about her life in London, but she felt he wasn't really interested so she didn't volunteer much information.

'I'll wait for you,' he said when they reached the shop. It was a small shop specialising in bridal wear.

'I'm afraid we can't possibly change it, Madam,' the shop assistant said. 'It's not our policy to exchange goods.'

The shop assistant was ash-blonde and slender as a flower. Laura felt large and shabby amongst all the wedding finery on display. She glanced at her shoes, wishing she could have left them outside.

'I've got the receipt,' she said, handing it to the girl.

'Madam, this purchase was made in October. We've had several new lines since October; new fashion-lines from London and Paris.'

'I'm not asking for anything newer; I just want a bigger size. I'm only asking for another exactly like this one.'

'It's quite impossible, Madam. As far as we know this dress

could have been worn already. You've had time to wear it several times over.' She tossed back her silvery curls and studied her profile in the long-length mirror. She was too indifferent to be disdainful.

'Won't you please look at it? You'll see that it's in perfect condition. It's been in the box ever since it was bought.'

'It won't be in perfect condition, Madam, if it's been in the box since October.'

'It's not at all creased. Let me show you.'

'Please don't get it out, Madam. We can't possibly help you.'

'I'd like to speak to the manageress.'

'The manageress is out, Madam.'

'I'll wait till she comes back. I'm not leaving till I get the dress changed; I can't.'

The assistant left her side and moved to the back of the shop where she busied herself unpacking some artificial flowers and small white head-dresses.

Laura couldn't see a sign of Peter through the white-veiled window.

She walked to the back of the shop. 'There's a dress just like mine in the window,' she said.

'It's not our policy to exchange goods, Madam,' the girl said.

'Could you please tell me the size of the dress in the window?'

'Certainly, Madam. It's a size thirty-six.'

'That's exactly the size I want.'

'It's not our policy to exchange goods,' the shop assistant and Laura intoned together.

Laura waited over half an hour in the shop; the shop assistant unpacking and pretending she wasn't there; no other customer appeared.

The manageress was about forty, hard-featured, smartly dressed.

During the long wait, Laura had considered many ways of getting the dress in the window; ranging from a direct appeal - with tears? - aimed at winning sympathy, to hard arguments, threats and abuse. The emptiness of the shop and a certain hopeless look in the manageress's eye gave her a different idea.

'I want to change the dress I have here for the identical but larger one you have in the window,' she said, speaking slowly and distinctly. 'I know that it's not your policy to exchange goods and I fully appreciate the trouble it entails, and therefore I'm prepared to pay half a crown for the trouble caused.'

'Certainly, Madam,' the manageress said. 'Have you your receipt? Naturally, I'll have to run my eye over the dress you're returning.'

She called the assistant. 'Would you get the dress from the window, Miss Glaze? Yes, this is fine. Would you pack it for Madam?'

The manageress moved to the back of the shop where she took off her coat and hat.

'You didn't tell me it was a cash transaction, Madam,' the girl said, taking her money and shrugging her shoulders. 'Good afternoon, Madam.'

Peter was still waiting.

'I couldn't face coming in,' he said. 'I knew I should have, but I couldn't face it. How was it?'

'I had to wait to see the manageress.'

'And she wouldn't change it?'

'Yes, she changed it.'

He gripped her by the shoulders. 'That's marvellous,' he said. 'You clever girl.'

'You take it,' she said weakly. He took the box from her.

'Come on,' he said. 'I'm going to buy you a drink.'

They walked about a hundred yards then across the road to a large hotel; to the lounge bar which was nearly empty.

He bought two half pints of beer. Laura had never tasted beer before. 'I'll remember this,' she thought, 'the way I feel now.'

It wasn't happiness exactly, but a sort of elation all the same. They didn't speak, but both seemed busy in imagination. Both were aware of how differently things might have been.

A shaft of sunlight entered the gloomy room; they both looked at it, the dust playing in it, the gold it lent the shabby armchairs in its path. They sat over their empty glasses.

'I've got to get back to work,' Peter said at last.

They walked down the hill into Corporation Street. 'What will you do now? Get the next train back?'

'I think I may go to the museum first. To see the Pre-Raphaelites.'

'I wish I could come with you.'

That was all he said.

'We're the same sort,' Laura thought. 'If only he could have waited for me, we might have been right together.'

He handed her the cardboard box and touched her hand as though he knew what she was thinking. 'Tell Susan I'll see her Saturday,' he said. For a moment their eyes met.

Then he was gone. She watched him striding away.

In the museum, during the afternoon, she walked from picture to picture in a daze of love and pain. All the paintings, it seemed to her, reflected her own rapture and her own anguish.

'She looks a bit like a Rossetti, herself, don't you think so,' one of the other visitors to the gallery whispered to his wife. 'She's got the same colouring and that same crazy look.'

'Only her hair's a bit tidier,' his wife said.

The dress fitted well, with half an inch to spare for the next fortnight's growth.

Laura saw Peter twice more during her holiday; once at her step-mother's on Christmas Eve, again during the wedding. On both occasions she held herself firmly in check, avoiding his eyes.

Being in love, she told herself, was irrational and self-destructive.

The next term, she worked even harder at putting Peter out of her thoughts.

It was a whole year, though, before everything became suddenly easier.

PART 2

Chapter Twelve

'We'll be at war in a month's time,' Laura told Kathleen and Edith when she came in, her voice seeming curiously detached. 'That's what Giles says.'

'Giles?' Edith said. She knew very well who Giles was; she and Kathleen had been discussing him earlier in the evening.

Laura looked up. 'He's got relations in the army; his uncle's a brigadier.'

'It's frightful,' Kathleen said, frowning at Edith. 'Chamberlain is the only one who won't see it.'

'She was always remarkably mature for her age,' Kathleen had been saying. 'But I think her two years with me have added something, don't you?'

Edith was afraid that Kathleen was becoming obsessed by her niece; it was natural, she knew, but dangerous; one's family, in her opinion, always let one down. 'Oh certainly,' she had said. 'She's an atheist now, and she smokes and drinks. She's improved no end. How is her love-life?'

'I don't think she has one, not exactly. After all she's still only twenty. She sees that Arthur Wilkins from time to time, but it's not serious, thank God.'

'You don't think he's good enough for her?'

'Of course he isn't good enough for her. He's dull. Oh, he's dependable and worthy and all those boring things, but utterly dull. I want her to have someone thrilling. There's one of her college lecturers, now, who used to walk her to the tube after various classes last term; they've been friendly since Christmas, I think; he's been here once or twice...'

'And he's . . . thrilling?'

'Oh yes.'

'Married, I suppose?'

'I don't know.'

'Then he is. The ones you don't know about always are, you can depend on that. What's his name?'

'Giles Summerton. Very urbane and handsome – very clever too. Just her type. He lectures on the metaphysical poets.'

'Does he now? What full and exciting lives we lead, Kathleen. Tonight, I shall rush home and look up metaphysical poets in my encyclopaedia.'

'I already have. I've even read some of their poetry. I've even prepared a sentence or two to throw casually into the conversation, should it ever become necessary.'

'Let's hear them,' Edith had said, settling back into her chair with all the appearance of rapture.

'It never seems to me that Donne is altogether a metaphysical poet. I rather agree with Dryden that he merely affects the metaphysics.'

'Is that it?'

'There's more, but I can't just reel it off in one breath, can I? Someone else would probably help me out at that point.'

'Yes of course. How interesting that you should say that, Miss Wells. Do go on.'

'Oh no, I mustn't go on; I become rather a bore on the subject, I'm afraid.'

'Oh please. You could never bore me on the . . . what were they called?'

Their conversation had fizzled out at that point because they'd heard Laura's key in the lock. She'd come home and had immediately started to talk about the war.

'Tell me about him,' Edith said. 'Giles. He sounds interesting.'

But Laura wouldn't be deflected. 'It's just as well you're moving to the country,' she said. 'The sooner you're out of London the better.'

'I don't retire till next April,' Kathleen said.

'All the same, the sooner you *buy* the better. Everyone will be moving out of London.'

'We'd been thinking of having a weekend in Warwickshire, to look around. Perhaps we should go this Friday.'

'You should. You definitely should.'

Kathleen and Edith were planning to buy a retirement cottage between them.

Kathleen wanted a small, easily-managed house near a pub and a shop and not too far from a decent-sized town. Edith favoured thatch, apple trees, crooked windows and a large garden; she had done no gardening in her life and very little cooking, but she imagined herself making apple jelly, and growing prize dahlias, while Kathleen imagined herself trying her hand at painting in oils and taking part in village affairs. They'd been studying brochures from various estate agents for months, but nothing had seemed to suit them both.

'Show Laura April Cottage,' Edith said.

'April Cottage? You must be mad. Three quarters of an acre of garden and windows no bigger than shoe-boxes.'

'I liked 3, Mill Lane,' Laura said. 'That was a good size, big enough for me to come to stay.'

'3, Mill Lane,' Kathleen said. 'Yes. It was the right sort of price. It had mains water and electricity.'

'And a summer house,' Edith said, 'and a lilac tree. We should certainly put it on the list. We could always call it Lilac Cottage, couldn't we? Why don't you come down with us on Friday, Laura, what a help you'd be. You've got such a clear mind.'

'I would, except for Giles,' Laura said. 'I'm meeting Giles on Saturday. It's all arranged.'

Laura had agreed to sleep with Giles Summerton on Saturday night. He had been trying to talk her into it for several months; it was during an afternoon at Lyme Regis the previous week that she'd decided on it.

She'd gone youth-hostelling in Dorset with a college friend, Mary Saunders; a quiet, sandy-haired girl who was reading French.

Meeting Giles on the Cobb had been sheer coincidence; he could have known nothing about her being there, the holiday with Mary not having been planned or thought of when they'd last seen each other.

She'd spotted him from quite a distance. 'That man looks like Giles Summerton,' she'd told Mary, 'do you know him?' And she'd thought, 'If it turns out to be Giles then I *shall*, and as soon as possible, because coincidences are surely significant in some way, and besides, the very thought of seeing him is making me happy and excited and a bit dizzy.'

It *was* Giles, extravagantly handsome in dark blue shirt and red tie, his black hair curling at the nape of his neck.

He was delighted to see her. His talk broke over her like a summer storm after Mary's still silences.

He'd taken them to tea in a sea-front café and over cream cakes and scones, Laura had signalled her message; and been understood.

They'd drunk cup after cup of tea. He'd talked about the imminence of war, the certainty of death, quoted despairing poems by Sassoon and Wilfred Owen; at the same time keeping up a steady grip on her legs under the table.

'I have to go now,' he'd said at last. 'I'm with my cousins, Charles and Marina; I'm meeting them for dinner. I'll write to you.'

'What interesting people you know,' Mary had said.

Afterwards, she and Laura had walked six miles to the next hostel where they'd made their simple supper and gone quietly to bed.

'Then come kiss me, sweet-and-twenty,' Giles used to sing to her. 'Youth's a stuff will not endure.' Dear, handsome Giles.

He was probably with Daphne and her parents, Laura decided. Daphne was his fiancée, beautiful, rich and a friend of the family. Well, Daphne or not, he was certainly not for her. Men like Giles didn't marry girls like her; she wasn't a fool.

She suddenly remembered her mother telling her about her employer's eldest son who had so embarrassed her with his attentions when she was in service. 'Oh, he was forever smiling and staring at me,' her mother had told her – she could only have been nine or ten at the time – 'It was hard on a girl. It wasn't nice.' And she, at nine or ten, had wondered why.

Well, things had changed. Unlike her mother, she could look after herself. Girls could have affairs nowadays as well as men, and if they were self-aware, expecting nothing more than pleasurable experience, they wouldn't get hurt.

It was at the departmental Christmas party the previous year that Giles had first picked her out. The men of her own age had never been attracted by her, probably finding her too serious and intense, so that she'd been grateful for Giles's attention. They'd had supper together and talked about modern novels. 'You've got an excellent mind,' he'd told her, his eyes fixed on her excellent chest; she was wearing Kathleen's best dress that evening, a holly-green crêpe, neither new nor fashionable, but tight-fitting with a low v-neck; she'd laughed. He normally sought out the small, pretty girls who cast down their eyes when he spoke to them; Laura had proved an exciting novelty; he'd hardly been able to keep his mind on *A Passage to India* and *Howard's End.*

She hadn't let him take her home that night; such familiarity with a member of staff didn't seem right.

She'd thought of him often, though, during the Christmas holidays. When Susan - they'd only met briefly on Boxing Day - had asked her whether she had any boyfriend other than Arthur, she'd admitted that there was someone else. 'What's he like?' Susan had asked, pinching her. 'Come on, tell me.' 'Beautiful as a Greek god,' Laura had said and they'd both giggled. 'Handsomer than Peter?' 'Heavens, yes.'

The next term he'd taken her out to meals and concerts and grumbled because she wouldn't ever go home with him afterwards. 'What are you afraid of?' he used to ask her.

In the summer term, his campaign had intensified. He'd accused her of being mean-minded and self-absorbed. He'd assured her that sex - sex with him - would enrich her life.

'Did you enjoy sex?' she'd asked Kathleen.

'I suppose I must have,' she'd answered, a little reluctantly. 'Sometimes it did seem as though it was something significant and life-enhancing; at other times, when I was tired or irritable, it just seemed a nuisance.'

'Does Daphne enjoy sex?' she'd asked Giles.

'She won't try it,' he'd admitted. 'She has this quaint notion of being a virgin bride.'

'Isn't that rather medieval?'

(Her reluctance, she'd come to realise, was class-based; it was because Giles was too rich and self confident, and engaged, not just to any girl, but to a girl of the same class.)

'She's not modern like you, she's very conventional; religious too. She believes that marriage is a sacrament; that sort of thing.'

'"The outward and visible sign of inward and spiritual grace." Will you feel up to that?'

'Certainly.'

'She doesn't expect you to be a virgin too?'

'I confessed that I'd had one or two lapses and she forgave me.'

'And now you're asking me to be another lapse?'

'Oh, please.'

Well, she'd always put him off; now she'd said yes. Because they'd met by chance, because she'd been excited to see him, because of the fear of war, because it was August, because... what did it matter? She turned in her sleeping bag, trying to get comfortable. She put her hand under her cotton nightdress. Her triangle of hair was thick and soft like fur. When she opened her legs a little, lips sucked at her fingers and closed on them. Her breasts ached.

On Saturday morning she got up early, washed her hair, put on her newest dress, a grey and white voile with a large ruffled collar, and got ready to go to meet Giles.

In the hall downstairs she found a letter from Susan; the first she'd had for months.

Susan had two children by this time, Julia, one and a half, and Tony almost six months. She hadn't seen her since the previous Christmas.

> I went home last week because Mum hadn't been well and imagine my surprise when I heard about you and Arthur! He told Mum you were getting engaged Christmas! Fancy not letting me know after all we've been through together!

As you can imagine, I'm in the Seventh Heaven. I only hope you'll come back here to live so that we can all be together. As you know, I've always had plenty of time for Arthur, even if he is my brother, and I always thought you two would decide on it finally. When are you coming to see Tony? He's really gorgeous. We're going to move soon and we'll have an extra bedroom so please come. (You can bring Arthur if you like!! I won't tell!!) Oh and thank you for the christening mug for Tony. It was just what he wanted.

Your ever loving and devoted friend, Susan.

Laura sat down heavily on one of the chairs in the entrance hall and frowned at the letter.

She hadn't seen Arthur for several weeks and couldn't imagine what she'd said or done to make him feel that there was anything between them.

They met about once a month, sometimes twice. They'd never talked of love or marriage, never kissed on meeting or parting, never held hands. She hadn't realised he was serious about her. Marry Arthur? Why was it so inconceivable? He was a decent sort, he had a good job, he'd surely make a satisfactory husband. He was certainly very proud of her; she remembered his proud little cough as he'd introduced her to his boss at some party he'd taken her to. Oh God, perhaps meeting him once a month and going with him to the office party had been courtship in his mind. It must have been.

Laura felt cold and frightened. Should she write him a letter, she wondered, regretting that she couldn't meet him again. No, that would be too brutal. What could she do?

Susan's letter had managed to destroy all her confidence. From feeling free and light-hearted, a modern young woman about to embark on her first love-affair, she was depressed and guilty. She hadn't been careful enough of Arthur's feelings, hadn't even taken the trouble to be aware of them. Everything was fraught with danger, nothing was easy. Why had she imagined that she should be allowed to play at love?

Giles suddenly seemed a menacing figure. She wouldn't meet him that day but would try to contact Arthur instead.

That's what she had to do. Damn Susan. Damn her.

She went back upstairs and let herself into the flat. Arthur worked in North London; she knew the name of the firm, she rang the exchange and got the telephone number. Employees were probably not allowed to receive calls in working hours, she realised that, but the letter from Susan seemed an urgent matter. She couldn't let him go on deceiving himself.

As she waited for the operator to get the number, Arthur was suddenly vividly before her; his best navy-blue suit – bought for Susan's wedding – shiny and short in the sleeve, showing his large red wrists. His nature was mild like his mother's, but alas his angular body was terribly like his father's. He'd worked hard, not only at marine engineering, but also at keeping abreast of books, art and music. He was an admirable man in many ways, intelligent too, but unexciting as milk.

'I want to speak to Mr Arthur Wilkins please. Yes, it *is* urgent. His sister: Susan Glover.'

While she waited, she looked round at the flat which she'd tidied with such pleasure earlier on, getting it ready for Giles. She'd pictured him lying on the leather sofa, his long legs stretched over the arm, listening to Kathleen's newest records, humming to them, but looking at her. He excited her, there was no doubt about that. His mind, too; she admired his mind. Arthur's studying had given him little parcels of knowledge about this and that, but Giles seemed to know everything. Not only about literature, but about what things meant. She could ask him questions about anything. 'Why do I like this?' 'Why not that?' And he could tell her. He was helping her get to know herself.

'Susan, what is it?'

'It's not Susan, Arthur, it's Laura. I thought I'd better say I was your sister. I had a letter from Susan this morning and it's worried me, and I'd like to see you as soon as possible. Do you think you could meet me this afternoon? Just for a short time?'

'Yes, of course. It must be urgent. Is it my mother?'

'No, nothing to do with your mother and nobody's ill.

Half past three at Charing Cross station?'

'Yes, that's fine. I'll be there.'

Arthur's voice was thin and unattractive; that was irrelevant; he was important, he'd been a good friend for years.

Giles would be waiting for her. Still, they were meeting at the college library where he always had work to do, so it wouldn't inconvenience him too much.

Would he ring her? She couldn't concentrate on anything. She walked about the flat. She changed her dress. She tried to read. She had hours to kill before meeting Arthur.

At one she got herself a sandwich and a glass of milk.

At two-thirty the bell rang and she found Giles at the door. 'Where the devil have you been?' he said.

'What do you mean? We always agreed to wait ten minutes for each other and then go. Last term you failed to turn up several times.'

She felt irritated that he'd come to the flat, that he'd pushed himself in without being asked, that he was looking at her so angrily, a spot of red burning in his cheeks. She was annoyed that he was so handsome and self-assured. The gulf between them was too wide. If he had only been half as attractive, poor instead of rich and in a different social class, she'd be less afraid of him, altogether less confused.

'Where's your aunt?'

'In Warwickshire.'

'Why didn't you come?'

'I changed my mind at the last moment.'

'You can't change your mind. It's not allowed. I've come up to Town specially.'

His voice, usually so smooth and urbane, was agitated and rough.

He put out his arms for her, but she dodged them.

'Do you want to sit down?' she asked him. 'Would you like a cup of tea? I had an upsetting letter this morning, that's why I didn't meet you. I have to meet someone else.'

'I can see you're upset,' he said. 'Sit down by your Uncle Giles and tell him what's wrong.' He patted the sofa by his side, but Laura remained standing.

'I have a friend from home whom I meet occasionally.'

'And?'

'I have to meet him this afternoon.'

'No, you don't. Not if this letter arrived this morning. We made our plans over a week ago. If you remember.' He tried to take her hand.

'There's been a misunderstanding between us. I have to meet him.'

'Are you in love with him?'

'No.'

'Then let him sort out the misunderstanding on his own. The world is full of misunderstandings and most of them, believe me, are quite beyond resolving.'

'Would you like to see the letter?'

'You obviously want to show it to me.'

She fetched the letter and sat down by his side.

'You funny girl,' Giles said. 'I adore you.' The letter had completely restored his spirits. He started kissing her, delicate little kisses which amused her at first and then made her tremble. 'Lie down,' Giles said. The sofa wasn't very wide, they had to lie very close together. 'When are you expecting your aunt back?' Giles asked. 'Not until tomorrow evening.' 'Ah.'

'It's almost three o'clock. I've got to go out.'

'You're not going out: I'm not even prepared to discuss it.'

'I can't let him stand about waiting for me.'

'You let *me* stand about waiting for you. I waited hours.'

'No you didn't. You went to the library and worked till it closed. I know you. I'll make a bargain with you. I'll be back by five and I'll make supper for us here, and then we'll listen to music and then . . .'

'I want it now. You promised.'

'Oh please wait. You'll spoil it for me. I'm worried about Arthur, I really am. I can't think of anything else.'

He didn't seem to hear her.

When he raised himself from her, he was appalled at his impatience; he should have been prepared to wait, he should have let her go to meet the worthy Arthur. But it hadn't been possible, that was the trouble, she was too lovely.

She opened her eyes and smiled at him, actually smiled.

'Forgive me,' he said. 'When you didn't turn up this morning I felt desolate; lovesick and hopeless as a schoolboy. I couldn't face the possibility that you'd evade me again.'

She smiled at him.

'Did I hurt you much?' he asked her.

'No, not much.'

He laid his dark blue shirt over her. She lifted one side of it so that he would come back to lie at her side.

After a moment or two he did. She smiled at him again. He smiled too. She meant to forgive him. He put his arm under her shoulder and watched her. After a short time her eyes closed.

She slept for over an hour.

When she woke, they put music on the gramophone and he sang to her; he had a pleasant tenor voice. 'Greensleeves is my delight,' he sang, and 'Drink to me only with thine eyes' and 'Ye banks and braes o' bonnie Doone'; those songs reminded her of him for many years.

At seven o'clock when they were dressed and ready to go out to dinner, there was a ring at the door.

Laura was aghast to find Arthur standing there; he had never before come to the flat uninvited.

'I was going to come to tell you,' was all she could say. And Giles stood, a little behind her, saying nothing.

'I understand,' Arthur said. 'I quite understand.'

He left at once. Laura didn't even have to invite him in.

They stood listening to his footsteps fading away. 'I hate you,' she shouted at Giles. She got hold of him by his arms as though she wanted to shake him, to kill him. But after a moment she dropped her hands and did nothing.

'Let me get you a drink,' Giles said smoothly. 'Sit down, my love.'

She sat on the sofa and let him pour her a large whisky. They sat talking for almost an hour.

Giles spoke to her every seriously about the dangers of love, about the prime importance of self-preservation.

'He was fond of me,' Laura said. 'He's a kind, decent man.'

'Laura, those are the ones you must most beware of. They're the ones who'll break your spirit. They'll smother you with their kindness and decency and adoration and worship; kind and decent men always worship women, it's one of their most tedious characteristics, and they'll bind you to them, "and his banner over me was love". You surely don't want to be a slave, even to someone's love. No, you want someone who'll let you grow and develop in your own way, who'll let you be independent and untrammelled. I'm the one for you, Laura. I'm prepared to love you and respect you and treat you as an equal.'

'I hate you,' Laura said quietly. 'I should have gone after him. You know I should have. I behaved rottenly to him.'

'He behaved rottenly to you too; don't forget that. How dared he tell his mother that you were going to get engaged to him. How dared he be so presumptuous. Did he really believe that all he had to do was name the date and buy a ring and you'd be his beyond question? How dared he.'

'I suppose he thought we were courting.'

'How could he think he was good enough for you?'

'He's . . .'

'He's a booby, a prize idiot. If he'd even taken the trouble to look at you, he'd know you weren't for him. And now I don't want to waste any more time talking about him; he's not worth it. Now, I'm going to take you out and give you the best food you've ever eaten and the best wines you've ever drunk, and later on I'm going to try and make you about half as happy as you made me this afternoon.'

'I'm not happy,' Laura said, several times during the evening. All the same, she was beginning to feel a sense of well-being, she had to admit that. It was almost happiness. As long as she could keep her mind off Arthur's resigned expression as he stood in the doorway of the flat, she was very nearly happy.

They returned at about eleven. 'Are you sure your aunt won't be back?' Giles said. 'It won't matter if she is, she's very broad-minded.' She certainly wanted him to stay. In spite of the high-handed way he had overruled her plans, the contempt he'd shown Arthur, she certainly wanted him to stay.

'Of course you want me to stay,' Giles said. 'How could it be otherwise? Look at us together. Don't we look right together? Of course we do.'

He undressed her very slowly and lovingly as he had in the afternoon. Her body slowly began to respond to his kisses, his tongue, his hands, the words he called her.

But when he was about to enter her, she suddenly pushed him away with all her strength, turned over on to her stomach and cried.

It was a long time before she stopped and wanted his comfort.

When Kathleen came back at about five o'clock the next day, Giles had only recently left.

Kathleen and Edith had opened negotiations for a cottage. They hadn't liked any on the agents' lists, but while looking out for 'For Sale' notices on their way back to their hotel on the Saturday evening, had seen a likely looking one and called there. It was a three-bedroomed, black and white cottage in the centre of a village with marvellous views to the Cotswolds.

For some time, they talked about damp courses, dry-rot, wood-worm, cesspools and rateable values.

'Giles was here last night,' Laura told Kathleen afterwards. 'I hope you don't mind.'

'I think you know what you're doing,' Kathleen said. 'Life seems to have taught you a fair amount of sense.'

'If so, it's knocked it into me,' Laura said. 'None of it's been easy.'

Chapter Thirteen

Exactly a week later, war was declared.

Giles, who had planned to come up to London that day, phoned Laura to postpone the visit.

It was a hot day for September. In the afternoon, Laura and Kathleen went to Regent's Park and walked through the late roses in Queen's Garden and saw barrage balloons floating like whales in the still sky.

Kathleen, who had lived in London throughout the previous war, talked resolutely about the hardships they were likely to be up against: air raids and black-outs and food shortages. Laura felt numb and frightened, unable to respond in any way; she had persisted in the belief that war would somehow or other, and against all the odds, be averted.

'My grandmother lost two sons in the last war,' she said after a long, heavy silence; two out of three. I suppose two out of three of all the men I know will be killed in this one.'

'That's a very shaky piece of reasoning,' Kathleen said. 'And it doesn't say much for your university education.'

'I wish I hadn't had a university education. What good will it do me now? I think I'd better leave as soon as I can and learn to do something useful like nursing.'

Kathleen, realising that no good would come of arguing while her niece was in her present mood, turned her attention to the roses and her own affairs.

She was heartily glad she'd be able to leave London the following April. The purchase of the cottage was proceeding satisfactorily. The plan was that Edith, who had retired the previous month, would move there as soon as the sale was completed, she joining her for weekends whenever she could. In the spring, when she herself retired, Laura would move to a hostel until the end of the summer term; cheaper for her than keeping on the flat, as well as easier for Laura than having to fend for herself during her final examinations. None of their plans need change as far as she could see. The war, of course, would bring its share of unpleasantness and inconvenience, she was quite aware of that, but she and Edith, surely, would be spared the worst hardships.

They encircled the gardens in silence. Everyone out walking seemed silent that afternoon.

In the evening Edith called and they listened to the news on the wireless.

'Of course *we*'ll have some, Kathleen, won't we?' Edith said, when they heard the plans for evacuating London's children.

'Of course,' Kathleen said, with hardly a second's hesitation.

'We'll find all sorts of things to do,' Edith said. 'What a pity you have to stay on here till April.'

'I feel depressed and nervous,' Laura said.

She went to bed early.

The way to combat war-nerves, Edith had said, was to plunge into the attack: to find things you could do to help and do them to the best of your ability.

Laura was sure she was right.

But if you didn't believe in war, how could you get any satisfaction from helping the war-effort?

'You'll change,' Edith had said, when Laura had propounded this view. 'You're young, now, and idealistic; your judgement will mature.'

And Christ would have changed, I suppose, Laura told herself savagely. At forty, 'Blessed are the patriotic ready to defend their country,' and at forty-five or fifty, 'Blessed are the glorious war-leaders.' He was simply young and idealistic when he told us to love one another.

As soon as she was in bed, images of the last war, 'The Great War', crowded in upon her: the long lines of blinded soldiers, their hands loose on the shoulders of the man in front, men and horses sinking in the black mud of the trenches, the acres upon acres of nameless graves. Even her father's anecdotes, half-lies probably, now seemed poignant and terrible; for the first time she could understand her mother's sympathy for them.

And now it was come again; millions more to suffer and die. And Kathleen and Edith, both nice, ordinary women, were talking about it as though it was rather an exciting adventure.

'Feeling superior to everyone else isn't going to help me,' she told herself at last. She wished she'd stayed in the sitting room with them, planning the safety and defence of the realm.

She turned and yawned and fidgeted and couldn't sleep.

At about midnight, she heard Edith leaving the flat.

It was at least an hour later before Kathleen tiptoed past her door on her way to bed.

'I can't get to sleep,' Laura called out, sounding - and feeling - like a small child.

'I don't suppose I'll sleep either,' Kathleen said. 'I suppose plenty of people are lying awake tonight. Would you like some whisky and water?'

'I think I would,' Laura said. It was company she really wanted, but Kathleen had sounded distant, even unsympathetic.

It seemed a long time before she returned.

'We've drunk all the whisky,' she said. 'We seem to have drunk all the whisky. Also, we seem to have drunk all the gin. Damn shame. You could have done with a little nightcap. Damn that woman. Have to watch her.'

Laura looked hard at Kathleen. She'd never seen her the worse for drink before.

'Don't worry,' she said. 'I'm not sure I want a drink anyway.'

'Damn shame. Damn shame Giles couldn't make it today, too. Told Edith it was a damn shame. It's all a damn shame.'

Kathleen turned and walked carefully towards the door. 'Goo' night,' she said. She raised her hand, seemed to regard it with some surprise, and then dropped it again. 'Goo' night.'

Laura giggled and cried into her pillows. She still couldn't sleep but she no longer felt so alone and isolated: it was some comfort.

She wasn't altogether sorry that Giles hadn't come up that day. She knew she was in danger of falling in love with him and wasn't prepared to abandon herself to it; she felt she'd be more in control of herself given another month or so. By the beginning of the next term she was determined to be friendly but cool towards him as she'd been before. Their weekend together was only a pleasant interlude for him, she knew that; he'd been honest enough about it.

'But what can be lovelier than pleasant interludes?' she could hear him say. 'Damn it, you're not a Victorian maiden facing ruin and shame because you've let a man seduce you. Anyway, I didn't seduce you, you seduced me quite as much. Do you think I've forgotten that café in Lyme? If we hadn't had that little Mary Saunders with us, God knows what would have happened to me. Why can't you accept that women need experience as well as men? Yes, I'm eight years older than you; that means you're eight years newer than I am; eight years more ruthless and demanding. I'm already nearing matrimony and a settled middle age while you've still got baby-blue in the whites of your eyes.'

He'd kissed her again, then, and they'd started making love for the seventh or eighth time in two days. 'I hope these damned things are safe,' was all she'd said and afterwards he'd mocked her, 'All alone on Airly Beacon,' he'd said, 'with his baby on my knee.'

'Ho-w could you treat a po-or mai-den so,' he'd sung to her as they were getting dressed.

A few days later she got a letter from him saying that he was joining the army; taking the plunge without even waiting for his call-up papers.

She was outraged. She'd always known he wasn't an out-

and-out pacifist as she was, but to be so eager to be at war seemed deeply offensive. How could a man who considered himself a poet - he'd shown her several poems which he'd had published in highbrow literary magazines - be prepared to kill? Where was the vision and sensitivity in that?

'He simply realises that it's a wise move,' Kathleen had said. 'To be in first, with a chance of choosing what to do. Perhaps he'll become an officer in the Education Corps, that will only be a different sort of teaching, won't it? He's being very sensible if you ask me.'

Laura had no time for such opportunism, if that's what it was, and wrote a sharp letter telling him so. 'I'll be sorry to miss your lectures,' she wrote in a post-script, 'I always thought them very stimulating.' (It was true. They had been by far the best of the last two years. However flippant he might be in private, he was serious about teaching and intense about poetry. Occasionally - she remembered this with particular sadness - he'd become quite inarticulate for a moment or two, as though knocked off balance by the beauty of a line or stanza.) 'Anyway, this seems a good time to make a break.'

That's what's called burning your boats, she told herself as she posted the letter.

In spite of her disappointment in him, she was very sad to lose him. She thought of him often but always with a sort of pride that she'd recognised the danger and managed to break away before she'd got too badly hurt. 'Work,' she told herself. 'What I've got to do is work and put everything else out of my mind.'

But Giles was too charming, too handsome, too remarkable to be easily dislodged.

She wondered whether she'd ever fall in love with a suitable young man, neither married nor engaged.

A fortnight after the outbreak of war Laura was informed that her college was being evacuated to Bristol, that she was to write there at once concerning accommodation.

'But I don't want to go to Bristol,' she told Kathleen when she got back from work that day.

'You don't seem to have much choice.'

'At least I don't have to stay in a hall of residence. There aren't enough places available for the third years. Mary Saunders rang up offering to let me share her bed-sitting room; her parents have already found her one.'

'That sounds convenient. You get on well with her, don't you?'

'She certainly won't keep me from my work. If I don't get a First, it won't be her fault.'

'So that's fine.'

'Fine? Oh no. I don't like to leave you here on your own.'

'I've always been on my own. Besides it's only until April when I go to Kingsbury.'

Laura liked Bristol immediately: its self-confidence, its bustling, prosperous air, its manageable size.

As she had imagined, Mary Saunders turned out to be an ideal room-mate, well-organised and quiet.

The bed-sitting room her parents had found them was a basement room, but large and adequately furnished and in a fine Georgian house in a residential area. Having a substantial midday meal at the college six days a week, they did the minimum amount of cooking - very little but toast and tea in their room. On Sundays they had dinner with their landlords, a retired Major and his wife who kept a maid and two Irish setters; Mary Saunders was terrified of the dogs and Laura, never having encountered one before, of the maid, but they managed to avoid all three most of the time.

Laura worked very hard, much harder than she had in her first two years. Her professor began to discuss with her some likely subjects for post-graduate research. 'Oh yes, you'll be an eccentric old don, yet,' he used to tell her. 'Your walk is already becoming a self-absorbed academic lope.'

She supposed it was true. She knew she often went to and from college without noticing anything or anyone on her way. Work cut out the war - and other problems.

Chapter Fourteen

Laura was surprised not to hear from Giles; there was no word from him even at Christmas. She hid her disappointment very well, though Kathleen was not deceived; Kathleen couldn't believe her niece wanted a complete break from such an attractive man.

'There was no future in it,' Laura told herself. 'I always knew that. This heaviness in my stomach, this feeling that I've swallowed a stone, is at least better than being in the grip of a hopeless romantic love... All the same, he could have sent a card, just a Christmas card.'

Apart from the black-out everything was fairly normal in London when she returned there for the holiday; the expected air raids had not materialised, the secret weapon not been revealed. She and Kathleen went to a theatre and to a concert and despite fears to the contrary, ate and enjoyed a traditional Christmas dinner.

On Boxing Day, Kathleen drove down to see Edith, taking Laura with her as far as Oxford. From Oxford Laura took a train to visit her father and step-mother whom she hadn't seen since the previous Christmas.

The little house was full. John, Mabel's eldest son, was home with his fiancée, Maureen, and there were also many other relatives, some of whom Laura remembered from the wedding.

'I should have let you know I was coming,' Laura said, 'but I wasn't sure whether I'd manage it. Kathleen's been very short of petrol.'

'There's always a bed for you, here,' her step-mother said, 'even if you have to sleep on the sofa. I'm only sorry Peter and Susan had to go back; they'll be so disappointed to miss you; Susan was sure you'd turn up today. You've never seen our little Tony, have you? He's as plump as a pudding, his little round arms are a picture, and Julia, well, she's so clever it isn't natural. She does love your Dad, too. "'Arry, 'arry, 'arry," that's all we hear from her; she won't have anyone else. It was such a shame Peter had to go back today.'

'Why did Peter have to go back so early?' she asked her father, when Mabel had turned her attention to someone else.

'He only had twenty-four hours leave.'

'He's in the army already? I'd no idea. Susan didn't mention it in her letter. I suppose she thought I knew.'

'He was with the first lot called up. He's training in Wiltshire now; he reckons he'll be in France in a month or two. John's off next week, South Coast ready for overseas posting.'

Laura took a gulp of the sherry she'd been given and tried to steady herself. She very seldom let herself think about Peter but she'd relied on seeing him that day, relied on that one dangerous glance which always passed between them when they met; counted on it.

'Where in Wiltshire?' she asked her father.

'I don't know off hand, lass. You'll have to ask his mother.'

'I won't bother,' Laura thought. 'Oh yes, I may dream of making my way there to visit him but I'm not brave enough or ruthless enough to do it.'

She spent some time looking at the studio portrait they'd sent her step-mother. Such an ordinary little family they seemed: pretty mother, pretty children, heavy-browed, unsmiling father.

'It's lovely, isn't it?' her step-mother said, at her side again. 'Such a shame to split up a lovely little family like that.'

'Terrible,' Laura said, so passionately that tears sprang from her eyes.

She stayed a week with her father and step-mother. Susan returned after Peter had gone back, and stayed the night. She had decided to give up her house in Birmingham to go back to her parents.

'I'd be so lonely without Peter,' she told Laura when they were getting ready for bed. 'When I'm home, Mum can look after the kids in the afternoon and I'll help Dad in the shop. It'll be a bit of life for me; better than being cooped up with the kids all day.'

Laura remembered how much Susan had hated being in the shop, how she had complained of the cold, the way handling potatoes ruined her nails, the way the customers watched her like hawks, the way her father criticised the time she took giving change. She didn't say anything.

'And how's life treating you?' Susan asked her.

'I live in a bed-sitting room which I have to share with another girl. I work in a cold library most of the week and have my midday meals in a canteen. On Sundays we have a posh dinner with our landlord and his wife: a big white table-cloth and three sorts of forks, while he tells us about his bravery in the last war and accidentally touches our knees under the table.'

Susan looked at her sorrowfully. 'Why did you turn down our Arthur?' she asked. 'He's got a very good job now, he won't even have to join up. He bought Mum a sewing machine for Christmas; she's always wanted one.'

Laura watched Susan undressing. She was still attractive, but her clothes were neat rather than pretty, she wore far less make-up, she was plump, her breasts full; she'd turned from girl to woman.

'What about you?' Laura asked her. 'You look very well and the children are gorgeous.'

'The children make up for everything,' Susan said. She sounded meek and sanctimonious like her mother.

'What do you mean? Isn't marriage as marvellous as you thought it was going to be?'

'You have to take the good with the bad,' Susan said primly. 'It's lovely sometimes. Sundays used to be lovely till Peter went away. He used to look after Julia while I made the dinner, and afterwards I'd change the children and we'd go out to the park, and when we got back we'd have ham salad for tea and when the children were in bed, Mrs Smithson next door would come in and we'd go to the club for a couple of hours.'

Laura smiled and waited for her to continue.

'In the week-day evenings, though, Peter could be very moody. Sometimes he'd just want to sit and work even though I'd been by myself all day and was dying for a bit of company. Sometimes he can be as dull as you.'

'All the same, he is working for a better job isn't he? You should be pleased. Mabel told me he'd won a prize for one of his designs.'

'That wasn't a prize, it was just a certificate. Oh Laura, I can't be friends with him like I can with you. I'm always having to keep him at arm's length otherwise I'll only have another baby; he can't leave me alone.'

'Susan, you must get a contraceptive. A Dutch cap or something.'

'Oh I've got one of those. But I hate it. It makes me sick just to look at it. It's a great fat thing and I'm supposed to use this horrible jelly with it, and it's revolting, so sticky, oh I can't bear it.'

'Well, you'll have to, won't you,' Laura said crossly. 'Have a little practice with it every night when you go to bed so that you get used to it.'

'You must be mad. When I'm on my own?'

'Yes. Because otherwise you'll either have six or seven children or you'll become frigid and frightened like your Auntie Beth.'

'I'm frigid and frightened already.'

'Don't be silly. You're wicked to say so. It isn't so long since you and Peter used to embarrass me so much in the pictures. You didn't seem very frigid then.'

Susan turned her round blue eyes at Laura. 'Those were the days, weren't they? I was so happy then.'

'You're still happy, Susan. You have to be. You wanted Peter and you got him. You have to be happy.'

'All right, all right, there's no need to shout, I am happy. He's very good to me except for that one thing. Oh Laura, you don't understand what it's like; he's always wanting to do it and I'm so tired all the time. Tony is still waking every night and I just can't cope with both of them.'

'Why don't you do it early in the evening as soon as the children are in bed?'

'Oh, I tried that, but he thought that was extra and wanted it again when we went to bed. Oh Laura, do you think he's normal?'

'How should I know? Yes of course he's normal. He's young and in love with you. Of course he's normal.'

'I don't know. I'm sure Arthur wouldn't be so... well, such a nuisance. Why did you throw him over? Have you got someone you like better? Come on, you can tell me.'

'No. Go to sleep now. I've got no one.'

January was very cold that year with heavy snowfalls.

Laura had long spells of being unable to work, and as a result, became very despondent. She couldn't stop herself thinking of Peter.

Since Christmas she'd realised that she was still in love with him however much she'd tried to fight against it. Peter was her type, her equal, so that her feelings for him seemed truer and more down to earth than her feelings for Giles. It's Peter I'd choose, if I could choose one of them, she told herself. By this time Giles seemed a fantasy figure, remote as a film-star or a matinée idol.

Peter. Giles. One or other of them was forever in her mind. Why couldn't she live her full, absorbing, satisfying life without having to dream of any man? She wasn't, she told herself, a mindless chit of a girl, but a grown woman with proven intellectual ability. Why was life so degrading? Of what 'use' was being in love? She could be studying hard, absorbed in a Jacobean play or a nineteenth-century novel, but the moment she put down her text, the characters she should still be pondering about, slipped out of her mind, and she'd be thinking of Peter again, visualising him in his khaki uniform, imagining their meeting. Would she have him stationed somewhere near Bristol and arriving at her digs to look her up, or would she project the action into the future and have him in an army hospital – not too badly injured – where she'd be his constant visitor. She was entirely honourable in her dreams, nothing passing between them but the burning look, the recognition of their deep and abiding love.

Sometimes her dreams made her snort with laughter – which should, God knows, have cured her – but a few minutes later she'd be at it again, changing the circumstances but never the end result. It was pathetic; sheer indulgence. What was the matter with her?

Her step-mother had begged her to write to him. 'You know Susan will never have the time to write,' she'd said, 'and letters are so important when you're away from home. I write every week but all my letters seem to be the same; it's a letter I learnt at school, I can't seem to write any other sort. I can do book-keeping and business letters, but with family letters I can never think of anything different to say. Now you could write to him about books and that; he was such a book-lover as a boy.'

'What sort of books did he like?' Laura had asked, simply to go on talking about him.

'I'll show you his books. They're still in the cupboard in the spare bedroom; he won't let me give them away.'

Laura had spent almost the whole afternoon in the cold back bedroom with the books: *Robinson Crusoe, Tom Brown's Schooldays, The Three Musketeers* (very well thumbed), *Stalky and Co, Swallows and Amazons, Round the World in Eighty Days, Swiss Family Robinson, Journey to the Centre of the Earth*; the usual boys' books. His name was written in them all, occasionally his address and his age. She got pleasure out of handling them. She wished she could take them away with her.

'I'll write to him when he's sent abroad,' she'd promised his mother. (She'd feel safer with a sea or two between them.)

'He'll be so pleased. He thinks you're so clever. He tells everyone that you're at university.'

Towards the end of January she had flu and had to stay in bed for a week. Mrs Croom's maid, Joan, brought her some lunch every day, Bovril or a soft-boiled egg, stopped to talk to her while she ate it, and then brought water and a flannel and washed her face and hands. ('Do you like working here?' Laura asked her one day towards the end of the week. 'It's better since you and Miss Saunders came.' 'Why is that?' 'Miss Saunders is very friendly. She comes to the kitchen to see me almost every day. I do her ironing, you know, and she brings me a little present sometimes, toilet soap or a handkerchief.' 'I certainly haven't been any help.' 'Oh, I don't expect it. I know you haven't got any money.')

It was February before she was able to get up and resume college life.

In the middle of February she received, re-addressed from Camberwell, the long-expected letter from Giles. It was very short. It made no reference to her last letter to him or to the intervening time.

He was in the Intelligence Corps and stationed in Carlisle. He'd very much like to spend his next weekend leave with her. They'd stay at a large, impersonal hotel, he'd have work to do, she could bring her books. He missed her.

How wonderful she thought; the luxury, she'd never stayed at a hotel before, the excitement, the only men in her life were her professor and Major Croom. The thought of seeing him again flared into the dullness of her life.

When Mary had gone to bed she wrote, giving him her Bristol address, and saying she'd be delighted to see him.

It was the second week in March before she heard from him again. In this letter he gave her a telephone number and asked her to contact him at nine o'clock that evening.

When she heard his voice she was stricken by a terrible shyness. When he said he was arriving at Bristol the next day, she almost dropped the receiver. 'Oh Giles,' she said, 'I'm not sure that I'll be able to see you; not this weekend.'

'I've booked us a room at The Grand,' he said. 'Do you know it?'

'I know where it is.'

'I'm not sure what time I'll arrive, I may be very late. I told them we'd be arriving separately. I'd like you to get there by nine or nine-thirty, sign the register as Laura Summerton, get yourself a drink and stay in the lounge till I come. Will you do that?'

'I'll never have the nerve. I don't look like anybody's wife. I haven't got a ring. I haven't got a decent coat. I haven't got a handbag. What if they ask me where I've come from? What if they turn me away? I'll never have the nerve.'

'The Grand. They're expecting you. I'm expecting you.

You'll be there won't you? It'll be such fun.'

The pips went and they were cut off.

Around her, the street was in total darkness; even the moon and stars seemed to have been blacked out. The war news was grim, food was getting short, because of her illness she was behind with her work, but suddenly she was embarked on an adventure. 'It'll be such fun,' he'd said. Of course she'd go; nothing in the world would stop her.

She walked briskly back to Merchant's Crescent and burst in on Mary Saunders who was making cocoa on the gas ring. 'I've got to be away for the weekend,' she said. 'I hope you don't mind.'

'Of course not,' Mary said placidly and without a spark of interest or curiosity. 'I'll be quite all right. Do you want a cup of cocoa?'

'Yes please.'

Chapter Fifteen

'Mrs Summerton,' the hotel receptionist said. 'A telephone message for you.' He glanced at a note-pad in his hand. 'Owing to train cancellations, Lt Summerton will not be arriving until after midnight.'

'Thank you,' Laura said.

She folded the newspaper she'd been trying to read and returned it to the rack. It was already eleven and the lounge was almost empty. She went upstairs to the room she'd been given on the first floor.

Her arrival had caused no raised eyebrows at the reception desk. 'No one but a wife would turn up here looking so dowdy,' she told herself, catching sight of her reflection in a full-length gilt-framed mirror on the landing. 'I look about thirty and virtuous as flannelette.'

The bedroom was vast. The heavy mahogany furniture was elaborately carved and scrolled, there were floor-length velvet curtains and thick carpets and the bed was big enough for a family.

She rang the bell which she found under the light switch.

After a few minutes, a porter arrived. 'Could I have an electric fire?' she asked him. 'The radiators are cold.' She gave him a sudden happy smile. She'd always wanted to stay in a hotel and ring bells.

'The heating goes off at ten, Madam,' the porter said. 'It's the war, Madam.'

'My husband's been travelling all day.'

'Yes, Madam. I'll see what I can do.'

He arrived back carrying a large mock Tudor electric fire.

He plugged it in and waited for it to heat up. 'That's better, Madam,' he said.

'Much better,' she said. 'Thank you.'

She gave him a shilling, which was half the money she had, after the obligatory purchase of a gin and orange in the lounge.

'Thank you, Madam. Would Madam like a pot of tea? I think it could be arranged.'

'Oh, please. Could sandwiches be arranged as well? Or biscuits? Both perhaps.'

When he'd gone, she pulled the huge armchair up to the fire and got her books out of her suitcase. She put her coat over her shoulders and waited for the tea. She started to read some Anglo-Saxon.

The tea arrived with three soft biscuits, no sandwiches, and she gave the porter her last shilling.

Laura wished she could have asked him to stay; she was nervous as soon as she was alone. Being in a hotel wasn't as exciting as she'd supposed. The tea was no better than tea she made herself in her room, hardly better than refectory tea. The room was certainly luxuriously furnished and fitted, but lit only by a single central light, it looked almost as dismal as a railway station. 'He should be here to cheer me up,' she thought crossly, 'because I certainly shouldn't be here at all.'

She suddenly felt guilty and rather angry. Like Annie and Kathleen, she seemed to have discarded conventional morality. All the same, she'd have liked to believe that she was acting according to some guiding light: she seemed in the dark.

'I've come here to have fun,' she told herself. The word seemed old and sad, like a ball without bounce.

'Your wife is upstairs waiting for you, Sir,' the porter told Giles when he arrived just before one o'clock. 'I managed to get her an electric fire from the basement. She's quite comfortable.'

Giles gave him a shilling.

*

'I was afraid you wouldn't be here,' Giles said. He sounded gentle and happy.

Laura, who had tucked a blanket round her knees, struggled up from the chair.

Giles looked completely different. He was thinner, his curly hair cut close to his scalp, she'd forgotten that he would be in uniform. She wanted to cry at the change in him.

He held her tightly for a long time. Even after he'd released her, neither he nor she seemed to have much to say to one another. It didn't seem a light-hearted adventure they were embarked on, nor anything light-hearted.

She sat down on the edge of the bed.

'What's the matter?' he said.

'Are you married?' she asked him.

He didn't answer for a moment. 'Yes,' he said then. 'Yes I am.'

He suddenly looked very tired. She saw how he would look when he was an old man.

'Do you mind?' he asked. 'Do you mind . . . much?'

'Yes. I'm not sure I want an affair with a married man.' Her voice trembled.

'You knew I was getting married.'

'I knew you were engaged. That's not the same. An engagement is a kind of trial period, I thought. Not nearly as final as marriage.'

'I should have let you know, but I didn't have the guts. That's why I didn't write to you. I couldn't.'

He sat down next to her and took her hand. 'Nice hand,' he said, 'capable and . . .' His voice cracked to a stop. She heard him swallow, but she couldn't take pity on him.

'When did you get married?' She couldn't look at him.

'A few days after Christmas.'

'Less than three months ago?'

'That's right.'

'You should be with your wife this weekend.'

'I know I should.'

She took her hand away. 'Oh Giles, didn't it turn out as you expected?'

'It turned out exactly as I expected.'

'I don't understand. How could you get married to

someone and want to be with someone else in less than three months?'

'I don't know.'

'I'm going back to my digs, Giles. It's not far. I don't want to intrude on your marriage. I mustn't.'

She sprang to her feet, strode over to the wardrobe, pulled it open and got her coat on, pulling the belt tightly round her waist as though to stiffen her resolve. Her cheeks were burning.

Giles stood between her and the door. 'Please stay. I couldn't bear not to see you again, that's why I didn't tell you I was married, I couldn't risk it. Keep your coat on if you like but please stay with me.'

Laura's outburst of energy was spent. She slowly sat down on one of the armchairs and he sat opposite her.

He, too, had lost all his vivacity; he seemed a different person.

For a moment Laura was reminded of her father in his self-pitying mood.

'You can't possibly sit up all night,' she said. 'You look terrible. You must go to bed. I'll sit up.'

'I got engaged when I was twenty,' he said. 'Daphne was twenty-one. Our mothers were school-friends. Our fathers played golf together. I was very much in love with her for two or three years. I still love her. There's never been a time when it seemed at all possible to break it off.'

'Thank God my father doesn't play golf,' Laura said, her voice dry.

'It's easy to be cynical. You've never met Daphne.'

'Have you got a photograph of her?'

'Yes.'

Giles took out his wallet and passed Laura a small photograph. Laura shivered as she took it from him.

The face was a sweet oval, down-slanting eyes, hair drawn back in an almost Victorian style.

'Thank you,' Laura said, passing it back to him. 'She does seem a person one wouldn't want to hurt. I certainly don't want to hurt her,' she added more aggressively.

She looked at Giles with some severity. 'I might have an affair with a married man if I knew his marriage was sterile and hopeless, but I can't get involved with someone who hasn't given it a chance. You have this lovely wife and...'

'Don't preach,' he said.

'I'm sorry.'

'For Christ's sake, do you think I don't know what a cheat I am? I'm very well aware of it. That doesn't alter the fact that it's you I think about. Daphne is a gentle, loving woman, but when I'm away from her she doesn't exist for me. There's only you. I don't know why. It doesn't seem to be my fault.'

It was two o'clock and suddenly very cold.

'Giles, I'm sorry,' Laura said. 'Everything's a mess for me too. I'm in love - half in love - with my best friend's husband. Nothing can be worse than that. Sometimes I catch myself, not wishing she were dead, but certainly day-dreaming of a time when she's somehow ceased to exist. Nothing can be more despicable than that. Yet I didn't choose to fall in love with him. I tried not to.'

A weary silence fell on them. To Laura, the dimly-lit room with its looming furniture seemed like a room in a dream. She sighed.

Giles leaned forward and took her hands again. 'Aren't you the least bit in love with me?' he asked.

She laughed, though without much joy, at the chagrin in his voice. 'I'm certainly excited by you,' she said. 'I was too excited to sleep much last night. I got up at half past six this morning to sneak a bath; we're only allowed one each a week, but the maid promised not to split on me. I cut lectures to have my hair set this morning; I've spent all my money; I won't have any lunches now till Wednesday.'

Giles looked at her as though trying to memorise her face.

'I'll have to make do with that, I suppose,' he said. 'I excite you, and God knows you excite me. And God knows it's the most... it seems the most... the most vital thing.'

'Not love?' Laura mused.

'Sexual excitement is real.'

'"The truth of imagination"?'

'"For God's sake, hold your tongue and let me love."'

'You shouldn't have left and abandoned me to the Romantics.'

'I'm here now.'

Yes, he was real enough. He gripped her hands so tightly that she almost cried out.

'I'm expecting to go abroad soon,' he said then.

The war was all around her again. Occasionally it seemed – though always an outrage against humanity – distant.

'We'd better go to bed, I suppose,' Laura said. 'I can't see what else we can do. We're already committed to it.' She twined her fingers with his. 'Isn't this intimacy?' They looked wide-eyed at each other, filled with awe at the hunger they felt.

She unfastened her hands from his and took off her coat and then, more slowly, her dress. 'We mustn't meet again,' she said. 'I think we both realise that.'

'I don't realise it. I couldn't leave you without the thought that we're going to meet again. I must have that to keep me sane.'

'He's got what he wanted again,' Laura thought. 'He wants me as a bit on the side, that's the truth of it.' All the same, she knew it wasn't the truth, or at least not the whole truth.

When it was light, she looked at the face on the pillow beside her. It didn't seem the face of a scheming man, a triumphant man. It just seemed full of ordinary human perplexity and trouble.

He would never have married her, even if he were free. She knew that. People of his class didn't marry people like her. The gulf was as wide as it had been a hundred years before. But it was his tragedy as much as hers. She realised that, too.

He woke as though at the intensity of her gaze. 'I thought you'd gone,' he said clutching her. 'I dreamt you'd gone.'

'Have you had enough sleep?' he asked her.

'Plenty,' she said. She'd got all her life to sleep.

After a late breakfast, they walked round the quiet back streets of Bristol, sad and loving. Laura wondered if they would meet again. It was a very cold morning; they held each other tightly as they walked.

Giles had to catch a train back to Carlisle at eleven-fifteen.

Chapter Sixteen

In the Easter holidays, Laura spent a few days helping Kathleen to pack and move, and almost a week in the new cottage.

Both Kathleen and Edith stressed that she was to regard it as her home; all the things she had left in the Camberwell flat were arranged in the third bedroom, a long, low room with pale grey walls, which was to be her bed-sitting room and study.

In fact, she didn't feel at all comfortable there. She had the town-dweller's fear of the country. The air was fresh and she had peace to work, but it was too silent, the noises in the night too abrupt and frightening. She was pleased to get back to Bristol. After the exuberant vitality of Kathleen and Edith setting up home together, arguing over the placing of every piece of furniture and every picture, she found Mary Saunders's sober presence a great relief.

But being back in Bristol, the ordeal of waiting for a letter began again. Every morning she rushed to get the post and every time was disappointed. She had begged Giles to try to put her out of his mind, but the thought that he seemed to be succeeding was hard to bear. Had she, then, meant so little to him?

What do I really know about him, she'd ask herself, time after time. Only that he's a married man and a philanderer.

Yet, he seemed to need me; seemed heartbroken when I said I couldn't stay. It was a dangerous time. Of course, I should have left the hotel and thought things over.

How could I have left the hotel and thought things over? With him standing there, looking so desolate, so beautiful, and talking about being sent abroad. Well, what's done is done.

And what's more, she'd tell herself savagely, I wouldn't have it undone. But only done again. Oh, why doesn't he write to me?

It was only by getting involved in her room-mate's affairs that she found some relief from her own.

Mary's parents visited her on the first Sunday of every month, and since Christmas had taken Laura as well as Mary out to lunch when they came.

Laura liked Mary's mother. She was a musician, playing the organ at their church in Guildford and the viola in an amateur quartet. She was small and shy like Mary, but came alive when talking about music and relished the chance to do so since both her husband and daughter were tone-deaf. 'I don't understand why you never had piano lessons as a child,' she had told Laura on one of their first meetings. 'You have a pianist's hands. It seems cruel that a person who loves music should be deprived of an instrument.'

'Laura's an orphan, Mummy, don't go on at her,' Mary had said. Laura hadn't bothered to correct her and ever since Mrs Saunders had treated her with great kindness, knitting her lumpy jumpers and hoods and mittens and always including her name in the parcels of cakes and biscuits she sent Mary.

Mary's father, a solicitor, very rich by Laura's standards, was a formal and rather formidable man who always wore black suits and stiff wing collars.

During the visit they made at the beginning of May, Mr Saunders approached Laura about her plans for the following year.

'I won't be staying on at Bristol,' Laura told him.

'Why is that? We want Mary to do teachers' training. She thought you might be offered a research-lectureship.'

'My aunt wants me to take the Civil Service exam.'

'Mary thought you'd be choosing an academic career.'

'No, I don't think so.'

Laura was always disconcerted to find that she answered Mr Saunders in the clipped, precise tones he used. Fortunately, he never seemed to notice it.

'We thought we'd get Mary a year's lease on a flat here, a decent sort of place. We'd like you to share it with her. You'd have a bedroom of your own as well as the sitting room, bathroom and kitchen you'd share with Mary. It would give you a real chance to work.'

'We could get you a piano,' Mrs Saunders said.

'Mary won't have any difficulty in finding a lodger,' Laura said.

'We wouldn't want her to have a lodger, but a friend. We know you. You're steady and dependable. A lodger might bring men into the flat, soldiers even, we've heard plenty of tales, I can tell you. We couldn't take the risk.'

'Mary could look after herself, whatever her lodger did.'

'Mary's very young for her age; you seem years older. Please think about it. Your rent would be no higher than in Merchant's Crescent.'

'I've even thought about taking up nursing,' Laura said. 'At least until the war's over.'

'A very impractical thought, if you'd allow me to say so. If you want to be of help to your country, do a job you're suited for. If you joined the ATS they'd at least find you a job commensurate with your qualifications.'

'I couldn't join the army,' Laura said.

They were having their Sunday lunch in a country hotel surrounded by beautiful lawns and gardens. The smell of wall-flowers drifted in through the open french-doors. The war seemed a world away.

'I may become a landgirl,' Mary said.

Everyone looked at her, small and unsmiling in her plain, cashmere dress.

'Shall we go into the lounge?' Mr Saunders said.

'Were you serious about joining the Land Army?' Laura asked her when they were back in their bed-sitting room that evening.

'Yes. I'm definitely not staying on here. Anyway, I probably won't be able to. I'll fail or get a Third. Do you know what I got for that essay on *Andromaque* last week? C double minus. After all that work I did. And anyway I love farms. My grandmother had a farm in Essex. I used to go there on holidays.'

'Being a landgirl won't be quite the same, though, will it? Are you strong enough to do tough, physical work?'

'I'm very strong,' Mary said, looking about as strong as a medium-sized lamb.

'Why don't you do the year's teachers' training course first?'

'So that I'd have something to fall back on after the war? Is that what you mean?'

'Well, yes. You wouldn't want to stay on the land all your life would you?'

'I'll probably get married,' Mary said.

'But you can't depend on it, can you?'

There was no answer.

Laura looked across at her room-mate and saw that her face was lit up. For the first time she noticed how lovely her eyes were, how gentle. She had no claim to beauty or even prettiness, but Laura was suddenly aware of her soft and affecting femininity.

Their year together had been the smoothest possible co-existence of two reserved, independent people, their conversation restricted to practicalities: who could pick up the groceries, who the bread, and who would be in when the laundry was delivered. Suddenly Laura wanted to know more about her, much more.

'Are you going to church tonight?' was the only question she could bring herself to ask her.

'Oh yes,' Mary said.

Laura went on looking at her, willing her to reveal a little of herself.

'I wish you'd come to church sometimes,' she said at last. The curate is so nice . . . I'm awfully fond of him,' she added in a rush. 'Don't make fun of me, will you?'

'Of course I won't. Why should I make fun of you? Have I ever made fun of you? Tell me about him. What does he look like? How old is he? Does he know you're fond of him? Is he fond of you?'

Mary looked down at her hands. 'I think so,' she said. 'Well . . . yes he is. We've been meeting every Sunday evening and every Thursday after Bible class . . . Oh Laura, he's asked me to marry him.'

'And you've said yes,' Laura said gently.

Mary raised her eyes and pleated and twisted her small lace handkerchief.

How strange the lace-handkerchief class was, Laura thought, as afraid of emotion as her own class was of debts and bailiffs.

'Of course he'll have to join up. I mean, he wants to; he thinks he should. I suppose he's right, but at least we'll be engaged before that. Oh Laura, we're getting engaged next month, I haven't told anyone else. I've met his parents. They're awfully nice. His father's a vicar, quite poor, you know, but awfully nice. He's got two brothers and two sisters, the two brothers are older than he is and the two sisters are younger, one of them is only six months older than me.'

'What is she like?'

'Oh, awfully nice. She's only somebody's secretary but she's much more intelligent than I am. I mean, she's not clever like you are; not intellectually clever. Neither is Francis I don't think. I mean, he doesn't have time to read all that much as far as I know, but, the thing is, he strikes me as being, well, rather wise. I've got the feeling that he knows a lot about people and about life. Do you know what I mean?'

'He sounds . . . awfully nice,' Laura said feebly. 'I think you should tell your parents about him, though. I really do.'

'Oh no. They wouldn't think he was suitable. I had a boyfriend once before but they didn't think he was suitable. I've got some money when I'm twenty-one. I shall probably get married without even telling them about it.'

'Oh, you mustn't. I'm sure your mother would approve of a curate. Wouldn't she?'

'No. He's thirty-three and just the sort of person . . . well . . . he'd let my father bully him. Would you like to meet him, Laura? I wish you would. I mean, I don't want your opinion of him or anything like that, because my mind is quite made up and settled, but I'd love you two to meet. I've told him a lot about you.'

'I'd love to meet him. You could bring him back here. I could make some supper for us one night.'

'Oh, I couldn't bring him back here. It wouldn't be right. Major Croom might not like it. He might say something to Daddy. I couldn't risk it.'

'You are a one, aren't you?' Laura said admiringly. 'And here was I thinking you thought of nothing but Racine and Corneille.'

'You're rather secretive yourself though, Laura, aren't you? Don't worry, I won't give you away. You see, I saw you that Saturday you said you had to be away for the weekend. I was helping at a jumble sale and I happened to see you passing the Church Hall with Lt Giles Summerton.'

Laura concentrated on her breathing and managed to keep it steady.

'Oh, I was very pleased,' Mary continued. 'I knew you two were fond of each other. I could tell that when we were having tea together in that café in Lyme Regis. I hope everything will go well for you. At least you don't have parents to worry about.'

Laura decided not to overwhelm Mary with the news that Giles was a married man. She smiled at her and watched her getting ready to go to church. Life was certainly full of surprises.

The following week Laura was invited to meet Francis Cosgrove, Mary's fiancé. He had enough petrol to drive them to Cheddar Gorge, which neither of the girls had yet visited. It was a warm, bright afternoon.

Francis turned out to be much as Laura had imagined him. He was tall and pale with dark, rather blank eyes, and as he spoke he inclined his head as though used to placating people, or God. His voice was gentle as softly-running water. Laura couldn't imagine him in the army, praying before battle or comforting the wounded, she could only visualise him with a congregation of elderly, upper-class ladies with loud cheerful voices and overbearing ways.

The Somerset countryside was beautiful. It was half-way between spring and summer, the air sweet with lilac and lime blossom.

'Look, a cottage with a pear tree,' Mary moaned gently as though she had toothache.

'One day I'll have a country parish,' Francis said. 'A country vicarage with an acre of garden, a stream and an orchard. One day . . . after the war.'

'Geese and chickens,' Mary said. 'A border collie.'

'And what about you, Laura?' Francis asked at last. 'What will you have?' They'd almost forgotten their passenger in the back seat.

Laura didn't answer. 'Oh, she'll live in London and have an important job in an office,' Mary said sharply.

All afternoon as they scrambled over the hills and explored the caves, Laura was struck by how well-matched Mary and Francis were, both so mild and well-mannered. Mary seemed fashioned to be a clergyman's wife; it surprised Laura that it hadn't occurred to her before, she had a pious little smile and her clothes, though expensive, were always unobtrusive, even staid.

'A penny for your thoughts, Laura,' Francis said when they'd been walking along in silence for some time.

'I was thinking how lucky it is that Mary believes in God,' Laura said.

Francis seemed a little disconcerted by the remark, but decided to smile it away.

Laura was glad when the afternoon was over. She was delighted that her room-mate was happy; all the same, being in the company of a pair of lovers for three or four hours had been a punishing experience.

They'd been back in their room for only a minute or two, when Joan, Mrs Croom's maid, knocked at their door. 'A telegram for Miss Brown,' she said. 'It came about an hour ago. I hope it's not bad news.'

She waited at the door while Laura slit open the little yellow envelope. 'Please meet Bristol station tomorrow four pm one hour only embarkation leave Giles.'

'It's all right,' she said. 'It's not bad news.'

Joan still waited at the door.

'It's from a soldier friend,' Laura said. 'He wants me to meet him tomorrow.'

'Will you go?' Joan asked.

'Yes, I'll go.'

'Good.'

Joan left and Laura passed Mary the telegram.

'You poor thing,' Mary said with tears in her eyes. 'Embarkation leave. Oh you poor thing.'

Chapter Seventeen

There was a trio of very pretty girls sitting on one of the station benches. Dressed for summer, carefully made up, hair curled and waved, they were laughing together, their faces turned to the sun.

Laura looked at them without pleasure. She went into the ladies' cloakroom to look at herself and comb her hair. In her brown skirt, brown blouse, she looked untidy and uncared for; she'd had no money to have her hair done, she'd forgotten to bring her lipstick. 'I'm nervous,' she told herself. 'My hands are clammy and I'm hot and cold at the same time. Whatever's the matter with me?'

She rushed out on to the platform as she heard a train arriving. Several soldiers got off, but Giles was not among them.

For over an hour, two, three, she stood or sat on the platform watching every train that came in. 'He couldn't get away,' she thought. 'It's foolish to stay any longer. What am I doing here?'

At last it was seven and the day getting chilly. 'If this isn't love it must be madness,' she told herself. Soldiers came and went on the platform, some whistled at her, one or two tried to engage her in conversation.

'He'll write to me,' she told herself. 'It's not as if he's standing me up. I'll get a letter from him tomorrow or the next day.'

But it wasn't a letter she wanted nor an explanation; she wanted his arms around her, his body pressed down on hers. Almost in tears she walked the length of the platform, sat on a bench, walked again.

The long wait had made her realise how much she loved him: it suddenly seemed desperately important that she should tell him that she loved him.

'Please, please don't send him abroad without letting me see him,' she prayed to someone looking vaguely like Mary's curate, but bearded.

It was after eight when he arrived. For a time they held each other without saying a word.

'I couldn't contact you,' he said, then. 'The plans were changed. We're not leaving now till tomorrow morning.'

Laura had travelled a long way since their last meeting. No longer reluctant, her moral scruples gone, 'Oh good,' was all she said. 'Oh good.'

They kissed again and then hurried from the station to find a hotel.

'I'd better let my room-mate know I won't be in tonight,' Laura said. 'My landlord will give her a message.'

'Where will you say you are? Are you sure he won't ask you to leave if he knows you're staying out over night?'

'I won't phone. Mary will know I'm all right. She knows I'm meeting you.'

All the big hotels in the city centre were full. They finally got a room in a small, run-down commercial hotel near the station.

As she stood at the hotel desk waiting for Giles to sign the register and pick up the key of their room, Laura noticed the manageress looking her up and down with a contemptuous expression. 'She thinks I'm a pick-up,' Laura thought. 'And I don't mind in the slightest.' She had accepted, completely accepted, her role as the other woman; why not a common tart?

They were too late for dinner in the hotel. There was a staff shortage - it was war time, they were reminded - so they had to go out to look for a meal. The best they managed to find was sausage and egg and tea, but they sat close together, their knees touching. They were very happy.

'I really thought I'd manage to leave without seeing you,' Giles said. 'I honestly did try to put my marriage first.'

'I tried not to think about you,' Laura said. 'But I kept on hoping you'd write.'

'It was the fear that I might never come back,' he said.

He gripped her arm so tightly that she almost cried out.

'You'll come back,' she said. 'You have to come back. This is a mess, I know, but things will sort themselves out. When we meet next, all this will be behind us. We're lucky that we've got to part.'

Giles groaned. 'It doesn't seem lucky to me,' he said.

'Would you rather I went back to my digs now?' Laura asked him. 'I don't want you to go abroad feeling guilty and upset.'

'I've been through all that,' he said. 'I can't do without you.'

As they walked back to the hotel the light was fading. In the rose-coloured dusk they stopped to listen to a blackbird singing in an ornamental cherry tree. The war news was grave: Norway had been defeated, Denmark and Holland had surrendered, Germany was poised to enter France from a Belgium still scarred from the last war. They stood as still as shadows listening to the bird. 'I'll remember this,' both of them were thinking. 'This May evening, this bird.'

'You're very beautiful,' Giles said. 'You make other girls seem like dolls.'

Laura glanced at herself in the wardrobe mirror; she always looked better without her clothes. 'I'd like to be small and dainty,' she said, but it wasn't true. She liked being large and feeling powerful. She suddenly felt like a goddess - Juno - with blessings to bestow. She wanted to give herself to Giles in some dramatic and ridiculous way. Because he was miserable, because he was leaving home the next day, because her body was all she had.

'Being in love is the only magic left in the world,' Giles said when it was morning. 'Not sex. I don't mean sex. Sex is perfectly straightforward. Easy to understand. Love is straightforward too; comfort, warmth, tenderness. But this is something else. Oh, I'm drawn to you by a most mysterious force.'

*

'I love you,' she said gently when it was morning. It was true. She felt magnified by her love.

She could bear anything. He was married, would probably have a family quite soon, the time he could spare her would always be strictly limited: they loved each other, that was enough.

Giles left Bristol at half past nine. Their parting was tender, not at all agonised.

For several days and nights afterwards Laura felt peaceful and fulfilled.

'You and Giles, I think you've reached some understanding, haven't you?' Mary asked gently.

Laura looked at her and smiled. It was an understanding, she supposed.

Giles wasn't sent to France after all. The British Expeditionary Force was suddenly in the process of withdrawing from Belgium and it was considered too late to send reinforcements. His unit remained on the South Coast preparing for the German invasion.

Chapter Eighteen

By June that year, the worst seemed inevitable. France had capitulated and Germany seemed ready to invade Britain.

Laura worked for her examinations. Whether she passed or failed, got a First or Third, seemed a matter of laughable indifference, but work seemed what she had to do to get through the long, hot days.

As relaxation, she wrote to Giles, but tried to keep her letters friendly rather than passionate. She told him about Mary and her curate - Mary's parents had reluctantly agreed to their marriage - about John Glover, her step-mother's eldest son who'd been one of the soldiers evacuated from Dunkirk, and who was now, after a fortnight's leave, back on the South Coast, about Kathleen and Edith busily Digging for Victory and knitting khaki socks. Reading over her letters before posting them, she was surprised at how carefree they seemed.

Late one night, Laura was overcome by the realisation that she was pregnant. (She thought afterwards that it had been lurking in the dark of her mind for some days.) She got out her diary, though without really needing it. Compared to the gravity and weight of her intuition, other evidence - that her period was a fortnight late - seemed irrelevant.

For over an hour she sat at the table over her books, sweating, trembling, seeing nothing.

At last, she undressed, put out her bed-side light and lay on her bed as though physically hurt. Her heart was pounding with terror. If it hadn't been for Mary, asleep on the other side of the room, she would have groaned aloud.

She was pregnant, there could be no doubt of it.

All the next day and the next she felt diminished, as though she'd lost her own identity and become someone inefficient, weak-minded, 'a mere woman', 'a little woman', 'only a woman'. Giles had insisted that birth-control had brought about the equality of the sexes, but when it went wrong there was no equality but a chasm dividing them.

After a few days, outrage took the place of fear and despair; on the whole it was a slight improvement.

She sat her examinations in a white hot anger, her mind like a razor. She knew she had done well but it hardly seemed to matter.

The examinations over, she visited the doctor who had, four months earlier, fitted her with a contraceptive cap, and he confirmed that she was pregnant. He was sympathetic but brisk, reminding her that he had not promised her total immunity. 'You'll get married?' he asked her. (She had told him she was engaged to a soldier.) 'Perhaps.'

The answer seemed to satisfy him. 'Well, take good care of yourself,' he said as she left the surgery.

The confirmation of what she already knew made her feel faint again. She had to go into a café to sit down.

'Are you all right?' the waitress asked her.

'I've just had bad news. Could you bring me a glass of water?' Her knees were shaking the table.

She was brought some water and then a pot of tea and she sat for half an hour staring at the tablecloth and trying again to get to grips with the situation.

It altered everything. She had been able to accept the limitations of an affair because she had never really wanted marriage, not even with Giles. What she had wanted was a high-powered career. 'With a good degree, you could begin where I finished,' Kathleen used to tell her. She had wanted her independence like poor Annie, and like poor Annie, she was going to be thwarted, and in the same way. She had intended repaying Kathleen in full for all she'd spent on her education, now she'd have the greatest difficulty in looking after herself and... the baby.

A baby? It seemed totally incredible. She felt her heart

thumping again. She remembered a terrifying evening in the Christmas holiday when she'd been left in charge of Susan's little son. When he'd woken up and cried, she'd stood on the stairs smitten with the knowledge that she was completely out of her element. Her instinct had been to run to fetch someone else. She remembered the child's convulsive sobs at seeing her instead of Susan, his body rigid with protest as she'd lifted him out of his cot, his hot tears against her cheek as she'd tried to comfort him. A baby was the last thing she wanted, the last thing she could cope with.

She left the café, walked back to her room and cried for what seemed like hours.

Fortunately she was on her own. Mary had already gone back to Guildford to prepare for her wedding, Major and Mrs Croom were at the seaside for a fortnight and even their maid, Joan, had gone to her home in the country.

'By tomorrow, I've got to be myself again,' she told herself over and over. 'It's not a bit of use being either angry or frightened.'

In the evening, slightly recovered, she went out for a long walk on the downs and afterwards had a good night's sleep.

But when she woke, instead of feeling refreshed, she felt sick and frail. 'Morning sickness,' she told herself savagely. 'Oh hell, it's no use. I can't bear it. I'll have to contact Giles and he'll have to give me the money to get an abortion. There's no other way. I can't go through with it.'

Previously, whenever she'd been brave enough to think of any future, she'd imagined herself keeping Giles in ignorance of the situation; had visualised herself with Kathleen in the country, doing odd jobs on the land to help support herself; she certainly didn't want to burden Giles with the knowledge of an illegitimate child. But if she could reconcile herself to having an abortion it would be a different matter.

Abortions in private nursing homes were expensive and illegal, but safe; she simply had to stop herself thinking of Annie. But how could she? She seemed to be back in the horror of that period of her life.

Overcome with weakness and sickness and misery and on the point of breaking down again, she heard the postman at the door. Almost absent-mindedly she pulled herself together and went upstairs to the hall to see if there was a letter for her.

There was. It was from Giles. His unit had been notified of an immediate posting abroad.

During the weeks that followed, the Battle of Britain was fought and won. Laura could never think afterwards of that historic time without recalling the nausea and panic of the first stage of her pregnancy.

Chapter Nineteen

Professor Dobson wasn't over-fond of his students; those who were prepared to work were usually lacking in wit and intuition, those who had occasional flashes of perception were usually lazy or undisciplined. Laura was an exception. For the three years he had taught her, she had worked steadily without ever losing her clear judgement, her vision.

'She's no genius, Good Heavens, no,' he told his wife over dinner one evening. 'She's simply a good student, the first I've had for four or five years, and when I invite her back to do research she calmly tells me that she'll be unable to because she's going to have a baby.'

'Good Lord,' Ruth Dobson said - she'd met Laura on one or two occasions and had liked her - 'I didn't know she'd got married.'

'She hasn't. At least, I don't think so. She didn't mention it. She doesn't wear a ring.'

'Invite her to tea tomorrow,' Mrs Dobson said. 'I'll have a little talk with her.'

'Nonsense. It's nothing to do with you. Anyway, I can talk to her myself, she's not one of these girly types. By the way, I've offered her Prisey's old job, she can index my book for me and so on. I suppose we could put her up for the time being?'

'No dear, we couldn't,' Mrs Dobson said firmly. She was curious about the girl, but war was war, and the food shortages were beginning to sting. 'Madeleine and the children will be here next month and it's quite likely that they'll stay on with us when Charles is called up.'

Professor Dobson sighed. Madeleine was their eldest daughter. Large and exuberant, married to an insurance salesman he disliked, her three children took after her with rude health and strident voices. 'I'd rather the Germans came,' he said.

His wife ignored him.

'Look here,' he told Laura the next day. 'My wife thinks you must get married.'

'Really,' Laura said, bristling a little. She'd come to discuss the details of the job he'd offered her and wasn't expecting to be greeted by moral precepts. 'And what do you think? Do you agree with her? Almost every marriage I've ever come across seems rather a miserable affair.'

Professor Dobson, very large and composed, stared out of the window. 'Oh, I wouldn't say that,' he said. 'Many marriages may seem unsuitable, but when you *are* married, the incongruity of it doesn't strike you; you settle down, you accept it. It's rather like being in the army, I suppose.'

'Many people aren't able to accept it. Most of the married people I know show the most obvious signs of failure and disillusion.'

'Failure and disillusion,' Professor Dobson said, as though hearing the words for the first time and trying to get to grips with them. 'Failure and disillusion. No I can't say I've ever felt much sense of failure and disillusion. Over my academic output, yes, but not over my marriage. Oh, it's hardly important enough for such grave words. My dear Miss Brown, I think you're being too much of an idealist. Marriage. Children. Look at it like this; without marriage you have no one to support you so you have to take a lowly, badly-paid secretarial job. Where's the freedom in that?'

'I don't mind struggling a bit. I shall quite like being different. I've always been different; I've always been proud of it.'

'Hm. You're like my sister, Hermione,' Professer Dobson mused. 'Not that she had a baby, of course, which made things easier for her. She also had a small income. Hermione Forrester. She took our mother's name, you may have heard of her. She was a suffragette.'

'No, I'm afraid not,' Laura said. Suffragettes had never interested her much; women of the upper classes, sick of being cossetted at home, making a fuss about nothing, or at least, very little. 'Women of my class had no time for that sort of thing,' she told the professor.

'Yes they did. Read R. Scobie, *Suffrage and the Working* Class Woman. I'll lend you a copy. He'd reached safer ground. He gave her a bright open look. It's time for you, now, to catch up with the twentieth century, Miss Brown. I suppose you've smirked your way through some Lawrence and Joyce, but what about Wells and Bennett, Conrad, Galsworthy. In fact, that's what you can do for me during this next month. If you're going to be any use to me you'll have to fill in some of the gaps in your reading. English literature, you know, didn't end with the demise of George Eliot.'

'So you're going to pay me for reading novels?' she asked him, fixing her eyes on his.

'Gissing,' he said. 'Victorian in form but definitely twentieth century in matter, Moore's *Esther Waters*, Virginia Woolf if you must. And of course you'll need to be able to type, too. You can take my portable machine with you when you go. By the way, my wife wants you to come to one of her dinner parties next week. No doubt you'll find it boring, but think how much excitement you'll be causing everyone there. Next Tuesday. Seven-thirty. No need to dress.'

By September Laura was feeling fit again. She hadn't heard from Giles since he'd left Portsmouth and though she'd written him several letters, she hadn't mentioned the baby. She wasn't sure how long she'd be able to keep it up.

It had been quite an ordeal to tell Kathleen. 'I find that I'm going to have a baby,' she'd written to her a few weeks earlier. 'I suppose one ought to be a little pleased that procreation flourishes in spite of war's alarms – and the best contraception. I mustn't let you accuse me of flippancy. I've worried a very great deal in the last weeks, not least about the fact that I shall take much longer now to repay my debt to you.

'By the way, I got my First, so I hope you'll feel that the

chance you took with me has not been wasted. Professor Dobson wanted me to remain here to do research and when I explained why I couldn't, offered me a job indexing a book for him, two pounds a week, so that I'll be able to keep on my room here. I have to learn to type during the vacation. Next week I'm going to Guildford to attend my room-mate's wedding. I shall visit you and Edith as soon as I can.'

For reply she received only a telegram. 'Many congratulations Kathleen.'

As a week, and then two, passed, she got increasingly agitated that there was no letter from her.

In the third week of September she spent a few days with her father and step-mother. Her father was ill with bronchitis and her step-mother busier than ever, so that she decided not to burden them with her news.

On the Sunday afternoon her step-mother's sister and brother-in-law were expected to tea, so she decided to go and visit Susan who was still living with her parents on the other side of the city.

In the bus, on the way over, she felt quite proud of the fact that she, at last, had some exciting news to tell. She imagined how surprised and self-righteous Susan would be. 'You don't mean to tell me that you're not getting married. I don't believe it. But, Laura, your baby will be *illegitimate*, have you thought about that? Do you remember poor Betty Hampton in Eversley Road School? Do you remember how pink she used to get when Miss Moorland used to mention fathers? Do you remember how everybody used to spin round and stare at her? Of course you could have it adopted, did you know that? In my opinion every baby should have a father. Anyway, you'll be a rotten mother, your head in a book all day. Looking after a baby is a full-time job, let me tell you. As soon as you're able to sleep a bit at night, they're running about all day, so you're always tired. And have they told you about labour? It's terrible, Laura. You feel like an animal. Everybody comes round to prod you. They tell you you're doing fine and they won't believe it's killing you.'

Though she'd amused herself by anticipating Susan's reaction to her news, she didn't get a chance to reveal it. Peter had that very afternoon arrived home on leave and naturally was the focus of Susan's attention.

Laura hadn't seen Peter for over a year. Now that her infatuation for him was over, she found him an ordinary, pleasant person and easy to talk to. He had put on weight in the army, he seemed older and more relaxed. He'd lost the restless, boyish look she'd found so attractive. He was delightful with the children. Very proud of them, but careful not to over-excite them, he spent his afternoon playing sedate little games with them.

Laura and he were alone for a time while Susan put the children to bed.

'And what are you going to do with yourself now that you've left university?' he asked her.

'Nothing very exciting. I'm staying on for a while helping my professor with a book he's writing.'

'It sounds very exciting. I was glad to hear you'd got a First. I thought you would.'

'I look like a blue-stocking?'

'No. You just look different; intelligent. When is your graduation ceremony?'

'It's already been.'

'I didn't know that. Did Mum go?'

'No. I didn't expect her to. How could she have left the shop?'

'Did your Dad go?'

'Of course not. Do you honestly think he'd have wanted to travel to Bristol for a graduation ceremony?'

'You've never been very fond of your old man, have you?'

'I'm fonder of him now than I used to be. I don't know why. He's getting less dangerous, I suppose.'

'Dangerous? He was never a danger to you, was he?'

'Oh no.'

'Well, what did you mean? Less dangerous?'

'I was exaggerating. I always felt my mother was frightened of him, though. I may be wrong. She died when I was eleven, but that was the impression I had. Anyway, your mother seems more than a match for him. She's tamed him.'

'Perhaps. She's quite forceful in her own quiet way.'

Peter bent to pick up a toy rabbit from the floor. He looked at it thoughtfully and put it on the table.

They were silent for a while.

'Do you think marriage has tamed me?' Peter asked.

'I never felt you were particularly dangerous.'

'Yes you did.'

Laura caught her breath. 'Yes, I suppose I did. But it's I who's changed, not you.'

'Why did you change? I loved that spark between us.'

'I was never happy about it!'

'Why?'

'Because you were Susan's husband of course.'

'Do you remember that afternoon in Birmingham just before the wedding?'

'Of course I do.'

'We had a drink in that pub in New Street and I knew that if you as much as touched my hand there wouldn't be any wedding.'

'What a foolish thing to say.'

'It's true.'

The door was pushed open. 'What's true?' Susan asked. 'Peter, they want you to kiss them good-night. What's true?'

'That I always wanted to go to university,' Peter said.

'Oh that,' Susan said. 'I've heard that hundreds of times.'

'I'll go up.'

'I'd better come with you or you'll stay too long.'

While Peter and Susan were still upstairs, Susan's parents came home from chapel and Laura went to the kitchen to help Mrs Wilkins make sandwiches for supper. Mrs Wilkins took the opportunity to talk to her about Arthur's new job – as a marine engineer he wasn't eligible for call-up – and his new car. 'He still hasn't forgotten you,' she said, rather plaintively. 'He'll be pleased you've done so well. Whatever went wrong between you two? Arthur would never tell me.'

'Nothing went wrong. We were never anything but good friends.'

Laura knew that Mrs Wilkins wasn't satisfied with her answer but she couldn't bring herself to elaborate. She still couldn't bear to think of the afternoon he'd turned up at the Camberwell flat and found her with Giles.

'He's always asking about you.'

After supper - when the conversation was all of Julia and Tony - Mr Wilkins offered to run Laura home in his van and she was delighted to accept.

No longer in love with Peter, she felt she had nothing to fear from him. All the same, she wasn't quite ready to put her theory to the test.

Chapter Twenty

Back in Bristol, Laura received the long-awaited letter from Kathleen.

Kathleen excused her silence by listing all the things she and Edith had been doing; they'd joined the Home Guard and been away on a week's course learning how to deal with mustard and other toxic gases, they'd dug up the lawn behind the cottage and planted the ground - excellent black soil - with leeks and winter cabbage, they'd joined a working party of ladies, drawn from the residents of Kingsbury and three neighbouring villages, which was meeting weekly to provide comforts and entertainment for the forces, they'd made twenty-four pounds of blackberry jelly.

On the second page of the letter she confessed to being disappointed that Laura wouldn't, in the immediate future, be able to embark on a career in the Civil Service, but added that she - and Edith too - had come to the conclusion that a new baby was always good news and more especially so in the midst of so much death and destruction. She insisted that she'd never wanted or expected any repayment, that she had as much money as she needed, even hoped to be able to provide a little financial help when the baby was born. 'And of course you can come here whenever you want to. Just let us know and we'll get the bed aired.'

It was a kind letter but Laura couldn't help being aware of the effort behind it, the time it had taken her to get it written. She had imagined Kathleen responding to her news by driving down to Bristol to be with her.

*

Her first letter from Giles arrived shortly after Kathleen's, and for a time it comforted her. 'I feel we're as close as two people have ever been. I find myself avoiding company so that I can have peace to think about you. God help me.'

Further letters she received were in much the same vein, chronicles of love and longing. He didn't mention the war or the work he was doing, though he occasionally sent her a page or two of an essay he was writing on Henry Vaughan which must have puzzled the censors.

She knew he must be disappointed with her letters to him, which were almost entirely about the research she was doing for Professor Dobson; she found it impossible to write on a more personal level without mentioning her pregnancy or the coming baby. Yet, she loved him. She no longer brooded about his relationship with Daphne nor considered trying to break with him.

The weeks dragged on. Her pregnancy still caused her spells of disbelief and despair, but most of the time she was able to accept it with something like composure.

She was enjoying the work she was doing, but since she realised it would be finished well before Christmas, she became more and more concerned about what she was going to do when the baby was born at the beginning of February. It didn't seem that she had any alternative but to accept Kathleen's invitation, however half-hearted it might have been. She knew she couldn't stay on in her bed-sitting room even if she had the money to do so. Major and Mrs Croom were not the sort of people to put up with any irregularities.

After losing the air battle in the summer, Germany had begun the heavy bombing of Britain's industrial centres. In mid-November, Laura's home-town was the target of their attacks, the area where her father and step-mother lived being particularly badly hit. She was naturally very anxious about them as well as about Susan and her two small children.

After the second bombing raid she received a hurried note from Kathleen telling her that an empty house in their village was being comandeered for evacuees and suggesting that she contacted Susan about it.

Laura tried to phone the Wilkins's shop as soon as she got the letter, but all the telephone lines were down so that she had to write instead.

She described Kingsbury in glowing terms. 'It's heaven, Susan, pretty thatched cottages just like the teapots, and a village pub with a garden full of roses and little old men who say "arh". I haven't seen the empty house, but Kathleen says it will be ideal for you. Get your Dad to take you as soon as you get this. It's only about thirty miles. Just go to Kathleen's - Cowslip Cottage, immediately opposite the village green - and she'll do everything else. If you go on Thursday or Friday, I'll come to visit you at the weekend and help you settle in.'

She posted the letter on her way to work.

'You're looking very pleased with yourself this morning,' Professor Dobson said when she arrived in his room, late and excited.

'Yes,' she said. 'I've been rather worried about where to live when the baby comes, and now I think I've found somewhere.'

'My dear girl, you shouldn't have worried. My sister Hermione has offered to have you live with her. She's got a great barn of a house near Oxford with living-in staff. I'd have mentioned it except that I didn't want to unsettle you before you'd finished the book for me. You and Hermione would hit it off, I think. Never mind, if you've found somewhere else we'll have to disappoint her, won't we?'

'It was good of you to think of it,' Laura said.

'Oh, it was my wife. She likes to arrange these things you know. She's also got you a job as a tutor in a correspondence college run by some chum of hers in Knightsbridge. She's negotiating your salary at the moment; she says it will be at least as much as you get from me, perhaps a bit more.'

'Please thank her,' Laura said, a little stiffly.

Ruth Dobson was the type of woman she most disliked: loud-voiced, bossy, self-confident, patronising. Whenever she'd been to a gathering at their home she'd felt she was being exhibited: the forties woman, bohemian and fast. She was never encouraged to mix on equal terms with the other guests, Mrs Dobson always managing to steer the conversation to subjects outside her range, foreign travel, previous members of the department, celebrities that only she hadn't met, and if Professor Dobson ventured to talk to her about books or poetry, his wife would beg him not to be boring.

'She likes to run people's lives. Always has,' her husband said.

'She's very kind,' Laura managed to say.

The professor busied himself with some papers. 'She's fond of you,' he said. 'She'll miss you.' For a time he hummed under his breath.

'That goes for me too,' he said, then, looking as embarrassed as if he'd made a declaration of undying passion.

He left for his lecture before Laura could make any response. 'Damn it all,' she heard him muttering as he closed the door. 'The fools they make of us.'

Early on Saturday, hoping to find Susan and the children already there, Laura set off by bus to Kingsbury. Cross-country buses were infrequent and very crowded, and the sixty-mile journey lasted four jolting and uncomfortable hours.

Kingsbury was very different from when Laura had last seen it in early summer. It was a dark depressing day, the clouds hanging low over the grey hills, the large elms in the centre of the village already bare. Rain was falling steadily.

There was no one at home in Cowslip Cottage, but the door was unlocked and the low fire carefully banked, so that Laura assumed that either Kathleen or Edith would soon be back. She took off her wet coat and set about making herself a cup of tea and finding something to eat; she'd had nothing all day but a piece of toast.

The kitchen was clinically clean, quite unlike Kathleen's at Camberwell, and had small urgent notices taped up in strategic places. 'Turn out that light.' 'Save gas.' 'Save waste paper.' 'Pig bin.' 'Keep tinned food for emergencies,' so that she felt too nervous to touch anything and went back to the sitting room out of harm's way. She was suddenly very depressed. It was obvious that Susan hadn't arrived and she wished *she* hadn't. The rain fell and fell and fell. She picked up a book, it was a civil defence manual, the daily paper was full of horrific pictures of devastated cities and homeless people; she burst into tears. She had no right to be bringing a child into such a terrifying world. She hadn't heard from Giles for nearly three weeks. And even if he was still alive she had no claims on him.

'What's the matter love?'

Kathleen was on her knees beside her before she could make any attempt to compose herself. She put her arms tightly around Laura and let her go on sobbing against her cold wet mackintosh. 'There, there, love. What is it? What is it?' Kathleen repeated over and over again. 'Tell Kitty what it is.'

For several minutes the two women rocked against each other, steaming gently together.

At last, Laura broke away, wiped her face with her hands, sniffed and said, 'This is not like us, is it?'

'No,' Kathleen said. 'But I wish it were. I wish we were closer. I wish ... we could be.'

'You didn't write to me,' Laura said. 'I thought you were disappointed in me, ashamed of me.'

'*You* didn't write to *me*. Not for weeks. Not until you'd got every blessed thing worked out and settled. I know I shouldn't expect you to turn to me first or anything like that, but all you wrote about was money, how you wouldn't be able to pay back the money I'd given you - which I'd never asked for or wanted. You didn't even invite me to your graduation. Edith and I expected you here in the vacation; I'd been missing you all the year. I haven't the right to expect very much from you, I know that: I ignored your existence when you needed me as a child, so I forfeited that right, but I thought we'd become friends, I expected *something*. And I wasn't ashamed of you, of course I wasn't. All I felt was pity. And love.'

'Oh Kathleen, I didn't consider your feelings, I see that now. For weeks and weeks I felt so let down, so furious at what had happened, that I had no thoughts for anyone but myself. I *do* feel close to you. I *was* upset at your silence. I *did* need your support, I realise now how much. But I felt like a trapped animal, unable to do anything or even think clearly. I *had* to tell Professor Dobson, I had no option. I haven't had the guts to tell anyone else.'

'Not even Giles?'

'Least of all Giles. How can I tell Giles? He seems to have enough on his plate at the moment. I think he's somewhere in occupied France. I don't suppose I'll ever see him again.'

'Of course you'll see him again.'

'I haven't heard from him for almost three weeks.'

'Three weeks is no time at all. A neighbour of ours didn't hear from her son for over three months and then she had six or seven letters together. Three weeks is nothing to worry about. Let me make you a meal. You'll feel better when you've had something to eat. Can you stay for a while to let me look after you? Can you come here to have your baby? I do hope you can. I've been thinking a lot about it.'

'I've only got a few more weeks with Professor Dobson. I thought I might come to share that empty house with Susan.'

'Oh good. That's why I wrote to you about it. I'm afraid I wouldn't have thought about Susan otherwise; I was just casting about for a way to get you here. The house is in a pretty bad state, but Edith and I are doing all we can to make it habitable. We've managed to get some help too, a woman who was in service there years ago. She works like a horse.'

'I thought Susan might be already here. I told her to come straightaway.'

'Oh dear, did you?' Kathleen's expression told Laura more about the state of the house than she wanted to know. 'Well, let's have some scrambled eggs. Edith's coming over in a few minutes. We'll all feel better after some food. If Susan does arrive we can easily have her and the children here. We had some evacuees last spring, a brother and sister, but their mother and some aunties came and took them back to Birmingham after a few weeks ... I wonder how they are now?'

'I wonder if my father and Mabel are all right?'

'I'm sure they are. You'd have heard otherwise.'

'What lovely brown eggs.'

'We have plenty of eggs. Have you been short of food?'

'No, not really. I don't have Sunday dinner, though. Not any more. Major and Mrs Croom couldn't manage it, they said; their joints were getting too small. The real reason is that I'm not patriotic enough for them. I can't seem to love the war as they do. I can't seem to rejoice when German planes are shot down and German pilots killed. I don't know what's the matter with me. I just wish it would stop.'

'So does everyone, dear,' Kathleen said firmly. 'That's why we've got to work hard for a quick victory.'

'The Crooms don't want a quick victory. They want the lovely war to go on till there's not a German left alive.'

'Here's Edith,' Kathleen said. 'Don't let Edith think you're a peace-lover, dear, will you,' she added in a whisper.

'Edith dear, I keep forgetting, are egg-shells pig-swill, or compost?'

The empty house was perched on a hill behind the village. Its name, Larkshill, was the only pretty thing about it, Laura thought as they approached it. It looked as though it had been abandoned for years. The gate was off its hinges, the garden completely overgrown, two of the upstairs windows were cracked, one badly, all the paint was peeling. It was uncompromisingly grey and gaunt.

Edith and Kathleen took Laura through the echoing hall into the kitchen.

'We've done this room,.' Kathleen said, looking round her with a satisfied smile.

'I always think a kitchen is the heart of a house,' Edith said. 'When we've made some nice black-out curtains, this will be very cosy won't it?'

'We got the table and chairs at an auction,' Kathleen said. 'The vicar's wife gave us the sofa. It's been in a summer house for years, but it's quite sound. I've got a plaid rug to throw over it and a couple of cushions.'

'The dresser was mine,' Edith said, 'but it was too big for the cottage. Wasn't it a good thing I didn't give it away? Of course we had a double lot of china and cutlery and linen when we moved, so you'll have plenty of those.'

'All we need now are some beds and mattresses. The

previous tenants left an old wardrobe in the front bedroom and six or seven washstands scattered about.'

'It's lovely,' Laura said.

It was terrible. It smelt like a disused church. She'd imagined a small pretty cottage like Kathleen's. She tried not to think what Susan would say when she saw it.

'It's got tremendous character hasn't it,' Edith said. 'It'll be quite different when Mrs Miller gets the range going; Kathleen and I can't quite get the hang of it. We haven't done the dining room or the drawing room yet, but I think the breakfast room could be quite useful as a play room when it's been brushed out. Would you like to see the bedrooms now?'

There were six large bedrooms, the two Mrs Miller had 'done' only slightly less awful than the rest.

'I'm sure we'll be able to pick up some pieces of carpet at the next sale,' Kathleen said as they trooped downstairs. 'Carpet makes all the difference, doesn't it? Look at the lovely curve of the bannisters. Look at the oak-panelling in the hall.'

Laura took a deep breath and steadied herself. 'It's wonderful,' she said. 'We're going to be very happy here.'

'Think of the vegetables you'll be able to grow in that garden,' Edith said, looking out at a piece of rough ground about the size of a tennis court.

Susan and the children arrived the next day at three o'clock.

'I can't stop,' Mr Wilkins said, when he'd carried out their cases and boxes from his van. 'Mother's nervous on her own. I wanted her to come along, only she won't leave the house. You wouldn't recognise the city centre, Laura, nothing but rubble, whole streets nothing but rubble. It's not so bad up our way. Your Dad and step-mum had a miraculous escape; Susan'll tell you; incendiary bomb ripped off half their roof. If they'd been sleeping in the back, they'd be being buried tomorrow, with all the other poor buggers. Three hundred people killed somebody said.'

Laura introduced him to Kathleen and Edith. 'I can't stop,' he said as he shook their hands. 'It's good of you to have them. There's some oranges in there somewhere and two or three pounds of best onions.'

'Your grannie'll miss you, my duck,' he told his granddaughter as he kissed her goodbye.

As Laura watched him hurrying back to his van, she was surprised to experience a moment's sympathy for him. 'I'm getting soft,' she told herself.

Chapter Twenty-one

Julia, two and a half, was letting Edith help her off with her coat. 'You *are* a pretty girl.'

'Yes, I know. Are you my auntie or a lady?'

'I'm . . . well, I'm Edith dear.'

Susan, nursing the still-sleeping Tony, was pale and subdued.

'Goodness, isn't he a big baby,' Kathleen said. 'Couldn't you put him down on the settee? I could get a little blanket for you.'

'He'd only wake up,' Susan said. 'I think I'll keep him on my lap for a bit.'

Mothers, Laura had noticed, were always terrified of their children waking. Anyone would think they hated them.

'Shall I get you a cup of tea?' she asked Susan, touching her hand and smiling at her.

'Yes, please. Oh Laura, it's wonderful to get away. The raids were absolutely awful. You've no idea. They've been going on for weeks but this last one was indescribable. The noise was deafening. It went on for hours and hours. Your stomach feels raw after it because you've been so frightened; all day it feels weak and raw, and then it's another night.'

'Were the children frightened?' Kathleen asked.

'No, the children were all right; they hardly woke up.'

'Mama,' Julia said, 'I'm having cake with Lady Ediff.'

'Lady Edith?' Kathleen said. 'Being an air-raid warden's gone to her head.'

As soon as Susan moved her arm to take her cup of tea, the large baby woke and became a small boy with a creased pink face. He started to cry loudly and went on and on with increasing passion until Julia, leaving her place at the table, marched up to him and tapped him sharply on the head, at which he immediately stopped and gazed round benevolently at them all.

'Should you let her do that?' Laura asked.

'No,' Susan said. 'It's probably killing off millions and millions of his brain cells. You mustn't do that, Julia, Mama's very cross with you.'

Julia accepted her mother's anger with little sign of concern. She went back to her cake. 'Are you cross with me, Lady Ediff?' she asked.

'She's an awful snob,' Susan said. 'I don't know where she gets it from. She wasn't a bit interested in You-know-who until Mum started calling him Lord Jesus.'

Susan was so upset when Laura said she had to leave that evening that she decided to phone Professor Dobson to let him know that she wouldn't be coming in to work until the Tuesday.

'You must be having a particularly good weekend,' he said drily.

'Yes. My aunt's just had three evacuees to stay and I'm helping them settle in.'

There was a short pause. 'Then I won't detain you,' he said.

'You said in your letter that you'd stay till I was settled in,' Susan complained later when they were putting Tony to bed in an old iron cot Kathleen had managed to borrow from a neighbour. I'd counted on you being here. I feel nervous with your auntie. Besides, I've got things to tell you. I haven't seen you for months.'

'I've got things to tell you, too,' Laura said.

Susan looked at her briefly but failed to notice the weight of meaning behind the words. She hugged her son with sudden ferocity. 'He's lovely, isn't he, this one?' she said. He, dressed only in a vest, gave her a small deprecating smile.

Laura studied him closely, his large head, the roundness of his body, the utter bonelessness of his legs.

'It occurs to me . . . ' she said, but stopped in mid-sentence. About to observe that primitive artists like Cimabue had got their babies all wrong because, being monks, they'd probably never seen any, an instinct had warned her that she was off the mark. She switched to, 'He's adorable, Susan, so soft and pink.'

'I'm glad you didn't say that he looks like Churchill,' Susan said. 'So many people say that. It's so silly. So affected. And they expect me to be pleased.'

'Saint Anthony,' Laura said, for no reason but that her mind had begun to run on religious paintings.

Susan, taking canonization in her stride, smiled gently. Suddenly, though, her expression changed. 'I'm pregnant again,' she said.

'Oh Susan are you? I *am* sorry. Are you very upset?'

'I'm devastated, absolutely devastated. Tony's just beginning to get a bit easier - and now it's all starting again. I was beginning to get my figure back too. I'd bought myself a lovely new dress, cherry red with a little round collar and puff sleeves, so pretty. I looked so nice in it, and then Peter had to come home on leave and that was it. Oh, I feel suicidal, I really do. And Peter is not a bit sympathetic. He says three children is not very different from two. It's all very well for him. Sometimes I wish I'd never got married.'

'Oh, Susan.'

'I do. Single girls can have a lovely time these days. I could join the ATS and have some fun. Everything's different now. Everything's changed.'

'*We*'ll have some fun, you and me. We used to, didn't we?'

'No we didn't. You were always telling me off for something or other. You always wanted me to be a stick-in-the-mud like you. You were always trying to get me to go to evening school and things like that.'

'I'm over that now. I've finished with studying. I'm going to give up my job and come and live with you.'

Susan turned to face Laura and examined her narrowly.

'That's right,' Laura said, standing up straight with her hands on her hips. 'Have a good look. Don't I look different?'

'Oh my God, I don't believe it.'

'Middle of February,' Laura said. 'When's yours due?'

'But you're not married.'

'It happens like that sometimes. Didn't you know?'

'How can you joke about it. Don't you mind? Can't you get married? Where's the father? Oh Laura, this is terrible. This is what comes of going off on your own to university. I told you how it would be. Oh, I don't know what to say.'

'You don't have to say anything, love. It's not your problem. You've got enough problems of your own, haven't you?'

'Of course it's my problem. You're my best friend aren't you, we've always shared problems. Of course it's my problem. Do you think my mother and father will let me stay with you now? The moment they know about this they'll come to take me home.'

'Will they think I'm more dangerous than bombs?'

'How can you joke all the time? Does your Dad know about it?'

'No he doesn't as a matter of fact. I can't see how it concerns him. Though I suppose I ought to let Mabel know. I'll write this week. I wonder how she'll take it? Gosh, my baby will have the same grandparents as yours, it'll make them cousins, won't it? Will you mind them having an illegitimate cousin?'

Susan refused to be deflected from the gravity of Laura's predicament.

'Does your auntie know?' she asked.

'Yes. I intended to tell you, too, when I saw you in September, but Peter had just arrived home and I didn't get a chance.'

'Oh God, what will Peter think? He was so proud of you, Laura. Are you quite sure your dates are right? If you're having a baby in February you must be ...'

'I'm over six months pregnant.'

'You hardly show at all.'

'It's all tucked up inside my cardigan.'

Laura opened this voluminous garment and revealed a skirt let out with a piece of elastic.

Susan finished fastening Tony's nappy and put him into his sleeping suit.

'I'm absolutely aghast,' she said, tucking him into the cot, pushing his thumb into his mouth and kissing his forehead. 'Aghast.'

'Will Julia be all right in this camp-bed?' Laura asked. 'Or would she be better off in my bed? I don't mind sleeping with you if you'd like me to.'

'She'll want to be in here with me,' Susan said, curtly dismissing Laura's offer.

'I don't think I shall bother to stay. If you're going to be in a mood with me, I may as well get back to Bristol. I'm paid for a five and a half day week and I'm not in the habit of taking time off. I may as well go back tonight.'

They were empty threats. Susan ignored them.

'Is he going to provide for you? The father? The baby's father?'

'I can provide for myself. I've got a job as a tutor in a correspondence college. I'll be marking essays and so forth. I'll be able to work from here.'

Susan's eyes narrowed. 'And *when* will you be able to do all this work, have you thought of that. When you have a baby, you don't have a minute to call your own.'

'I shall have a girl to take it out in the afternoon. If you're nice to me, she shall take yours out at the same time.'

'Where do you think you'll get a girl? People can't get help these days, you know. My Dad can't get a girl for love nor money. They all have jobs in factories now, making munitions. They get three pounds a week.'

'Not at fourteen, surely. Not in the country, surely. I'll go to the village school and ask for a little school-leaver.'

'I wouldn't let mine out with a fourteen-year-old, I can tell you. I remember what I was like when I was fourteen.'

Susan's voice lost its sharpness. 'I used to take out Mrs Swift's baby. Do you remember Mrs Swift? Her first baby was called Leslie John. He was ever so sweet. She used to make me promise not to get him out of the pram, but I always did. As soon as I was round the corner by the Mission Hall I used to rush him down the park and I used to have him stripped to his little vest before he'd had a chance to blink.'

'I could never understand why you wanted to – all that dressing and undressing – the poor little mite blue with cold.'

'It's a natural instinct, isn't it? It's the preparation for motherhood. You won't know anything about it.'

'I can learn.'

There was a short silence. Laura began to feel that the worst was over.

'Poor little Leslie John. He had a protruding belly-button. Mrs Swift used to put a sixpence over it and bind it with a piece of rag. Once I lost the sixpence; it rolled down a grating I think. God, I was so worried. She must have noticed, but she never said anything. Mine have got beautiful belly-buttons. Did you notice Tony's? It looks as though it's embroidered. Did you notice his willy? I couldn't keep my eyes off it when he was first born. He was a very small baby, only six pounds, and all mottled like a little trout - he wasn't much bigger than a little trout - but he had this huge willy. I felt quite embarrassed when I had to undress him.'

Her voice changed again.

'Julia's little fanny makes me want to cry,' she said. 'It's so pretty and sweet. I can't bear to think of her growing up and running after boys. She will. She's the sort. You can tell already. It's horrible. I can't bear to think of it.'

'Hey, she's only two and a half,' Laura said, 'you needn't start worrying yet, surely. But why worry at all? I thought you loved being a woman. You used to be so proud of your sex-appeal. Do you remember how you used to practice sultry glances in the mirror?'

She gave a demonstration of Susan's Theda Bara looks.

Susan refused to smile.

'Having a baby is a nightmare, Laura. I may as well tell you the truth. It's hell. I'm dreading having to go through it again.'

Laura couldn't think how to comfort her. 'Tony's asleep already,' she said at last. 'Isn't he a good boy?'

She bent over him. His eyelids were pale and glossy like the inside of eggshells and he smelt of milk.

'Don't wake him for God's sake,' Susan said.

When Julia was in bed and asleep, they had supper and listened to the nine o'clock news, and afterwards, while Edith and Kathleen earnestly discussed the progress of the war, Susan enlightened Laura on the subjects of labour pains, tearing, stitching, after-pains and engorged and impacted breasts.

Chapter Twenty-two

Laura finished the work she was doing for Professor Dobson at the end of November, and since even the departmental clerical work he was finding for her was drying up by the middle of November, she told him she wanted to leave.

'Nonsense,' he said. 'Stay till the baby's born.'

'I've got some money saved. Don't worry about me. I should go now.'

He arranged to drive her to Kingsbury at the end of the week.

'How we'll miss you, Laura,' Ruth Dobson said when they were on their way. 'Your unconventional attitudes, your determination to be different.'

'I never wanted to be different, not at all. Everything that's happened to me has been an accident. I didn't plan any of it.'

'Nonsense. You mustn't be so modest. You're the New Woman we all talked about when we were young: no money, no background, just guts and common sense and plenty of the Life Force. Alfred thinks you're a genius, don't you, dear?'

'Don't talk such rubbish,' he said. 'Now which way?'

Laura knew he was feeling upset to lose her. He'd been very bad-tempered for the last week, kicking drawers that wouldn't open, and scowling very childishly at students and members of staff alike.

'Through the village, left by the church and half a mile up the hill,' she said.

The sun was shining as they got out of the car. The gate had been mended, the garden cleared of bedsteads and tea-chests, the holly tree outside the front door seemed newly painted.

'It's a fine house, Laura,' Ruth Dobson said. 'I'd expected something more picturesque, I don't know why. But this suits you, it's just your style. Isn't it a fine old house Alfred?'

The church clock struck three in the distance and on the instant some wood pigeons whirred up into a sky pale as opalescent milk in the frail sunshine.

'It's too cold to stand here breathing,' Professor Dobson said. 'Let me have the key. I'll take the things in.'

He seemed anxious to go, but while he and Laura carried in the suitcases and the boxes of books, his wife insisted on seeing over the house.

He stood waiting for her, tapping his foot. He declined to see anything, even the kitchen. Laura looked at him; large, old and irritable. Is he a bit in love with me? she wondered.

'My life is full of disappointments,' he said, as though reading her mind.

She leaned over and kissed him.

'What good's that going to do?' he asked crossly. 'That's going to turn me into a handsome prince, I suppose.'

'It's charming,' Mrs Dobson said when she came downstairs. 'But, believe me, you won't be able to live in it for at least six months. Plasterers and decorators take such a time these days, even when you can get hold of them. Anyway, we must go, Laura dear. I'm giving a dinner party tonight. We'll be getting in touch with you over Christmas.'

'Nonsense, nonsense,' Professor Dobson said, though about what Laura wasn't quite sure. She watched him getting into the car and waved until it went out of sight. Her heart felt as though it was being squeezed.

When she went round the house she was amazed at the difference in the atmosphere. There'd been no radical change since she'd been there last, but there was a healthy smell of polish and wood fire instead of damp and drains. She opened the door into the kitchen; the range had been lit and the table spread with a blue and white cloth. This isn't going to be too bad, she thought.

She went in to one of the large front rooms, imagining a small table in the window as a desk, some shelves for books. Giles would like this, she thought, the tall Georgian windows, the elegant proportions. For a moment, Giles was vividly present in her mind.

Would he ever come here, she wondered. Would he ever visit her and her child; their child. Why not? She suddenly felt a rush of desire for him. Once, he had mentioned the possibility of having leave for Christmas: what if he did? Would he be able to spend a day with her? A night with her? She went to the window and laid her forehead on the cold glass; she seemed feverish. Not in the six months since she'd last seen him had she felt his presence so acutely.

She wanted to write to him, that minute, from the window of that house. I've found a house for us, she wanted to say, I've found a place where we can be together sometimes. It's up on a hillside surrounded by trees and the first time I stood in the front window, oh, I felt you by my side. Oh, Giles, you must come here. You must come as often as you can and stay as long as you can: I need you. I need you and want you with me.

Why did she suddenly feel that he was rightfully - if not legally - hers? Houses meant families; she supposed that was it. The house seemed already to have laid its claims on her.

It was a long time before she felt composed enough to leave the cold room and go down the hill to Cowslip Cottage.

That night, after some lively hours with Kathleen, Edith, Susan and the children, she did write to Giles, giving him her new address. 'It would be wonderful if you could come for a day or two when you have some leave,' she wrote. 'You'd love the house. I'm going to try to buy it.'

After she'd sealed the envelope, she wondered what had possessed her to mention buying the house: she had about six pounds in her Post Office book. All the same, she felt the house was going to be hers one day.

She wasn't usually given to dreams or premonitions.

It was just over a week to Christmas.

So far, only Laura was living in Larkshill; Susan and the

children, all having developed chest colds, had remained in the warmth and comfort of Cowslip Cottage.

Laura was spending her days helping Mrs Miller, the casual work-force of the village, to scrub out, polish and decorate.

They had spent two mornings on 'her' front room which had by this time acquired a saleroom carpet, a large oak bookcase and a country Chippendale elbow-chair (Edith had been to an auction sale at a private house and got seven old chairs, two of them antiques, for a pound) and were by this time busy on the upstairs.

Mrs Miller was a dark, wild-looking woman of seventy or so who worked in currents of fierce energy and whose conversation consisted of involved histories of some of the former occupants of Larkshill, fascinating to Laura whose interest in the house was rapidly becoming as fanatical as hers.

'This was the boxroom and this was where the boys slept. There was one bed 'ere, two more over there, and these bars on the winder are because they would climb out on the roof and try and kill the'selves. One of them's a parson now, they tell me, only nobody keeps in touch now they're dead.

This was my room, this one. It were little but it were a palace to me, a room to m'self. I 'ad me box in this corner and 'ere me bed. It were cold in winter and 'ot in summer, but it were a palace to me. And this one was the nurse-maid's room. 'Er name was Daisy Oliver, she was courtin' a farmer's lad from Cleeve. She was a pretty girl, Daisy, but not . . . well, let that go.'

They didn't spend long on the top floor. They carried down some loads of rubbish and burned it in the garden, swept and washed the floors, then moved down to the first floor: three large bedrooms and a bathroom. 'Of course, there was no bathroom in my day. I used to bring up jugs of water. That was me first job after the grates.'

'And this was Miss Rosamund's room. She was a beautiful young lady and she married the Major's son from Bickleigh, but that was after my time. This is the room I'd sleep in if I were you. It's warm over the kitchen. Of course the mistress always 'ad a fire, but who does fires nowadays? There was a beautiful flowered carpet in this room. It was like a garding.'

Mrs Miller's voice was suddenly sad.

'Was she the only daughter?' Laura asked her.

'Yes, but she was trouble enough for 'alf a dozen. Once, when she was thirteen or so, she ran away from school. That was a to-do and no mistake. The master 'ad only just come in, 'is 'orses only just rubbed down, so I 'ad to go with a lantern ... Just a minute. Remind me where I got to.'

Mrs Miller clattered down the uncarpeted stairs for something or other and Laura went on washing the paintwork of Miss Rosamund's room.

'You got a visitor,' Mrs Miller said when she got back. 'Very posh. "I'd like to speak to Laura Brown please"', Mrs Miller said in a radio announcer's voice. 'I thought I 'eard a car drawring up. I put him in the front room with the 'lectric.'

Laura dried her hands on her apron and hurried downstairs.

It was Professor Dobson. 'Ah, my dear,' he said holding out his hands to take hers.

She knew soemthing terrible had happened because he'd become so kind and gracious. He'd never called her 'my dear' before, let alone touched her.

'I've had some bad news,' he said, 'and I'm pretty sure it concerns you. I'm very sorry.'

She bowed her head and steeled herself to listen.

'Summerton, Giles Summerton, reported killed in this morning's *Times*. Do sit down, my dear.'

Laura sat heavily in the elbow chair and looked at him. 'Killed,' she said.

She almost lost consciousness for a time, seeing only the swirling patterns of the blue and grey carpet. Professor Dobson's voice seemed to be coming to her from a great distance. 'Terrible shock,' he was saying. 'Better to hear it from me, perhaps. That's what I thought.'

With an enormous effort, like a person surfacing after a too-dangerous dive, she raised her head.

He came round to face her and took her hands again. For a

moment he stood over her chafing her hands.

'Thank you for coming,' she said. She could feel sweat running down her body.

'I'll ask the charwoman to get us some tea,' he said.

She heard him calling Mrs Miller.

She got up and went to the window. At that window, such a short time ago, she had had a premonition of Giles coming to her.

It was some time later.

'Can you drink this?' Professor Dobson was asking.

'What is it?'

'Brandy. Mrs Miller fetched some from the "Star". I told her your news.'

She was in the kitchen sitting by the range, her legs up on a stool.

'Can you drink another cup of tea? It's got a lot of sugar in it. It will do you some good.'

She was aware of time passing, but only when he said he had to leave did she realise that the curtains had been drawn; that it was evening.

'Your charwoman had to leave. She said she'd go to tell your aunt what had happened. She'll come up, I'm sure. I'm afraid I'll have to go. You see, I came without telling Ruth. She would have wanted to come and I didn't think that was a good idea.'

Laura made a great effort and got to her feet. 'How did you know?' she asked him. 'How did you know about Giles and me?'

'Quite by chance. I was having tea in the Charing Cross Hotel the last time I was in Town and I was accosted by a friend of yours; your former room-mate, it seems.'

'Mary Saunders.'

'She had her new husband with her. They joined me for tea and she asked after you. You hadn't written to her, she said. And in the way of newly-wedded women, she wondered when *you* would be getting married; you and Giles Summerton.'

'I see.'

'And then it all slotted together: handsome teacher, clever student. It only surprised me that I hadn't thought of it before.'

Laura's interest in his explanation was short-lived.

'It's a nightmare. I don't know what I can do. Have you got the piece from the *Times*?'

'It gives no information. "Killed on active service" that's all. I'll ring his father in a few days' time to express my sympathy. Perhaps I'll hear something else then.'

'He hoped to have leave for Christmas. I wrote asking him to come here. I felt certain he would. He didn't know about the baby. Oh dear, isn't it sad? Isn't it sad?'

She started to rock herself backwards and forwards in her chair. Professor Dobson was loath to leave her on her own.

It was after eight o'clock before Kathleen came. She and Edith had been at the wardens' Christmas social.

After Professor Dobson left, Laura broke down and Kathleen held her in her arms as though she was a child. 'I loved him,' she said, over and over again. 'And we had such a short time together.'

Kathleen let her talk and cry for most of the night.

Chapter Twenty-three

The next day Susan and the children moved in with Laura.

'They're not really well enough to come to this great cold house, but they'll have to put up with it,' Susan said, 'because you're more important. I shall look after you, you'll see. I know you won't be able to enjoy Christmas or anything like that, I shan't expect you to, but I think having the children with you will do you a little bit of good. They're bound to cheer you up a tiny bit, aren't they?'

'I'm sure they will.' Laura managed to bring out the words expected of her, but her eyes were dead.

'And, Laura, you're not to worry about my Dad. I'm not going to desert you whatever he says. You'll need me more than ever now. Kathleen and Edith say you could live with them, but their cottage is much too small for you and a baby. I've felt terribly in the way there, and I'm much tidier than you are. Anyway, I'm going to enjoy it here. Think how lovely it will be up here in the summer with all this space.'

Susan kept Laura busy every minute of the next days. She felt relatively sane while she accomplished each small menial task, but as soon as it was finished she felt in a dangerous limbo, she felt she was nowhere, that she had no existence, that she was in that moment in the nightmare before you hit the ground, before you're able to scream.

She was set to scrub the larder shelves with Julia as helper, Susan supervising and chivying. 'Come on, I want to move all this stuff from the kitchen before dinner time. Now, wring out your cloth and dry the shelves. No, you need clean water, Laura. That's better. Can I leave you to finish while I put Tony to bed? Julia will carry in the tins for you. No, keep that shelf for flour and sugar and tea; the things we use every day.'

'Can you make a shepherd's pie? Well, honestly, Laura. You'll have to watch me then, won't you? You can chop up that onion for a start. No, we've got a vegetable knife in that drawer. Now, you can put this piece of meat through the mincer.'

'Now, I'm going to clean the front windows. Julia can help you unpack your books.'

'You got a lot of books, Lala.'

'Yes, I have.'

'There's no pictures in them. Are they story books?'

'Some of them are, yes.'

'Will you read me one of your books? This one?'

'Mine are rather long I'm afraid, and a bit dull. I'll read you one of yours if you'd like me to.'

'Shall I bring my books in here with your books? My books have got pictures in.'

'All right.'

But when Julia brought in her little book, Laura only opened it and then thrust it back at her. 'Another time,' she said, in such a tortured voice that Julia accepted it without question and going over to the window sill turned over the pages one by one, 'reading' to herself very quietly.

While Laura stood for several minutes as though reading the titles of the few books she had arranged on the top shelf, but seeing nothing.

'Pack these toys for me, Laura, could you? I want Julia to have a little Christmas stocking. She won't know what it's all about, but she loves unwrapping things. She'll get so excited. Oh Laura, you don't have to do it so carefully, just one little fold like this. And then a piece of coloured string.

That's it. I'm going to make some mince-pies now. Your auntie managed to get a jar of mincemeat this morning from the Co-op in Shipton.'

'I can't make any sense of it,' Laura said, her words so sullen and desperate that Susan couldn't ignore them.

She came round to Laura's side of the table and put her arms tightly around her. 'The vicar here is awfully nice,' she said. 'He came round to see me when I first came and he was so kind. He told me I could go to see him in the vicarage any time I felt lonely or depressed. I know you're not religious or anything Laura, but I'm sure he could help you. I mean, it's his job isn't it? Let me slip out and ask him to come. His son is in the army, he ...'

'No,' Laura said.

She freed herself from Susan's arms, looking round her as though for a way of escape. 'I feel as though there's a great weight on my stomach,' she said.

'Oh, I know,' Susan said, most gladly forsaking Laura's spiritual welfare, a dangerous zone for the layman, full of rocks and shallows, for the safety of a recognisable ante-natal symptom. 'You do feel that. In the seventh month specially. The baby's taking up so much room, you see, and it hasn't got its head down yet ... Oh Laura, you'll be much better when the baby's born. You won't have time to brood then. You'll have the baby to think about. However unhappy you are, however fed up with the way things have turned out, once the baby is born it takes over everything. I promise you.'

Laura didn't answer, only looked at her stonily.

'I'll make us some tea,' Susan said, faltering a little. 'Your auntie and Miss Simpson are coming up soon; you'll feel better to have a bit of company.'

'I'm going to bed.'

'Oh Laura, you mustn't. They'll be disappointed if you're not here, they're so worried about you. Stay to see them, even if it's only for a little while. And there's carols on the wireless after the news. Stay to hear the carols, they'll comfort you.'

Without answering, not even looking in Susan's direction, Laura went upstairs and shut herself in her room. She sat on her bed in the dark, cold bedroom until at last Kathleen came upstairs and helped her into bed.

'Will you have a drink of milk?' Kathleen asked her.

She shook her head. She felt heavy with tiredness.

'Shall I sit with you for a while?'

She shook her head again.

Kathleen patted her shoulder and left. 'Sleep then,' she said. 'Sleep as much as you can. You've had a terrible shock and sleep is the best thing in the world.'

It seemed the best thing in the world. Throughout the next day, Christmas Eve, Laura stayed in bed, pulling the bedclothes up over her head whenever Susan tried to reason with her.

'You're being very childish, Laura, and very selfish. Kathleen's brought up a little tree and we're making decorations for it. I would have thought you'd have liked to help with that. After all, Christmas only comes once a year. Julia keeps asking for you and even Tony's learnt to say Lala. I would have thought you'd have liked to be with the children.'

At tea time she brought up a boiled egg, a piece of bread and butter and a cup of tea. When she'd left the room, Laura drank the tea but left the food untouched.

'If you don't eat this soup I'm going to the village to telephone Dr Martin,' Susan said at supper-time. 'I'm not taking the responsibility any more. Think of the baby if you won't think of yourself. You're starving your baby. It'll be born thin and fretful.'

There was still no response.

Susan burst into tears. 'You'll die,' she said. 'That's what you want, isn't it? You've got no guts. What will I do, stuck up here on my own? I had my Mum and Dad at home. You asked me to come here and now you take no notice of me. What about me? I've always been your best friend, haven't I? Have I ever let you down? You owe me something, don't you?'

'I'll eat the soup,' Laura said from under the bedclothes, her voice muffled like a foreign correspondent. 'Please go now. I'll get up tomorrow.'

Laura got up at seven the next morning - before even Tony

was awake - and as soon as it was dawning, she went for a walk in the woods.

The woods surprised her; they were deep and full of strange sounds and smells.

She knew very little about trees and plants, almost nothing about wildlife; she should have felt out of her element, but she didn't. She even felt a little comforted.

Certainly her head felt clear again. Since the news of Giles's death, she'd felt her mind being subjected to enormous pressure, a dark tangled mess of thoughts which wouldn't be unravelled filled her brain. It had seemed like madness.

Now, in the woods, she could think lucidly. She found she was able to confront squarely the tragedy of Giles's death, could begin to grieve for the young man full of spirit and intelligence and their sweet flawed relationship. 'Let me come to terms, first, with his death,' she told herself. 'All the problems of going on living; I'll take those later.'

She thought of him, was able to think of him, without breaking down.

She saw him coming towards her as she'd seen him in Lyme on that summer afternoon. That day she'd felt his sexual intensity so acutely that she'd feared it, thinking it was all that attracted her. But she'd found that she loved him and had told him so. On that last meeting she had told him she loved him and he had shut his eyes and shuddered. 'I know,' he'd said. That was all. How sad it was.

But she was thankful for that last meeting. Even though she'd become pregnant, she wouldn't have a moment of it erased.

She found herself standing as still as a shadow under the dripping trees; her feet in the sodden leaves were cold and wet. Her coat had changed its texture and become felted like a badly-washed blanket. She felt as though she'd been standing there all night.

She turned and walked slowly back to the house. She realised that she was hungry.

For some reason she walked up the path to the little-used front door and banged on the knocker before going in. Julia and Tony, who were in the hall playing with their new toys, rushed up to her.

'Here's Lala,' Julia shouted to Susan in the kitchen. 'And she's all better.'

Laura kissed the children. Their breath was sweet. They were rosy and cold with excitement.

'I was just going to take you up a cup of tea,' Susan said. 'Good gracious, wherever have you been? Whatever have you been doing?'

She helped Laura out of her wet coat and shoes, took her to the kitchen and got a towel for her hair.

'You'll have a bit of breakfast, love, won't you?' she asked rather hesitatingly when Laura was sitting in the rocking chair in front of the range. 'What will you have?'

'Tea and toast will be fine.'

But Susan had heard the different note in Laura's voice and her response was immediate. 'Why don't we have some bacon? Let's use up all the ration. Shall we? Why not? After all we're eating for four, aren't we?'

Of course, Laura's brave mood didn't last. By the time Kathleen and Edith had come up after church, it was already faltering a little.

'I didn't know you went to church,' she said crossly to Kathleen. 'You never used to.'

'I know. It seems more relevant in the country, somehow.'

'A quaint pastoral custom, and certainly less objectionable than hunting.'

'Now, now, dear,' Edith said, 'please don't be naughty. Not on Christmas Day. Kathleen comes along with me. I'm a believer, Laura, and what's more I said a little prayer for you.'

'It can't do any harm,' Susan said quickly, putting her hand on Laura's arm and exerting gentle pressure.

'Have you heard from your father?' Kathleen asked. 'How are they?'

'I had a letter from Mabel. They're all right now. They've had their stairs mended.'

'Oh Laura, you had more than a letter. She sent you two

tablets of toilet soap. We haven't seen any for months. And a lovely card.'

'She sent me some soap,' Laura said.

In fact, she had been moved by her step-mother's letter. 'A baby is God's gift,' Mabel had written, 'and we all know marriage isn't always possible these days and I blame the war for that, separating people and sending our brave boys overseas. Whatever we can do we will. Always remember that you have a daddy and mummy and I have begun to knit already and we hope to see you as soon as we've managed to have the ceiling done, but they do take a time now everyone being in the same boat but we have our stairs now and our good health except for your Dad's chest, worrying as ever.'

'My father's always chosen very nice women,' Laura said. 'It says something for him, I suppose. Not that I've ever understood what they've seen in him.'

'He was a very handsome man when I first met him,' Kathleen said.

'All the same, you thought my mother was throwing herself away on him; you said so.'

'That may have been my snobbishness, dear.'

'He's very happy with my mother-in-law,' Susan said. 'Anyone can see that. She's just right for him.'

Tears came to Laura's eyes again as she thought of Annie – who'd been altogether too much for him. Oh Annie, Annie.

'Who'd like to test the chicken?' Susan asked, pressing Laura's arm again. 'What do you *do* with the skewer, that's what I'd like to know? The vegetables are cooked and the gravy's made, but it's such a big chicken, p'raps it'll be raw inside. Thank goodness we haven't got visitors.'

'What about Edith and me?' Kathleen asked, pleased, all the same, to be counted as family.

'Spinsters don't count, dear,' Edith said. 'Have you lived sixty years without realising that? They put us at the bottom of the table with someone's ninety-two-year-old uncle, and in the afternoon we're expected to organise the costumes for the charades . . . I'm well out of it this year. I told my sisters I had no petrol.'

'Last Christmas I had my little home in Birmingham,' Susan said, 'and Peter came on leave.'

She lifted the sizzling chicken out of the tin and transferred it tenderly on to the heated plate.

What a strange assortment of women they were, Laura thought.

Edith, following a rule unbroken since earliest childhood, had put on her gladdest rags. Her dress, of lilac crêpe, was gathered across the chest and caught at the waist by a shiny purple rose. Her greying hair had a sweep of small waves across her forehead, as though to compensate for the rather military abruptness of the back and sides. Possibly owing to more efficient corsetry, she seemed well-built rather than plump like Mabel; Laura recalled being shown an all-in-one garment of considerable complexity which Kathleen called her hold-all.

Kathleen, tall and majestic, her thick brown hair in a bun, was wearing a rather severe woollen dress, dark green, but had attempted to dress it up with a salmon-pink chiffon scarf dotted with sequins. The effect was bizarre, like chocolate icing on seed-cake.

Susan was femininity personified in a pale blue maternity smock with a tiny lace collar, while Laura herself wore the trapeze-shaped jumper with grey and violet stripes she'd had for Christmas from the Dobsons, and a long brown skirt, and looked like a visitor from the Twenties.

'Still, I mustn't grumble,' Susan said. 'I have to think of the children.'

She hacked a leg off the chicken. 'How do you carve through bones?' she asked. 'It looks so easy on the diagrams.'

Kathleen remembered lonely Christmases - her lover with his family in Sussex - when she would eat a sandwich for dinner and read the newest thriller, terrified of getting to the end and having to face her thoughts. She wouldn't have admitted it, especially to Laura, but she felt happy now; as though she'd somehow come into her own.

Laura stood at the end of the table, her hands on her belly. 'Forget about the diagrams,' she said. 'Forget about legs and wings. Just cut off little bits wherever you can. If we don't get started, Tony will wake up.'

They had an excellent meal. Tony did wake and had to be

brought down, but he sat on the floor with a bone until everyone had finished and Julia was as good as gold, playing with her new doll and pushing all the tender pieces of white meat into her shiny new money-box.

At five o'clock, Laura and Susan, who were playing trains with the children in the study, saw the Wilkins's van drawing up outside the gate.

'I thought they weren't coming because of Arthur being home,' Susan said. 'Oh crikey, I'll have to tell them about you now. You've got so fat all of a sudden. What shall I say? Oh Lord.'

'It's Peter,' Laura said. 'It's Peter on his own.'

She fled into the kitchen.

When Edith and Kathleen, after a piece of greyish Christmas cake - very little dried fruit and reconstituted eggs - went home to their cosy cottage, their log fire and their wireless, Laura was tempted to go with them. Unfortunately, though, she was smitten with tiredness again. Besides, Peter was more or less ignoring her, so it didn't seem worth the effort.

'I think *I'll* go up now,' she said, after she'd helped to get the over-excited children to bed.

'What about a chicken sandwich?' Susan asked.

'No thanks. I've eaten too much cake.'

'I hope you're not going early on my account,' Peter said, addressing her directly for the first time.

'No. I sleep most of the time these days. It seems all I'm fit for.'

'I was sorry to hear about your ... boyfriend,' he said stiffly.

'I don't want to talk about it,' Laura said. She didn't care what Peter thought about her. He was mean-minded like most men. He'd been hot enough for Susan, how dared he show any disapproval of her.

Her bedroom was at the back of the house. For some time she looked out at the woods through the uncurtained window, trying to regain the composure she'd found there.

Susan cried when Peter left the next day, but she soon

cheered up. He'd bought her fur-lined gloves and a pink woolly scarf for Christmas and he was hoping to get a longer leave in a couple of months' time.

'There's only one thing I'm really miserable about,' she said. 'Dad wants him to take over the shop when he leaves the army but he won't hear of it. It would be so nice. It's a good life, working for yourself, being your own boss. But there you are, Peter can be very stubborn. Even his mother admits that.'

'He's an artist,' Laura said. 'A designer. I can't see why you should expect him to give it all up. He's done very well, hasn't he?'

'The money's very poor, though, Laura. It's all very well for you and his mother to go on about getting on well. He's certainly not getting on well as far as money's concerned. We never had two ha'pennies to rub together till he joined the army.'

'What did he say about me?' Laura asked, wanting to change the subject. 'He seemed pretty annoyed, I thought.'

'Perhaps he was. Who cares. "It's nothing to do with you," I told him. "She's got a good job with a jolly good salary. She's clever enough to look after herself." "So only stupid girls need husbands," he said. "That's right," I said. "Who else would have you?" ... D'you know, I didn't mind it too much last night.' She looked skittish for a moment, eighteen again. 'When I'm already pregnant it's too late to worry, so I don't mind it so much. I don't mind it when he takes trouble over me, do you know what I mean? When he talks to me as though, well, as though he loves me. Do you believe in love, Laura? Do you believe in true love? You know, the love that lasts for ever? Oh please don't make fun of me. Give me a serious answer for once.'

'I don't know. I loved Giles but I've no idea whether it would have lasted for ever. I think we suited each other. It might have lasted a while.'

Her words seemed to burn in her brain, but she remained dry-eyed, outwardly calm.

'What about Peter and me? I don't think we suit each other, do you? I mean, we didn't know anything about each other, did we. We didn't bother to find out anything. We just met at your dad's wedding; I had a new dress and I was happy; and I was looking for a boyfriend and he noticed me staring at him.'

'Of course you suit each other,' Laura said, floundering, though, when she tried to substantiate the assertion. 'Of course you suit each other,' she said again.

It reassured Susan. She flung her arms around Laura and kissed her. 'I suppose we do,' she said, 'if you say so. After all, you're an old cleversticks aren't you?'

They went to Cowslip Cottage for lunch and tea.

Chapter Twenty-four

A few days after Christmas, Laura had a letter from Giles. It had been originally posted at the end of November and readdressed from Bristol.

'Perhaps it's best you don't read it,' Susan said. 'You've been so much better. It will only upset you again.'

'I'll leave it till later,' Laura said. Seeing Giles's small, beautiful handwriting had frozen her blood.

For an hour or so she and Susan carried on with their chores, Susan washing nappies, she cleaning and chopping up vegetables for a soup, both occasionally glancing at the letter as though it was a little coffin lying on the table.

'How was he killed?' Laura suddenly asked, her voice harsh. 'I don't know anything. How can I find out? I must get to know something. Could I write to his parents, do you think? I've got his home address.'

'I don't think you should,' Susan said gently. 'You must think of his wife.'

'Why?'

'Why? Oh hell, why make things worse? Why should you want to harm his wife? She's suffering as well, you know.'

Laura looked at Susan as though she hated her. At that moment she couldn't bear to think of his wife, couldn't bear to admit that there was anyone suffering as she was.

She snatched up the letter and went upstairs, flinging herself on to the bed to read it.

It was different from every other letter she'd ever had from him. The danger he was in, though not mentioned, was tacit in every line. There was no comfort in it.

'What a miserable cad I am. I'm writing to two women tonight and unable to feel close to either of them. So many regrets. I should have had the strength to sort out my life, but instead I let events overtake me and harmed all three of us. I feel stricken tonight. Truth matters because what else is there? Forgive me. Try to remember the times we were happy.'

There was no mention of love. Oh love, where had it gone?

Laura lay on her bed, too anguished to cry.

'Please come down,' Susan was saying outside the locked door. 'I'm sorry I upset you.'

'It's all right,' Laura called back, her voice unnaturally calm. 'I'm all right. Carry on without me for a while. I'll be down soon. As soon as I can.'

She wished she had told him about the baby, but now it was too late. She had shielded him from the truth, but truth was important because what else was there?

She read the letter over and over again. How had he died? In what pain and fear? She was frightened by her imaginings.

For days, thoughts of Giles's death were the reality of her life. 'Wake up,' Susan would say from time to time, but it was no use. Susan, Kathleen and Edith, Mrs Miller, even the children, were shadows.

It was work that forced her to face life again.

On the twelfth of January, her first batch of completed question papers arrived from the Knightsbridge Correspondence College and then there was nothing for it but to get down to marking them.

They took far longer than she'd expected. Unless she dropped her standards or learnt to work much faster, she'd have to keep at it all hours of the day for the £2 a week they were paying her.

The pupils she'd been allocated seemed uniformly dull. They'd been taught a formula which could be adapted to suit each one of the always straightforward questions; there was never any originality to lighten her task. There were ten questions on each paper, each carrying ten marks, and as well as totalling the marks she was expected to write a page of tutorial comment for each pupil. It was soul-shrivelling work since it was difficult to believc that such a mechanical question and answer technique would benefit anyone but the directors who were pocketing the substantial fees.

'Do you think I should go on with this?' she asked Kathleen on the second day, showing her the folder she was marking.

'It's work. It's relatively well paid.'

'Isn't it immoral, though? Those pupils are asking for bread and they're being given stones. "Question 3. Write out the paragraphs in Lesson 13 which describe the character of Macbeth." They're not even encouraged to read the play, no, they're only required to reproduce some banal exposition in Lesson 13. I don't think I can stick it. I'd rather be a landgirl.'

'More difficult, though, with a baby.'

'Hell, I keep forgetting the baby. It should be born in about six weeks. Susan's gone to call on the district nurse this afternoon. She's getting quite excited - but I can't say I am. I can't even bear to think about it.'

'You must. I know your mind's still with Giles, but try to think of the baby as well.'

'I'm too frightened.'

'Nonsense. Having a baby is nothing these days, what with chloroform and all the new drugs.'

'I don't mind the actual birth - that might be grim for all I know, but I certainly can't be bothered to worry about it beforehand - I mean the responsibility for another life. That's what makes me sweat and gibber in the night.'

'You're not on your own, love. You've got me, and Edith of course. And dear Susan, who's such a brick.'

'And this rather sordid job.'

'If it worries you so much, give it up. I'll be able to help you. I'm not destitute.'

'I haven't got the guts to give it up. I can't afford the finer feelings.'

'Perhaps Professor Dobson could find you something different.'

'No, I don't think I should trouble him again. I think I've

troubled him quite a lot one way or another.'

Laura's baby was born at the end of January, nearly three weeks early.

Snow lay deep on the ground, the temperature was below freezing, the windows frosted over.

Susan, taking Laura her morning cup of tea, found her already sitting up in bed. 'I'm in labour,' Laura announced. 'Isn't it a beautiful day? I feel I'm in a church. That window, look, it's like stained glass all in pure white. Do you see the angel's wings, do you see the Virgin, the shape of her robe and her halo?'

'Shut up,' Susan said, setting down the tea on the bedside table. 'You're trying to frighten me, aren't you? No one will be able to get up here today and you're just lying back and talking about angels. You should get up this minute. If you are in labour, which I doubt, you'd be much better to walk about for the first few hours.'

'I have been walking about for the first few hours. It started last night. Just after we'd gone to bed. I starting having this nasty jabbing pain in the small of my back. I thought I'd been sitting too long over those damned question-papers so I crept downstairs to make myself a cup of tea, but I still couldn't get comfortable. Then, with the pains coming and going pretty regularly, I realised what it was. I remembered what you'd said about keeping active, so I scrubbed the kitchen floor – I suppose you thought the fairies had done it – and then finished the rest of my marking. Guess what, I feel quite excited now; exhilarated. Just as I used to feel before an exam.'

'You're not in labour,' Susan said. 'You've just got yourself worked up over nothing. If you'd been in labour since last night your waters would have broken by now.'

'That happened hours ago. At about two o'clock. Isn't it an extraordinary feeling, this warm gush that you can do absolutely nothing about; incredible really. That's when I began to resign myself to it. There's nothing in the world I can do now, I thought, but let it happen.'

She lay back on her pillow and let out a protracted groan and for the first time Susan took her seriously. 'What can I do? Oh my heavens, what can I do? Who can I fetch? How can I get to the village?'

Laura groaned again.

'It's all right,' she said afterwards. 'You'll be able to cope beautifully. What time is it?'

'Half past eight. The children aren't even dressed. I gave them breakfast, but they're still in their dressing-gowns.'

'Go and dress them and boil some water.'

'I've got a kettle full of boiling water. What the hell do you want it for? Midwives always want boiling water and newspapers just as though they're going to spend their time making papiermâché.'

'It's to sterilise the scissors before cutting the cord. That's all as far as I know. I've been reading all about it in Edith's *Home Doctor*. It's quite simple. I'll tell you what to do as we go along.'

Laura groaned again and Susan groaned with her.

'They're coming every two or three minutes,' Laura said afterwards. 'You'd better hurry. Give the children the cooking tins to play with and a lot of water, all the spoons as well and the saucepans. They'll be fine. Don't bother to dress them. Just fetch the scissors and a basin of the boiling water.'

Laura wanted to throw back all her blankets but felt too cold. She'd tried to make a fire in the bedroom the previous night; she'd laid it but hadn't been able to find any matches.

She'd had two more pains before Susan came up with the scissors and a pile of old newspapers.

'I've put newspapers under the sheet,' Laura said. 'And I've aired the baby clothes. What I need is matches to light the fire. Oh, don't go again.'

'I'll just go to fetch the hot-water bottle. It's ready for you.'

'Good girl. My hands are frozen.'

Susan took her hands and rubbed them vigorously. 'If I opened the front door and shouted for help, do you think anyone would come?'

'No. Save your breath. The milkman may come later on and he'll go for Kathleen.'

'I'll fetch the hot-water bottle and the matches.'

When Susan arrived back Laura had pulled up the blankets

and was sitting up in bed with them round her shoulders. 'If I had a feather in my hair I'd look like a Red Indian,' she said.

Susan forebore to smile. She gave her the hot-water bottle to hold and then knelt down to light the fire.

'I think it's coming,' Laura said, her voice suddenly cracking. 'I can feel the head pushing out and, oh, it feels as big as a horse. Ahh,' she groaned. 'This is terrible. Terrible.'

'Yes, I can see the head,' Susan said. 'Oh, Laura, let your knees drop right back to give it room. Oh God, it looks as though you're coming apart.'

'Light the fire,' Laura said. 'I can manage this. Light the fire.'

'It's done. It's alight. Now I'll have to rush down to wash my hands. Do stop groaning, it makes my blood boil.'

'Bring a bowl of water with you. I'm fine. Don't worry about me. Oh Christ, I can't stand much more of this. Ahh. Ah, that was a long one. Is the head further down?'

'No, just the same. It always takes an age, this part. When you have a pain you have to push as hard as you can, that's what they told me. I'll be back in half a minute. For God's sake don't push when I'm away.'

'The fire's doing well,' she said when she got back.

'So am I. I've got the hang of it now. Is the head further down?'

'Well, not much. Don't worry though. When the head's out the rest is easy.' She mopped Laura's forehead with a flannel.

'When it's born, don't panic about cutting the cord. The most important thing . . .'

Laura gripped Susan's arm, raised herself up and gave a long animal cry. 'Ahh,' Susan echoed, pulling herself away.

'Oh good,' she said. 'Good. Oh you clever girl. The rest will be easy. Grip the sides of the bed now, I've got to stay here ready to take it.'

'Ahh,' they both cried together.

'I've got it, Laura. It's a boy. It's a beautiful little boy.'

'Beautiful,' Laura echoed, lying back on the pillows.

'Just lay him there over my thigh,' she cried then, her voice suddenly sounding frail and distant. 'I think you have to suck the mucus from his mouth,' she said, after a few moments. 'Do you think you can do that?'

'Of course I can.'

Now Susan was in charge. She knelt on the bed by Laura's legs, took the baby's face in her hands and sucked his mouth and his nostrils.

The baby took a breath into his lungs and let out a strange, high, separate, living cry. Both women shut their eyes, breathed deeply and re-gathered their forces.

'A shawl over him,' Laura said. She shivered, frightened for the first time. It was very cold in the room.

While they were still resting - the baby quiet, the women listening to his breathing - they heard someone trudging through the snow to the back door.

'I'll go down, it'll be the milkman,' Susan said. 'I'll send him to get help.'

But it wasn't the milkman. It was Edith. She was up with them in a minute or two.

'I thought something was going on when I saw those children on their own - they're having a whale of a time. Yes, you can leave it all to me now. I've done this in my First Aid. I'll just run down to sterilise a pair of scissors, the baby's breathing beautifully, there's no need to rush. I'll have to scrub my hands, too, but I won't be a minute.'

Though counselling calm, she was talking rapidly in little breathy spurts and her cheeks were flooded with colour.

'I've got the scissors here,' Susan said. 'They are sterilised. There's clean water there for your hands and a clean towel.'

Edith cut the cord with what seemed a practised hand, wrapped the baby in a shawl and put him into Laura's arms. Susan's eyes were full of tears but Laura seemed calm. 'Isn't he big,' she said. 'No wonder I've been uncomfortable with this life-sized baby stuck in my belly. What a badly thought-out process it seems to be.'

'He's gorgeous,' Susan said. 'Look at his little arms.'

'My God, he's looking at me,' Laura said.

Edith got the afterbirth away, washed Laura's legs and dried them and made up her bed. 'Kathleen made me come up to find out how you were. She thought you might be needing something. She's got second sight but unfortunately no wellingtons.'

Susan made up the fire. 'How can we weigh him?' she asked. 'He's got to be weighed. That's a part of it.'

'I'll go to make us some tea,' Edith said. The flush had drained from her cheeks leaving them crepy and unnaturally pale.

'I did the most important part, didn't I?' Susan said, bursting into tears as the door shut behind Edith.

'You were absolutely wonderful. I'll never forget how wonderful you were. Come and sit on the bed again. Edith will see to the children. Don't cry any more.' Laura wiped the tears off Susan's face with her sweating hands. They had never been so close.

Susan lay down on the bed and looked at the baby. 'What are you going to call him?' she said, the tears welling up again. 'Do you think I'd better dress him now. I've got his little vest and nightie.'

'Not yet. Let him have a little rest. When the room's really warm you shall dress him.'

'When he wakes up you can put him on your breast. There won't be any milk, but he'll be able to practise a bit of sucking. I wish he was mine. He's much handsomer than Tony was.'

'Nonsense,' Laura said, but feeling the words curling round her heart. 'Oh, I do hope Edith's making us some breakfast.'

He was a big demanding baby. Laura named him Alexander which was Giles's second name. He looked like Giles. From time to time that comforted Laura a little.

Mabel came to visit as soon as the weather permitted, bringing bootees and pilches and matinée coats and two dozen new nappies. She thought the baby looked like Laura's father.

'Why didn't Grandpa come with you?' Susan asked.

'He's not well, dear. His chest's bad. He goes to work but he shouldn't really. His chest's that bad. Wasn't he in the trenches in the last war, Laura?'

'Yes. Hasn't he told you?'

'No, he don't mention it.'

Their house was more or less repaired, the city more or less back to normal. There were still bombing raids, but compared to the November onslaught, they were insignificant, and everyone was determined to cope, even to make light of them.

'When we hear the bombers coming over I can't sleep for worrying,' Susan said.

'You mustn't worry, dear. We've got used to it. We don't even go under the stairs any more.'

'Mum doesn't seem to have got used to it.'

'Doesn't she, love? Ah, there's some that don't. What does she say in her letters?'

'Only that she can't pull herself together. My Dad has to finish the letter usually and he just puts "Hoping this finds you well as it leaves me at present" which isn't very helpful.'

'I'll go over to see her, dear. Wouldn't it be nice if she came to stay here for a time? In all this country air?'

'I'd love her to come. It would do her so much good. My Dad could easily bring her over one Sunday. I've written to tell them about the baby. I told them how Giles had been sent overseas before he and Laura could get married and that they weren't to refer to him.'

By this time, Susan quite believed the story she had fabricated and was affronted whenever Laura reminded her that it wasn't altogether true.

Chapter Twenty-five

'I'm down the bottom,' a little tired voice said. 'I'm right down the bottom. I'm the wrong way round.'

Outside the children's bedroom, Laura stiffened and sighed. If she went in to Julia, Tony might wake and begin to bawl, and what if that woke Alex who didn't care to know night from day and whose needs were simple and fierce. For a moment or two she stood quite still, waiting.

Julia must have sensed her presence on the landing.

'My arm is stickin' out the side,' she said. 'My head is the wrong way round . . . I'm fractious,' she concluded with great feeling.

Laura opened the door and tiptoed over to her. 'Poor little kipper,' she whispered. 'You must have had a nasty dream. I'll lift you up and make you comfortable. Do you want to go on the pot? No, I don't think you do.'

'Am I too late?'

'Never mind, love. I'll get you a nice dry nightie and a dry sheet. I've have to go downstairs a minute.'

The night-light flickered as Laura collided into the cupboard next to Tony's cot. Tony shuddered and then for a moment his regular breathing seemed totally suspended. Laura waited for the storm to break but eventually he turned and seemed to go back to sleep. She walked backwards down the stairs, clutching the bannisters. 'Please, please don't wake,' she was saying.

There was a nightie hanging on the airer, but no damn sheet anywhere, though she'd been washing clothes, clothes and more damn clothes every day. Don't go to pieces, she told herself sternly. Improvise. Improvise. She'd have to use a towel as a sheet, that was it.

'I come down to help you,' Julia, in vest and furry slippers, announced from the door.

'Love, you mustn't walk downstairs in the dark. You know you're not allowed to.'

'I left my nightie with Tony,' Julia said, 'because he's awake now. He likes it wet. My vest is wet as well. I don't have my vest on when Mama puts me to bed.'

Laura peeled off the wet vest and pulled the nightie over her head. Julia wriggled her body into its warmth.

'I'd better stop a little while, bett'n I? Otherwise Tony won't settle.'

'Sit here then and put my cardigan round your shoulders. That's it. Do you want a drink of milk?'

Julia put her thumb in her mouth, contemplating the proffered drink with little enthusiasm.

'A biscuit?' Laura amended hastily. 'Or would you like to sit on my lap?'

'I want my Mama,' Julia said, her face suddenly clenching up with dismay.

There, it was out. For the last three, or was it four, days she'd been unnaturally quiet, unnaturally good, unnaturally helpful: she wanted her mother.

'I want her, too,' Laura said, taking her on her lap and attempting to smooth out the little face which seemed to have puckered up like darning; Laura's darning. 'I can't manage without her much longer, but we've got to be brave, haven't we, because your Grandma's ill; Grandma Wilkins. When she's a bit better, Mama's going to bring her back here and then you'll have both of them: Mama and Grandma.'

'And Ediff?' Julia asked.

'Oh, certainly.'

Good old Ediff, Laura thought. Who'd have believed that that slightly caustic upper-middle-class spinster would prove so thoroughly adaptable, so much a mainstay, so indispensable. 'You can have *her* tomorrow. Listen, we'll put the boys in the pram and we'll take them for a walk to Cowslip Cottage and you shall stay there for dinner.'

Could she manage an hour's marking, she wondered, in

between Tony's twelve o'clock jacket potato followed by short nap, and Alex's two o'clock feed which was rapidly working round to half past one? Last week the course director had written commending her on her full, conscientious assessments; perhaps very skimpy ones would pass once in a while.

'Shall I wash up?' Julia asked.

'Now?'

'No, silly. With Ediff.' Julia giggled at the thought of washing up in the middle of the night. Little did she know of woman's work, Laura thought. She still had a bucket full of nappies to deal with as well as several days' ironing.

For a time they sat together, leaning on each other.

'There's Alex,' Julia said then, sliding off Laura's knee as she heard the sudden high wailing from upstairs.

'But I fed him a couple of hours ago,' Laura said. 'He can't be hungry again.'

'P'raps he is,' Julia said; adding with some asperity, 'P'raps he wants some bread and butter or custard. P'raps he gets fed up with sucking your elbows all a time.'

'Do you want to nurse him a minute?' Laura asked, deciding to ignore both Julia's shaky grasp of infant welfare and adult anatomy.

'Oh no, I'm much too tired,' she said. 'I'll just pop back into bed.'

'There, there, my son,' Laura said, plugging the little searching mouth with her nipple. 'That's better, isn't it?'

She wiped her forehead with the back of her hand. She was too tired even to read. Her life had taken another plunge.

Mabel had written a frightening letter when she'd been to visit Susan's mother. 'I think you should come home at once, dear, because your Mummy's not at all well. It's her mind, dear, but you can't blame her, always over-sensitive as your Daddy says and Arthur with a job of national importance so what can be done. But these places are not what they were and they say the electric treatment can work miracles, but you'll see her and judge for yourself and I'm here to help you, you know that and PS I'm sending money for the bus and the train because I know how things are and what a mercy Laura is there with you to look after Julia and little Tony.'

Susan had left that day, three or was it four days ago, and there hadn't been a word since.

Of course, Laura felt desperately sorry for Susan and her mother. All the same, she felt that she herself was near a breakdown, both mental and physical. She simply hadn't realised how much help Susan had always given her with Alex, now two months old. He seemed so little trouble when she was around. As for running the house, Susan hadn't ever let her know it needed running. Laura had performed certain allotted tasks, yes, but she'd known nothing about the racing one needed to do simply to stay on the same spot. She washed clothes but couldn't get them dry. She made meals but couldn't get the children to eat them. She ran out of really vital items like tomato ketchup, and by the time she'd got all the children into trouser-suits and bonnets and mittens, and treked into the village, the shops had closed. She wanted to be back in Merchant's Crescent with her gas ring and her quiet books. Or if not that, oh, she wanted Susan back.

When Susan did return a fortnight later she was a different person. Her mother had made so many suicide attempts that she'd had to be committed to an asylum.

'She's lost her mind,' Susan repeated over and over again on the evening she returned to Larkshill. 'It's so sad, Laura. So sad. I always thought people in asylums were mad, you know, crazy, saying crazy things or reciting nursery rhymes. Why do people make fun of them?'

'Because they're frightened, I suppose.'

'Oh Laura, it's just as if she's wound down and we can't start her up again. She just sits in a little chair with her hands in her lap and doesn't recognise anyone. She thought my Dad was one of the doctors. She asked him not to ... not to ...'

'Never mind, love, tell me later. Try not to be too depressed. She may get a little better.'

'I don't think she will. I mean, it's not like somebody being injured, is it? Her mind seems lost not injured, it seems to have slipped out of her eyes. It's horrible. Her eyes are empty; they're like holes. Oh, I shouldn't have left her to come here.

I should have realised what was happening to her.'

'Don't cry, love. Nobody could have realised that this would happen. Don't make things worse by blaming yourself.'

'I think I'll have to go back home to look after my Dad.'

'Did he suggest that?'

'No. Auntie Sarah is looking after the house for the moment, but he's never got on with her.'

'Stay here for a little while anyway. I don't think you should go back for at least a month. It wouldn't be right for the children. And in any case, you're not strong enough yet.'

'How have you managed without me?'

'Do you want the truth or a comforting lie?'

'A comforting lie, I think.'

'We've been fine. Apart from missing your company, we've all been absolutely fine. When did you have the miscarriage? Was it awful?'

'Terrible. Very, very painful. I'd no idea a miscarriage would be as bad. It was as bad as being in labour. You wouldn't think so, would you?'

'Most things are worst than you expect. Why didn't you get your Dad to contact me?'

'I knew you wouldn't be able to do anything. You had enough to do here.'

'Oh, I dare say I could have managed a bit of nursing at odd moments.'

'What my Dad did was send a telegram to Peter and he got twenty-four hours compassionate leave.'

'Oh good. That was much better.'

'He wasn't very sympathetic, though. Oh, he brought me some tea in bed and he got me some chocolates and some magazines, but, well, he couldn't understand why I minded so much. "But you didn't want another baby," he kept saying. They don't understand, do they?'

'How could they?' Laura said.

'I mean, as soon as the baby moves, well, it's alive for you, isn't it? I mean, it's a part of you, you have this relationship with it. It's not just a thing, is it?'

'Of course not. When Alex was born, what I felt wasn't love so much as recognition. I just felt he was someone I knew. Someone I'd known all along.'

'How is he? Has he grown much?'

'Yes. Julia's been feeding him Tony's rusks.'

'Oh Laura, he shouldn't have solid food till he's at least three months old.'

'Rusks aren't solid food. Not when Tony's been sucking them for half an hour. Oh yes, our standards have slipped I'm afraid, but we've all survived.'

'How is Tony?'

'He's lovely. Do you want to go upstairs to have a peep at him?'

'Do I have to get your permission then?'

It was Susan's turn to be looked after. For a long time she remained weak and very depressed.

In spite of it, she insisted on visiting her mother every other Sunday - alternating with Arthur who drove down from London once a fortnight.

'Does it do her any good, do you think?' Laura asked, after the second visit. 'It wears you out, I know that. Does it do her any good?'

'No, I don't think so. She doesn't even recognise me. Oh, it's awful. She isn't even dressed in her own clothes any more. She's quite clean, but she has anybody's clothes on, things that don't fit her, awful things she'd never wear. I know it doesn't matter, but I made a hell of a fuss about it.'

'I think you were right.'

'Do you? I felt ashamed of myself afterwards. All the nurses seem so busy. They say she's very good, very contented. She's certainly quiet compared to most of them.'

'She was always quiet.'

'My Dad keeps on saying little prayers for her. "Gentle Jesus, meek and mild," things like that, but she's never responded at all. But this time, as soon as he'd sat down and bowed his head, she suddenly said a very dirty thing. He was awfully shocked, so was I really, it seemed so out of character.'

Laura wondered what very dirty thing poor Mrs Wilkins could have come out with, but Susan wasn't forthcoming.

'Will I ever get used to it, do you think?' she asked.

Laura couldn't find the words to answer her. She didn't know the answer.

When Peter's ten days' leave was due at the end of April, Laura insisted that he and Susan went away together for a week's holiday while she looked after the three children again. 'Only don't you dare come back pregnant,' she told Susan. 'Either fight him off or make jolly sure he uses contraceptives. Soldiers get them issued free, they say.'

'Whatever for,' Susan said. 'When they're hardly ever with their wives.'

They went to Weston-super-Mare and had fine, sunny weather.

When they got back, Peter went home to visit his mother. Laura and he were still very uneasy together.

'You seem to have weathered Giles's death wonderfully well,' Kathleen said, one lovely May evening when she and Laura were sitting in the garden together. 'You've been incredibly brave. Edith was remarking on it the other day. "Many girl would have gone under," she said.'

Laura reflected for a time before she was able to answer. She supposed it was true. She had accepted his death, and though she still thought of him every day, thought of him with grief and regret and love, she was able to think of other things most of the time. 'I never really thought of him as a permanent part of my life; I suppose that helped. Usually I thought of him, well, almost as a dream I'd had. He was too perfect, too handsome, too much out of my class – too good to be true, I suppose. It was only when we were together that I really managed to think of him as my lover. We hadn't any future together, not really. I see that now.'

As she spoke, she felt again the powerful sensuality of his presence, saw his rakish smile, his long hooded eyes.

'All the same, I don't think I'll ever forget him,' she said. 'I don't think there'll ever be anyone like him.'

Kathleen heard her sharp intake of breath. 'You once mentioned writing to his parents,' she said quickly.

'Did I? I never really meant to. Professor Dobson did, and they wrote a short letter back saying he'd been killed evading capture; that's all they knew. He was in occupied France. Spying I suppose. It seems a long way from lecturing on seventeenth-century poetry, doesn't it?'

'You never considered letting his parents know about Alex?'

'Of course not. How could I? It would be like asking for some sort of financial help, wouldn't it?'

'They're grieving parents, though, Laura. Think how they'd respond to the knowledge that they have a little grandson.'

'With horror, probably. Remember, they're very close to his wife. Her parents are their greatest friends. Giles told me it was one of the reasons they'd got engaged so young: because both sets of parents considered it such a happy match.'

'I think they should be told. Invited to come here. After all, they could always refuse. They could always ignore his existence if they chose to.'

'Kathleen, are you quite certain this has nothing to do with this morning's electricity bill? As well as our ever-pressing need for all those little luxuries of life like food?'

'My pension is so inadequate, Laura. If I help you - and God knows it's little enough - I seem to be living off Edith before the end of the month.'

Good old Ediff, Laura thought.

'I'm sure she doesn't mind,' she said. 'Anyway, I'm afraid she'll have to put up with it for a while. She's happy enough, isn't she? Of course she is. She's absolutely blooming. Bossing everyone in the village - about black-out or evacuees or salvage. She's come into her own; she admits it. And she wouldn't be able to do half as much, would she, if you weren't at home seeing to the cooking and the shopping and the gardening.'

'I don't think she's got much money, though. She likes to hint at how wealthy her family used to be, but I don't think much of it came her way.'

'I'll be supporting both of you in a few years' time. Is that it?'

Kathleen smiled, but without much joy. 'Everything's getting so expensive,' she said. 'I managed to get some sheets in Shipton this morning – they'd had a new lot in – and do you know, they'd gone up six shillings a pair since last year. Do you know how much they wanted for carrots? "No, thank you," I said. "Our own will be ready soon." Do you know how much a three-pound bag of flour costs now?'

'Don't worry,' Laura said. 'We won't starve. Something will turn up, you'll see.'

'I *hate* that skirt you're wearing and that jumper. Haven't you got *any* decent clothes?'

Laura examined the offending garments with mild surprise. 'Don't you know there's a war on?' she said.

Towards the end of the month Susan had a letter from Arthur letting her know that he was getting married the following week.

'Good heavens,' Susan said. 'He's marrying a widow with three young children. Can you imagine: taking over a breakfast-table like this one at a stroke.'

Laura raised her eyes and shuddered.

Julia's cereal dish was surrounded by four naked dolls, one of them eyeless, which she was feeding and smacking in turns.

Tony was eating, with much more gusto than seemed necessary, a slice of bread and a very soft egg.

Alex, half asleep in his high chair, belched gently as they looked at him, bringing up an unsavoury grey mess which had once been apple purée.

Susan returned to the letter. '"She's a little older than me, but a fine, honest, intelligent woman." Well really. A funny way to describe your bride: fine, intelligent and honest.'

'Not if you're Arthur,' Laura said, mopping up Alex and what she could reach of Tony. 'She sounds just right for him. He's the sort to fall for an older woman; someone reliable and steady.'

'He probably hasn't fallen for her at all. He's probably just not ruthless enough to escape her clutches. Widows shouldn't be allowed to keep lodgers. I wonder how old she is? At least thirty, I bet. Why isn't he inviting anyone to the wedding? It sounds fishy to me.'

'I don't suppose your Dad would go, would he. Not to London.'

'Why not? Auntie Sarah would certainly go. I think he must be ashamed of her. Or ashamed of us.'

'Don't be so uncharitable. People aren't having big weddings these days. You know that.'

Susan made a sudden swoop on Tony, removing him from the widely-scattered debris of his meal. Holding him as far away from her as possible, she'd plunged his hands into a bowl of water and soaped a flannel ready to tackle his face before he'd found breath to voice his objections. Laura looked on admiringly.

'I wanted him to marry you,' Susan said.

'Oh Susan.'

'He loved you. He told me so.'

'But that was years ago, love. And I wasn't in love with him. Even if he'd asked me to marry him, I wouldn't have.'

'I wanted you to be my sister. I wanted you to have a husband with lots of money.'

Tony was clean again, shining as morning and sweet as a pear-drop. Susan hugged him to her and nibbled his small pink ears.

'Oh Laura, we're so poor,' she said. 'All the money we get goes on food and rent, there's never anything over. I'd like some new clothes: pretty summer dresses and sling-back sandals.'

'I'll have to do something about it, then, I suppose,' Laura said.

'Whatever can you do about it?'

'Let me put Alex to bed first, then I'll think of something.'

'Queenie is fine, intelligent and honest,' Julia said, holding up the eyeless doll, large and pink, by her matted hair.

'OK. What does *she* think we should do?' Susan asked.

Julia considered the question gravely.

'She thinks we should wash-a-dishes,' she said.

'What about us keeping a lodger?' Laura suggested that evening. 'The new schoolmaster is looking for digs. There's a card in the Post Office.'

'We couldn't have anyone here.'

'Why not? The drawing room would make a lovely bed-sitting room. Mrs Miller would come and slap some distemper on the walls and I could stain the floor boards like I did in my room.'

'We haven't got any furniture for it.'

'We could send Edith to the Auction Rooms again. You know how she loves sales. She'd lend us the money. We could pay her back weekly.'

'Have you seen the new schoolmaster?'

'No. He doesn't start till September.'

'He can't be married, anyway, or he'd be looking for a house.'

'What do you say? Shall I answer the advert? It gives an address; somewhere in Herefordshire. Come on. It'll be a laugh.'

'It was new clothes I wanted, not a laugh. To think we've got all these clothing coupons and no money. I think I'll write to Peter. I'm sure he could afford to buy me a dress. He seems to have plenty of money to send the children things.'

'You do that. And I'll write to Mr Redfern. H.E. Redfern. Quite a nice name. H.E. Redfern, BA.'

Chapter Twenty-six

In spite of the war, life was peaceful at Larkshill that summer. Susan was strong and well again and also feeling happier about her mother, who'd been moved to a smaller and quieter mental home outside the city boundaries. The last time she'd seen her she'd been sitting out in the grounds, and though she hadn't recognised her, she seemed to be taking a close interest in the leaves and the clouds. 'She lets us know where she wants us to put her chair,' one of the nurses had told Susan and her father. 'She enjoys the garden.' That seemed something to be going on with.

Then, in the second week of July, they'd had another letter from Mabel, which had ruffled the calm of the lovely blue and gold days. John had recently had three days' leave, she said, and was very well considering, new potatoes were very dear, eggs seemed to have disappeared, and there was no sweets or chocolates to send the children. And PS she did think Laura should bring Alex for a few days to see her daddy, because he wasn't well at all; insisting on going to work, but not well at all.

'She's at it again,' Laura said. 'She's a nice little woman, but doesn't she seem to enjoy spreading gloom and despondency.'

'It must be his chest again,' Susan said. 'You must go.'

'Must I? Why?'

'Oh, don't be so unnatural.'

'Unnatural? What's he ever done for me?'

'He didn't do too badly by you, if you ask me. He didn't desert you, did he? He could have gone off and left you with his mother. Plenty of men would have.'

'You didn't know his mother. She was not a woman you took liberties with.'

Laura thought of Grandma Brown, dark, violent-looking and smelling of chickens. 'Thank God,' she said.

'Your father gave you much more freedom than I ever had. You could always do what you liked.'

'Because he didn't care what I did.'

'Parents can never do right. I resented my father because he never let me go out, you resented yours because he did.'

'I resented mine because he had double standards. Because he thought it was all right for men to behave in a certain way, but wrong for women.'

'Men *are* different,' Susan said.

'It doesn't give them a right to despise us for doing something they're proud enough of doing themselves.'

Now she was thinking of Peter rather than her father. He could hardly bear to look at her or Alex. Her father was no worse than most men, perhaps.

'I'll go tomorrow,' she said, her mood suddenly changing. 'It's too hot today. I'll go on the early bus tomorrow.'

'Your Dad will dote on Alex. He loves children.'

'Yes. He's got his good points, I suppose.'

'Don't stay away too long, will you.'

Alex was six months old, a large baby, placid enough except when he thought he was hungry. He had Laura's tawny hair and brown skin. For hours he sat, square and solid, on a rug in the garden, banging tins with a wooden spoon.

'In another two months, he'll be a terror,' Susan would say. 'Crawling everywhere and getting into everything. You just make the most of this stage.'

Julia and Tony were fair and fair-skinned and had to be protected against the sun. They'd both recently had a birthday; there was less than thirteen months between them, but while Julia was advanced for her age, talking and reasoning - and arguing - like a child of five, Tony seemed rather backward and wouldn't communicate at all except with smiles and nods and little flicks of the head. His hair was almost white and fluffy like down. 'This is never going to be hair,' Laura would say as she brushed it. 'I think he's a bird. Fly, Tony. Fly like a bird.'

Tony would smile at her and point to the birds on the grass. 'He's not unintelligent,' Laura would say. 'It's just that he's never going to talk and never going to have hair. You mustn't worry about him, though.'

The garden was lovely. They'd had a man in to scythe the grass, and the shrubs and bushes Laura had hacked down at the beginning of March, thinking them quite dead, had put on, first, a most magnificent show of tender leaves and then, more astonishingly still, a profusion of amazingly delicate and fragrant flowers; creamy honeysuckle, lilac, orange blossom. 'I could get to like gardening,' Laura had said. 'I could certainly get to like this garden - all this grass. It's soil I don't like. Soil is altogether too bare and basic. Once you expose your actual soil, it's only a step to things like giant cabbages and those repellent dahlias Edith is so fond of.'

'Kathleen and Edith have got some lovely lettuces. Perhaps they'll give you some to take Mabel. It would be a treat for her to have something fresh.'

'Can I come with you to see Mabel?' Julia asked Laura.

'No, love,' Susan said. 'Because tomorrow you have to help Kathleen with your new watering-can and your little trowel.'

'All-a-time I have to help somebody,' Julia grumbled. 'Anybody doesn't seem to know I'm only three years old.'

'Could you run upstairs and get me a clean nappy for Alex?' Laura asked her.

'Up and down, up and down,' Julia said. 'Anybody doesn't seem to remember I'm only little.'

Laura and Susan looked after her as she walked crossly towards the house, her shoulder-blades protruding like little wings.

'Isn't it a lovely house. Will you ever want to live in a town after this?' Laura asked Susan. 'Do you remember what summer was like in Mason's Lane; everything so dusty and parched? Do you remember how yellow the grass on the common used to get? It used to be like the inside of a circus tent. Do you remember that brook we used to paddle in? A trickle of tea-coloured water and broken glass.'

'It's nice here, but it isn't real life,' Susan said. 'I'll have to go back soon to help my Dad in the shop. The bombing is nothing like it was. I like towns. I can't help it. Shops and people. Noise.'

'Here you are,' Julia said, returning with the nappy. 'And now I suppose Mama wants the potty for Tony.'

'Yes please,' Susan said.

Like a very small conjuror, Julia produced it from behind her back.

'What a good girl you are,' Susan said, hugging her. 'What would we do without you?'

Laura was appalled by the state of her home town. Nothing she had read, nothing Susan had told her, had prepared her for the streets and streets of ruined houses, ruined cinemas and shops; whole streets of rubble. It seemed impossible to believe that people were still carrying on with their normal lives in such conditions, going to work and then fire-fighting at night. She didn't know where to get the bus to Longfield, all the landmarks in the city centre had disappeared: at first sight the entire city centre had disappeared.

Mabel's shop was intact, but inside, the shelves were almost empty. 'There's coupons for everything, dear,' Mabel said. 'It takes twice as long to serve anyone and I'm only making half the profits because I haven't got the goods. I feel like giving it all up, I really do. I'm beginning to feel my age.'

'I'll go through to the kitchen,' Laura said. Alex was heavy on her arm.

'Put the kettle on, dear. I'll be with you soon. I'll shut early and make us a spot of lunch.'

'I hadn't wanted to worry you, dear,' Mabel said, after they'd had a cup of tea. 'You've had enough on your plate, you and Susan. Oh, I went to see Susan's mummy the other day. It did upset me. She was dressed in a child's dress, blue and white gingham. Oh dear, I must try not to think about it. P'raps she's quite happy in her own way . . . She looked like . . . well, like a very old child.'

She took Alex on to her lap. She'd lost some weight, Laura noticed. Alex seemed almost too much for her.

'He's gorgeous isn't he, Laura? He'd win a prize anywhere, he would, in any baby show in the land. Who's a lovely boy, then? Who loves his Grandma?'

The baby-talk stopped abruptly. Her voice changed. 'Oh Laura, they break your heart,' she said.

To Laura's surprise, she pushed Alex back at her and slumped into her chair, dabbing her eyes with her handkerchief and suddenly looking old.

'What is it Mabel? Is he very ill?'

'Your daddy? No, he's all right love, just his normal bad chest. It wasn't your daddy I wanted to talk to you about. That was just an excuse, dear.'

Alex began to cry and Laura opened her blouse to feed him.

'Susan's mother?' she said. 'There's worse news about Susan's mother?'

'No, dear. It's about Peter. It's bad news about our Peter.'

Mabel's older son, John, had had the opportunity to look up Peter on his way home from Scotland and had discovered that he was seriously involved with a local girl. 'Plenty of people have a girlfriend when they're away from home, but this is different,' John had told her. 'The silly ass insists that he'll never give her up, that his marriage means nothing to him. I've never known anyone so determined and stupid. He's got his embarkation leave soon, but he's going to spend it with this girl and tell Susan he wasn't able to get any. He's going to go on sending money to Susan, but he says the marriage is over.'

Laura was stunned by the news. For a time she could say nothing. She just sat feeding Alex and from time to time touching her step-mother's arm.

'Thank God, he's being sent abroad,' Mabel said. 'I never thought I'd live to say that, but I mean it. It may knock some sense into him. I'm only frightened that he'll write to tell Susan something before he goes. John says he's in that state where he's dying to get everything sorted out. You must go to see him, dear, that's the only hope I've got. What I want you to say is that he mustn't do anything hasty. However he feels. If this girl he's met is any good, she won't want him to do anything hasty. You must tell him that.'

Laura moved Alex to the other breast. 'But John must have said all that,' she said. 'I'm sure he'd take much more notice of John than he would of me . . . Or why don't you go up to see him? I'll look after Dad and the shop to let you go. I'll stay here and see to everything. That would be the best thing. Honestly.'

Mabel looked at her with swimming eyes. '*You* must go, dear,' she said firmly. 'You've got a lot of influence with Peter. He looks up to you. Oh, he's had no time for me since he was thirteen or so. His father would have been able to talk to him, he was the same sort of person, quiet and clever, but I was never anything to him but a part of the furniture; never someone to talk to.'

'I can't go,' Laura said, almost to herself.

'You must, dear. I've got the train ticket for you. You must do it for Susan's sake. She'd do anything for you, you know that.'

'I'm the last person to preach to him.'

'I don't want you to preach to him, dear. What's done is done. I only want you to get him to promise one thing - not to be hasty. To say nothing to Susan, however much he wants to get it off his chest, to promise nothing to the other girl until he's far away from them both and having time to think.'

There was a heavy silence in the little kitchen. Alex, his pangs of hunger appeased, let go the nipple to smile up at his mother. Usually Laura found it an enchanting moment, but on this occasion she failed to respond to it.

'When have I got to go?' she asked at last.

'Not till baby's in bed, dear. I suppose he takes a bottle, doesn't he? It's high time he was weaned. You mustn't let him make you thin. I've got Maureen to mind the shop for me, so I can give him all my time. Maureen knows all about it. It was her made John tell me. She's a good girl. They're getting married in September.

In the afternoon while her step-mother was back in the shop,

Laura took Alex for a walk. It wasn't that she wanted to see more of the devastated city, but anything seemed better than being by herself thinking of the fool's errand she'd promised to undertake.

'Look, Alex,' she found herself saying. 'This is war. This is what it looks like. Try and remember this, won't you.'

Some houses were completely burnt down, only the front steps showing where the doors had been. One house had its entire front blown off; with the furniture still in place in all the rooms, it looked like a giant doll's house.

It was certainly grim. But after a while she noticed that the people who walked past her looked very much as they always had, some cheerful enough. Shops were still trading, though the windows might be boarded up, and the signs outside were vying with one another to offer humour if nothing else. 'No oranges, no bananas. Ask and it shall not be given unto you,' one said, and another, determined on a more positive approach, announced 'Fair shares for all. Bring your own bottle,' and underneath, in smaller letters, 'Vinegar 2d a pint.'

The strangest thing of all was that there were already wild flowers - poppies, willow-herb, campion - wherever the ground was cleared of rubble. Where had the seeds come from, she wondered. How had they taken root with so little sustenance; on brick dust it seemed.

That's what she remembered most vividly afterwards: the wild flowers covering everything in the end.

Her father was home by the time Laura got back.

He greeted Laura coolly enough but he warmed to his grandson. 'Ah, he's a great little fellow,' he said. 'Look at the back on him. Mabel told me he was a handsome lad.'

'Just like his Grandpa,' Mabel said, looking lovingly from one to the other.

'I'm glad you're not ill, anyway,' Laura said. 'I was worried about you.'

'I *am* ill,' he said, in the self-pitying tone she so well remembered. 'My chest's terrible. I cough for ten minutes when I first get up. You should just hear me.'

'Are you going to see her boy for her?' he asked as soon as

Mabel had left them to get their supper.

'Yes.'

'Good girl.' He sat back as though satisfied with her.

Laura realised once again that he wasn't really concerned about her. On the whole she was quite pleased.

'Do you think Alex will be all right with Mabel?' she asked, only to tease him a little.

He sat up with a jerk. 'What? *All right? All right?* He'll be looked after like a prince of the blood, that's what he'll be. He'll be spoilt to death, that's what he'll be. She won't take her eyes off him.'

Laura's train left at 8.15. She put Alex to bed in the cot Mabel had borrowed for him and felt as though she was deserting him for ever: for six months he had never been out of her earshot, she had lived by his breathing, his pulse had been hers, the rhythm of his hunger had ordered her life. She looked nervously at Mabel as she closed the bedroom door.

'He's with his Grandma,' she said firmly. 'And it's high time he was weaned. He took his bottle like a champion. I don't think you had enough for him. He'll be all right.'

Mabel had booked a room for her in the Station Hotel in Leeds. In the morning she was to get a bus to Falconridge, the small town near Peter's camp.

'I sent him a telegram,' Mabel said. '"Please meet camp gates midday Mother."'

'You think he'll be able to get away?' Laura asked.

'Yes. That's how John contacted him. He didn't keep John waiting long.'

'He'll be surprised to see me.'

'He'll take notice of you,' Mabel said, giving her the money she needed for the hotel and the return ticket. 'He thinks you're someone to be reckoned with.'

Laura felt very nervous on the train. She knew nothing of air raids. The warning went often enough at Kingsbury, but no bombs had ever been dropped except on one occasion when a stray plane, probably bound for Birmingham, had released its load of bombs in a field nearby, harming no one. She wondered what she'd do if the warning sounded when she was in the hotel. She'd left home without a dressing-gown and her nightie was a slip of a thing. It would be better not to get undressed she supposed.

'Is your journey really necessary?' the posters screamed out from all the stations. She was certain that her journey would prove a complete waste of time. John would have already tried to talk sense to Peter, so why would he listen to her? Why was she wasting her time?

But then she thought about Susan, so innocent of life's complications. The Saturday night play on the wireless had once been about marital infidelity and they'd had to turn it off because Susan had become upset and bewildered by it. 'But I don't understand,' she'd kept saying. 'I thought Trevor was married to Hilda, so who is June? It doesn't make sense.'

When shopping in Shipton, she'd once been stopped by a young airman who'd asked her whether she ever went to the Saturday night hops.

'What did you say?' Laura had asked.

'Nothing. I just pointed to my wedding ring and asked him to let me pass.'

Laura often pictured that incident. Susan, slim again since her miscarriage, her flower-blue eyes, her short curly hair, making her look so young, her pretty hands, always smooth and delicate however much work she did.

'You're a sweet duck,' Laura had said, hugging her.

'Why? Would any girl go to a dance, with her husband away in the army?'

Instead of answering, Laura had read her a passage from *Othello:*

> *Des.* Dost though in conscience think, tell me, Emilia,
> That there be women do abuse their husbands
> In such gross kind?
> *Emil.* There be some such, no question.
> *Des.* Wouldst thou do such a deed for all the world?
> *Emil.* Why, would not you?
> *Des.* No, by this heavenly light!
> *Emil.* Nor I neither by this heavenly light; I might do 't as

well i' the dark.

Des. Wouldst thou do such a thing for all the world?

Emil. The world is a huge thing; 'tis a great price
For a small vice.

And this had led eventually to Laura having to recount the whole terrible story, whereupon Susan had cried over Desdemona's death as though it had taken place that very afternoon.

Chapter Twenty-seven

'The thought that my mother was coming upset me,' Peter said, 'but this is a bloody farce.'

Laura felt his anger like a slap in the face.

It *was* a farce. She inclined her head to acknowledge the fact. During the journey to Leeds and for long stretches of the night she had considered and reconsidered her mission and had arrived at a very similar conclusion: she had been manipulated into taking a moralistic stand in a situation where she didn't know the rules and suspected that no one else did either.

He had turned up on time; a minute or two after twelve.

The other fifteen or twenty soldiers who'd emerged from the camp at the same time had all rushed to a bus stop a few yards from the gates.

He and Laura had walked past the jostling crowd. 'Hi, Pete,' some of them had shouted in the way of young men trying to embarrass another. There were one or two wolf whistles.

Peter's face was stormy. Perhaps girls didn't turn up at the camp. Laura wondered if he was ashamed of her. She suddenly felt uneasy about her appearance. She was wearing a plain, quite unexceptional grey skirt but a decidedly odd white blouse. 'I can't wear this again,' Kathleen had said a week or two earlier. 'Can you wear it?' 'If it fits me I can,' Laura had said. 'What's wrong with it?' she'd asked afterwards when Susan had sighed and looked pained. 'It's so old-fashioned,' Susan had said. 'All that material, that flounce and that collar.' For the first time, Laura felt dubious about it, unsure of herself.

The bus passed them but they carried on walking, walking hurriedly as though late for an appointment. The weather was very hot, even hotter than on the previous day. Laura felt her clothes sticking to her. There was no breeze.

'Can we sit down for a few minutes?' she asked, when at last they came to a seat by the side of the road.

By this time Peter was looking tense rather than angry. He sat on the extreme end of the seat and half turned towards her. He looked older and thinner than when she'd last seen him. She had once thought him handsome. Now he seemed a most ordinary soldier who didn't merit a second glance. His mouth looked petulant.

'It's the first time I've been to Yorkshire,' she said, in an attempt to break the silence between them. 'I suppose this can't be far from Brontë country?'

'Eleven or twelve miles,' he said.

'Have you been there?'

'Yes.'

'What's the village like?'

He turned away from her without answering.

'I'm sorry I came,' she said. 'I apologise. I never felt it would do any good.'

The moors stretched out for miles around them. The air was close and smelt of honey. There were harebells and bell-heather in the short grass and hundreds of small blue butterflies. There were so many bees that the whole earth seemed to be buzzing. Laura longed to take off her shoes and lay her feet in the singing grass, but she dared not. In Peter's present mood, she felt even more nervous of him than usual.

'We could go to Haworth if you like,' Peter said, after another long silence.

'It's all right,' she said primly. 'It wouldn't be appropriate. I didn't come up to enjoy myself.'

'We'll take the next bus to Leeds then,' Peter said. 'When's your train?'

'There's one at seven - the only one, I think. Oh Peter, couldn't you possibly come back with me?'

'No, I couldn't.'

'When are you going abroad?'

'We're sailing from Liverpool on Monday. And I don't want to see anyone before I go.'

Glancing at him, she saw that his eyes were glittering. She looked away quickly. 'I can understand that,' she said.

'It's all over, you know,' he said then, his voice gentler than before.

She realised from his blank, hopeless tone that he was referring to the affair, not to his marriage.

She said nothing. She wasn't sure she even believed him. She knew that affairs weren't over because the participants said they were.

'What was her name?' she asked. What daft things she seemed to be coming out with.

'Marguerite.'

Marguerite. She was to remember afterwards the weight of love he put into those three syllables. It conveyed more of the desperate passion he had suffered than anything he would tell her later.

'We'd better go on to the next bus stop,' he said. 'I don't think they stop here. I suppose we should have something to eat.'

But Laura was loath to leave the moors. 'I had breakfast late,' she said. 'I'm not at all hungry, are you? Let's sit here a bit longer.'

'When I met John, I wanted to shock him,' he said. 'I don't know why. Because he's so much the older brother, perhaps, and so bloody conventional. I suppose I exaggerated - not my feelings, I couldn't exaggerate those - but the probable outcome. I told him my marriage was over. I always knew it wasn't, that it couldn't be, that I wasn't the sort who could put it all behind me.'

'I honestly didn't think you were,' Laura said. 'God knows why I came up all this way.'

'Well, Mum persuaded you into it, I suppose. I never dreamed John would tell her.'

'He told Maureen. I think Maureen got him to tell your mother.'

'I'd forgotten Maureen.'

The midday sun beat down on them.

'*He* was married,' Laura said. 'My boyfriend. He would never have left his wife; I'd accepted that.'

He looked at her. 'You've had a tough time,' he said. It was a long time since he'd thought of anything except his own problems.

'I think I'll take my shoes off,' Laura said, immediately responding to his change of mood.

She leaned forward, unlaced her shoes and laid her feet tenderly on the grass. 'Lovely,' she said. 'Of course it will be worse when I have to put them back on. I go around bare-footed in Kingsbury these days.'

'Don't people think you're very bohemian?'

'No, they think it's patriotism; saving leather for bayonet cases and things.'

She decided it was no time for cynicism. 'Do you know where you're being sent?' she asked.

'Africa, according to the rumour.'

Laura's eyes widened. 'Africa,' she repeated.

'You promised to write when I got sent abroad,' he said.

'I will.'

'She doesn't intend to: Marguerite. She lost interest in me as soon as she knew I was going overseas.'

His eyes searched the sky as if for some understanding or help. 'I suppose you think she's a tart,' he said.

'I'm sure she's not.'

'Why do you say that?'

'I can't see you making a fool of yourself.'

'I *have* made a fool of myself.'

Laura felt unable to go on. Nothing she'd said, nothing she could say seemed of any help. Was it her own heartbeats she could feel throbbing in the silence? It seemed like something outside herself, something larger. Was there some spirit in the universe that took pity on human folly, she wondered. She rejected the idea, though not without regret.

Her eyes ached in the burning sun. 'Do you want to tell me about her?' she heard herself say.

'I'm mad about her, Laura,' he said, his voice breaking in a way it never would again.

There was another long, despairing silence. Laura found

herself thinking about Peter's great love, who, if not hard-hearted, certainly seemed practised in the art of self-preservation, and of Susan, who had no defences.

She was suddenly shivering and realised that the weather was changing. 'There's going to be such a storm,' she said. 'Look how these clouds are coming towards us. Are we anywhere near shelter?'

They both stood up. Laura took her cardigan from her bag.

A streak of lightning whipped across the sky. 'Let's go,' Peter said. The thunder growled in the distance and a few large spots of warm rain fell on them. 'I think there's a bus shelter just beyond those trees.'

He took her bag, she picked up her shoes and they started to run.

When the rain came, it broke over them like a huge wave; they laughed at the force of it. Laura's light-weight skirt was soon completely drenched, it flapped round her legs as she ran. The road which a few minutes before had been white in the sun was running like a river.

'You'd better have my tunic,' Peter said, slowing down, but Laura didn't stop running and laughing under her breath. She'd never experienced it before: the weather breaking. It was exhilarating.

They'd almost reached the clump of trees when a large car, a dark blue Daimler, drew up and a door was thrown open for them.

'We're very wet,' Laura said. 'Absolutely soaking.'

'Never mind. Get in.'

They shook themselves like two dogs and got in to the back seat.

The smartly-dressed couple in the front surveyed them with some amusement. 'You poor things,' the woman said. 'Did you miss the bus?'

'Yes,' Peter said, 'and then we thought we'd walk to the next stop.'

'They don't run very often,' the man said. 'We've been trying to get them to improve the service, but they keep telling us there's some damned war on. We've got a son in the camp,' he continued after he'd got a smile from Laura. 'Roger Carey. Do you know him?' he asked Peter.

'*Lieutenant* Roger Carey,' his wife added with a deprecating smile. She was younger than her husband; when she smiled her eyes became blue slits in her face.

'Yes, I know him,' Peter said, his voice expressionless. 'I'm Lance-Corporal Glover. This is Laura Brown.'

'Geoffrey and Elspeth Carey,' the woman said.

Mr and Mrs Carey had been to the camp to take their son some records he'd wanted for a party that evening. They seemed devoted parents, and their pride in their son overflowed on to the wet soldier in their car. When they heard he was on embarkation leave, they insisted on taking him and Laura back to their home to get their clothes dried.

'What a dreadful mess,' Peter whispered, when they were alone for a moment in the drawing room of the huge detached house they'd been driven to. 'Their son is a pompous twit; he'll be furious when he knows about this.'

Mrs Carey had given him some of her son's clothes to wear while his own were being dried on the airer in the kitchen and Laura'd been given a pink dress of her daughter's. 'Don't worry,' Laura said. 'You'll be in Africa.'

Mr Carey joined them, bringing a tray of drinks. 'I'm afraid it's steak and kidney pie for lunch,' he said gloomily. 'Carrots and potatoes and Oxo. Yes, you must stay. My wife's told cook to lay on some fruit salad.'

'Cook says she won't be able to get your uniform dry till this evening at the earliest,' Mrs Carey said, when she joined them later. 'Are you sure you won't take those flannels of Roger's? He won't mind at all.'

'Not at all,' Mr Carey echoed. 'He'll be tickled pink when he hears about your dousing. He's got a wicked sense of humour, our son. Elspeth, tell them about the time he came limping in with bandages half way up his leg. Eleven o'clock one Saturday night.'

'Of course, I panicked,' Mrs Carey said. 'His face was deathly, his ...'

The large glass of whisky Laura had been given was

making her pleasantly sleepy; she looked at Mrs Carey without hearing a word.

A little earlier, Mrs Carey had taken her to the largest bathroom she'd ever seen in her life - it could have housed a family - and had run a bath for her. The water was softer than ordinary water, the soap was pink and heart-shaped and smelt of strawberries, and the towels were thick and soft and warm. When she was out of the bath and wrapped in a towel, Mrs Carey had brought her some underclothes which were probably silk, and the lovely pink dress - 'It's a bit out of date, I'm afraid,' she'd said - and taken away her own clothes.

When she was dressed, Laura had felt like someone else. Her hair was curling as it always did when it was wet and she'd lifted it on to the top of her head and stuck some pins into it. When she'd come downstairs Mrs Carey had told her she looked like Josephine. 'A bare-footed empress,' she'd said, and had apologised yet again for her small feet and for her daughter's small feet. 'We have very small feet,' she'd said in such a way that Laura was almost forced into sympathising with her.

'A penny for them,' Mr Carey said, looking at her as though she was 'the real woman' he'd talked about all his life. (His daughter wasn't a real woman. His son's girlfriends would never be real women.)

'They're too sad; not worth a ha'penny,' Laura said.

Mrs Carey squeezed her arm. In the last war, her husband had spent two years in the trenches. 'Lunch is ready,' she said.

Peter was still painfully ill at ease. Laura saw him rearranging the food on his plate, eating hardly anything. When the meal was over, he got to his feet abruptly. 'It's been very good of you,' he said, 'but now I'm afraid we must go. Our clothes won't be dry, but they'll certainly be less wet.'

'And we've been fed and cossetted,' Laura added. 'So we won't come to any harm.'

Mr Carey looked as though he wanted to argue, but Mrs Carey rose at once. 'Of course,' she said. 'You must have a hundred things to do and so much to talk about. We've enjoyed your company, but you naturally want to be on your own. Geoffrey will drive you into town as soon as you're ready.'

In the car, Laura became apprehensive again. The whisky, the good food, the coffee, had been only an interlude which already seemed unreal. Peter hardly said a word. If anything he was looking more strained than before.

'Weren't they kind?' Laura said, after Mr Carey had dropped them off in the city-centre. 'Say what you like, the war is certainly bringing people together. Can you imagine people like that having anything to do with people like us before the war?'

Peter turned to her with a completely blank expression. His face reminded her of newspaper pictures of shell-shocked casualties. 'I had to get away,' he said. 'I had to. I've got to make a phone call.'

Without further word they walked to the Post Office and Laura waited while he found an empty kiosk. He was inside for several minutes.

'She'd already left,' he said when he came out. 'She goes to her parents at the weekend.'

'Perhaps it's all for the best,' Laura said gently. 'You told me it was over. What's the point of trying to contact her again?'

'It will be a bit easier when you've got away from here,' she said when they were out on the street again. 'Try not to be too anguished. It will pass. Everything passes.'

'Life passes,' Peter said. 'That's all we can be sure of.' His voice already seemed that of an old man.

'I'll go to the station now,' Laura said. 'You needn't bother to come with me. You go back to the camp. You'll be better with company.'

'Of course I'll come with you. All my unit is on leave. I'm lucky to have your company.'

They walked in the direction of the railway station. The violent storm hadn't succeeded in clearing the air; it was still warm and moist, the sky still threatening.

It started to rain again, not heavily as it had before, but in a steady drizzle that looked as though it would never end. They went into a café and ordered two cups of tea. It was a dismal place, with oilcloth on the tables and cigarette ends on the floor. The people there looked miserable and undernourished.

'I have to see her again,' Peter said. 'I'm going mad.'

'Come back with me to your mother's. It will give you something to do. You can go straight back tomorrow morning.'

'I can't bear to see anyone.'

'Wouldn't you like to see Alex?'

'Alex?'

'My son.' Her breasts ached as she thought of him.

'Your son. I'd forgotten about him. How are my children?' he asked as an afterthought. It seemed almost as though he'd forgotten them as well.

Laura searched her mind for some interesting or amusing anecdote. 'Tony's getting to look very much like you,' was all she managed to come up with.

He was deflected for a moment.

'Is he backward, do you think? He's certainly not as bright as Julia, is he?'

She couldn't think of much about Julia either. 'Julia's learnt a little song,' she said at last. 'And the greengrocer grew all around, all around. And the greengrocer grew all around.'

He didn't smile, but his expression lightened. 'You will write to me?' he asked.

'Of course I will. I'll write reams. I'll tell you all about them; everything they say and do. Do you want me to send you anything? Books?'

'Books? That would be a change. Mum keeps sending me balaclavas.'

'What sort of books do you like? I know the ones you liked as a boy. Your mum showed them to me.'

She suddenly remembered the afternoon she'd spent in his bedroom, sick with love for him.

'I loved botany when I was in school; I loved botanical drawing more than anything in the world. I got ninety per cent in my School Certificate - and the school prize. But what use was botany to a boy like me?'

'I'll get you books on African flora. I know a man in the botany department at Bristol. He'll help me.'

'You were lucky to get to university.'

'Yes. Perhaps you'll be able to make a new start after the war.'

'I'll be too old; I'm twenty-five already. Oh, it makes me sick to think of all the stupid oafs – Roger Carey for one – who went to Oxford or Cambridge simply because their parents had money . . . And Susan wants me to take over her father's shop.'

'No, I don't think she does. I think she's changed her mind about that.'

'Oh Laura, Susan is so boring. She's given up thinking. She doesn't want anything but . . .'

'No she hasn't, I promise you. She's bright and very quick-witted. And she's loving and generous and loyal.'

'Don't go on. It makes it worse. Oh Christ, I know how awful I've been to her. I don't need you to point it out.'

He's at least thinking about Susan and the children, Laura told herself. I've done all I could hope to do.

'Do you know why I made a pass at her in the first place? Because I thought she was you. No one introduced us properly. I thought *she* was the daughter of the man my mother had just got married to. And you see, I wanted to get back at him.'

'You were even worse than I thought,' Laura said quietly.

'I was despicable, I know. It wasn't even that I minded my mother remarrying. It was just the fact that she blushed and simpered like an eighteen-year-old, that she seemed to have fallen in love. And with such a very ordinary man.'

'It may comfort you to know that I certainly suffered with her,' Laura said bitterly. 'Oh Peter, do you even know the trouble you caused her? Did she ever tell you about the thrashing she got from her father? About her period being late? Oh Peter, to think of all she went through; all those steaming-hot baths, all the jumping off the slides in the park. All *my* fault. Because you thought she was *me*.'

'I fell in love with her afterwards, though. Afterwards, I kept on thinking how rotten I'd been to her.'

'I can hardly believe it of you. It seems out of character. I could believe that you were careless of people's feelings – you were careless of mine – but that you should have set out to seduce a girl out of dislike for her father seems ...'

'Rotten,' Peter said again. 'I've been ashamed of it ever since. Well, it can't be undone now. And if I'd only got the real you, things might have turned out quite differently.'

They both considered that. Laura remembered how much in love with Peter she'd once been, how conscious that they were suited, how jealous of Susan.

'You looked beautiful in that pink dress this afternoon,' he said. 'You looked a different person in that dress, in that room.'

'It seems like another world. I can hardly believe it happened.'

They looked about them at the mean little café, the cracked cups, the dirty windows, the people at all the tables who'd never known, and didn't expect, anything better.

'When the war's over things will be different,' Peter said. 'People won't put up with the way things have always been; rich and poor. There'll be a complete change.'

'Do you think so? Nothing changed much after the last war. But I hope you're right ... When will it be over, do you think?'

'Who knows! Our chances are certainly better than they were last year. Things might start going our way.'

'Are you pleased to be a part of it?'

'Not really. Just resigned. I haven't got any decisions to make, now. I'm a cog in a machine; mindless. I obey orders, nothing more. It's going to be very easy in a way. In a way, I'm quite looking forward to embarking.'

They looked at each other and realised that they might never meet again. Their hands touched on the greasy tablecloth.

'And what about you, Laura? You and your son? Susan says she has to go back to her father. Will you stay in the village or will you go back too?'

'I'll stay. I somehow feel I'm meant to. I advertised for an aunt and I got her, now I've answered an advert for a headmaster and I expect I'll get him too. He's thirty-three, unmarried, unfit for active service because of his eyesight.

H.E. Redfern BA. I expect he'll be very suitable. He'll be a little put out by Alex at first, but he'll manage to convince himself that I was only another war casualty. Oh, I'm quite looking forward to the future.'

'Yes,' Peter said. 'And so am I.'

Only their eyes gave them away.

Suddenly their fingers locked together in a grip which hurt them both. 'Can you stay till tomorrow?' he asked. 'I've got to go to Liverpool tomorrow. Will you stay till I have to go?'

He didn't need a reply. They looked out at the rain and sipped their tea.

That's all.

The night had passed. His lovely shoulders had spread over her body like wings. His dark chin had grazed her breasts. He had cried for Marguerite, and she had cried, too; for herself, for Giles, for Susan.

Appalling silence.

What did any of it matter? Oh yes, perhaps she loved him - as she had loved him before - but it would pass. He loved Marguerite and that would also pass.

If he comes back alive, she would be a staid married woman perhaps; perhaps with several children.

He would return to Susan and perhaps be a good and faithful husband throughout a long married life.

'Only please, please come back,' she found herself crying in the corner seat of the compartment, now empty.

Even at its worst, life was interesting; endless avenues, with occasional surprise, occasional delight. Death was the only tragedy. 'Please, please let him come back.'

The train rattled into a tunnel and she realised that her journey was almost over.

Loss and gain. Love and pain.

At least she'd be able to tell Mabel that Peter's affair was over, that Susan wouldn't get to hear of it. It was something, she supposed. Something.

She dried her eyes and rose from her seat.

She wondered whether Alex would have missed her.